To the magical girls that shaped my childhood, for without you, I would have never thought to take this series in this direction.

As always, I have to thank those of you who were around back when this series was up on Wattpad. This book is almost completely different now, and I hope that you agree with me when I say that every single change has been for the better. It is my goal to make this a series worthy of such long-term support.

For people who continue to be the person they want to be, in spite of the expectations from those close to you, whether that be family, friends, or some other similarly significant person in your life; those who do so despite experiencing horrible things that shaped you as a person, and most of all, never stopped being kind: this one is for you.

Prologue

There is always a dilemma facing those who fight for the greater good: is it enough to defeat a clear enemy? What should be done if defeating the opposition welcomes a greater difficulty?

As the sun rose upon Compositora, bringing with it a golden light that unfurled upon the lands, birds began to chirp. Gentle winds tickled the semi-dry grass around the town, as well as the sprouts of tiny flowers that had begun to sprout. Usually, this hour would be a time of serenity. Today, however, the defeated voice of a dark-haired young woman softly flowed through the dining room where she was seated, her head sinking into the open book sitting in front of her.

"I... haven't gotten any sleep..."

A sigh, as she pushed her hair aside and stood, beginning to leave the room. Even though she was dressed in the most comfortable pajama set she owned- a calming lavender set that was as soft as she thought the clouds would be- even that felt heavy and uncomfortable against her skin.

"*Did* I sleep last night? No... I don't think I did." She feebly continued as she walked down the hallway, toward the front door. "I can't now... there's no time."

She opened the door, and right on cue, the group of men she'd been expecting rushed through the door. As always, her first instinct was to visually scan the group for two distinct figures; seeing the dark umber tones of the largest man in the group's skin made her feel at ease, and seeing the silky black ponytail of one of the younger men made her feel even more relaxed.

"How many today?" she mumbled then.

"We were fortunate today. There's only two–"

The room grew silent as the two locked eyes.

"Phoenix, you look like hell," Thunder said then. "Are you sure you don't need a break?"

"Positive. Please, bring the injured to the infirmary. I'll treat them, as usual."

Usually, the sight of her mentor and her younger brother gave Phoenix a sweeping feeling of relief, knowing they were home safe yet again. And she did feel that way today as well, because it was always good to have them return; albeit on a smaller scale than she would normally be. But she was so tired that she didn't have the strength left to outwardly show that relief.

"You're positive?" added Logan. "Phoenix. You know I'll help if the workload is too heavy for you."

"I'm fine, Logan. I wouldn't be able to sleep if I tried, knowing so many of our own need my help." Phoenix began to continue to walk down the hall. "I'm expecting those patients in the infirmary by the time I get down this hall, boys. Do *not* prolong their healing process by being slow."

Logan just sighed as he watched her leave, and afterward, he and Thunder began to walk toward the kitchen. "She looks awful."

"I'd probably look worse if I were in her position. She's been working harder than hard this week," Thunder replied. "If I recall correctly, at this point, we don't have any other medics; they've all either been injured, or been going out to fight with us. I know you hate to see your sister like this, but she knows how important her role is."

"I know, too. But even still. Can we rest a second? I'm dying here." Logan sighed in effort as he sat down, grateful to rest his aching leg muscles. As he inspected himself– a new cut on his forearm, a dark bruise on his left thigh– he could only think of how much he ached. Thunder was in slightly better shape due to being more experienced, and a ranged combatant, but even he had a few bruises that were impossible to miss. There was a gash on his forehead that had scabbed over, but there still remained some dried blood that made a few stray hairs from his frontmost locs cling to his forehead.

"How are you feeling, Logan?" he asked then, in an attempt to calm the tension of the situation.

"How do I feel? Despite our best efforts, the village populace is still sustaining multiple injuries, not to mention the property damage, and the difficulty we're experiencing with trying to recultivate the plant life in this area. It's frustrating, devastating, it's crushing that no matter what we do, these... these *things* are ruining our lives!"

It had been two weeks now, since everything had changed. The first few months following the defeat of The Dictator had been peaceful, mellow. Everyone in the village had slept soundly every night, after a fulfilling dinner and periods of recreation. And with peace restored, the magic had gradually begun returning to the town; so far, this had enabled the rivers to become healthy and strong again, and for the native plant life to begin its rebirth. The grass had begun to turn green again. Flowers had been blooming once more. That was until two weeks ago, when hell had broken loose.

No one knew where the creatures had come from– and so far, they hadn't shown any sign of going back there, either. They'd descended upon Compositora suddenly one night, tearing through anything or anyone who was unfortunate enough to be in their paths. Although their forms seemed pretty human at first glance, there were ways to tell they weren't, the most obvious being their sickly blue-gray skin tone. They didn't seem to be capable of speech, but they ran at a fast enough pace to outrun a healthy adult, and seemed to have competent eyesight as well. The only natural occurrence that drove them away was sunlight, and even then, that only seemed to stun them, and signal a need to retreat; so far it seemed the only permanent deterrent was their own deaths, and so, the Resistance had immediately decided that the best course of action was to take up arms. The issue was that their opponents were more persistent than expected, and so, many members of the Resistance had been injured since they'd begun their battles.

"Oh, yeah. By the way, we have a visitor today," Thunder continued as he and Logan began to walk again.

"Yeah? Interesting choice in these times. Who is it?" asked Logan.

"If I were you, I wouldn't get *too* excited."

They'd reached one of the meeting rooms now, and Thunder gestured to where a teenage girl was sitting. Her dark brown hair fell halfway down her back, adorned with one yellow-blonde highlight that framed her round face, sharply contrasting her autumnal skin. She drummed her chubby fingers on the table, waiting somewhat impatiently, until her dark brown eyes noticed the two men entering the room.

"Oh! Logan! Nice to see you again, my guy."

Logan's response was to sigh yet again. "Nice to see you too, I guess."

"Thank you for joining us, Lisandra," added Thunder.

Lisandra was Logan and Phoenix's younger cousin; similarly to Logan, from a young age she'd wanted to assist the Resistance, but her parents had kept her hidden away from their operations–intending to let her experience life as a normal teenage girl. This was, of course, why Logan was confused as to why she was here now.

"I know," she said in response to Logan's obvious confusion, before he could get the question out. "I'm surprised too, utterly shocked, but I think the turning point of the whole thing was me mentioning that I'd heard Phoenix was struggling and could really use my help. You know Dad's always had a soft spot for her."

"You were certainly right about that. Have you seen her today?" asked Logan. "She's been walking around here like a zombie. I'm afraid to ask her when she last slept."

"Then, it's a good thing I'm here, right?" Lisandra smiled. "Although my healing powers aren't as strong as hers, I know I can at least alleviate *some* of her pain."

Thunder gave her a slight nod, smiling a bit as well. "We hope so, Lisandra. Now, I need to talk to y'all both for a second, okay? Logan, have a seat."

"Sure, Captain." Logan nodded, turning his chair the opposite way and sitting on it with a soft grunt.

"I'm sure that, at this point, it's no secret that the Resistance has our backs against the wall with this... mutant creature situation. Our current ranks are doing their best to keep everyone safe, but it seems like the situation is steadily getting worse. I'm tellin' you this, as the two youngest members affiliated with this organization, because your generation tends to be better at progressive thinking than your ancestors were, you know? So maybe y'all can help us put some thought into how to stop this at its source. Which would mean finding the source in the first place."

"Understood." Logan nodded. Lisandra nodded as well.

"Good. That'll be your first assignment; when y'all both have time, I'm trusting you to try and figure out the 'behind-the-scenes' of what's going on, and report any significant findings back to me. You can start immediately."

"Perfect! No time like the present, after all!" Logan hopped up from his chair. "How about I take a few of the guys and start looking for hints, and Lisandra handles the book-smart portions?"

"Shouldn't we reverse those? I mean, you are the smart guy, right?" asked Lisandra.

"That may be, but for the time being, while things are this dangerous, I'd prefer that you stay indoors as much as possible," replied Thunder. "Logan's absolutely correct. Let's not forget that the main reason you're here is to help out on the medic side of things, which means you need to be available to do that as often as possible, which means we can't have you running around out on the field. Speaking of that, I need to have a preliminary talk with ya before you start taking on work here– if you don't mind."

"Of course." Lisandra shrugged. "Not like I'd have much of a choice in the matter, anyway."

"Well, I know when I need to make myself scarce. Be back in a jiffy." Logan saluted the two, before heading out of the room.

"So, what's this extra-secretive conversation about?" asked Lisandra.

"I don't suppose your hearing has gotten any better?" asked Thunder.

Lisandra frowned initially, hearing this as an indirect insult– until the real reasoning behind the question sank in. "Oh. *That.* Yeah, I'm sorry I don't have better news for you."

"Don't be sorry. Besides, we can't really be sure that'd be helpful at all in this case..." Thunder sighed. "It's all so confusing. I never saw anything like this in all my years, and Logan says he ain't seen anything like it in his history books. This world is ancient, and yet, no trace of any explanation at all? It's... for lack of a better word, it's weird."

"Yeah, I feel you." Lisandra nodded. "But that just means that Logan and I will have to work extra hard in our research!"

"Speaking of that. How soon can you start?"

"Oh, Thunder. Immediately, my dude. The sooner we learn where these things are coming from, the sooner we can kick them off of our turf, and that'll be better for everyone. Phoenix will finally be able to get some rest, for one thing."

"You're right." Thunder nodded. "Then, once Logan is done with whatever busy work he took on to preoccupy his mind for now, you two can get right to work!"

"Yes, sir!" Lisandra saluted, standing at attention. "So, what do you have for me today? I'm expecting some mild to moderate blunt injuries, or disinfecting of wounds. Maybe even both. Anything harder, I can't guarantee that I can fix on my own, but I *can* guarantee that it'll only be approached with the best of care and highest level of diligence."

"Heh." Thunder chuckled a bit at her enthusiasm. "Actually, I got a patient I brought in personally that I'd like you to have a look at. Of course I put her on Phoenix's itinerary, but I'd like to hear your input too. This way."

"My input." Lisandra smiled, feeling important, before following behind Thunder.

The two walked down a few corridors of the Resistance's head-quarters before Thunder stopped for a second to remember what room he needed, before turning left and opening a door. Lisandra was shocked to see a fair-skinned, blonde girl lying in the bed. Between her plain but very obviously well-crafted blue fluffy hoodie and neat haircut, something about her just oozed an air of foreign nature; while it wasn't unheard of to see blonde hair in this area of the world, this girl even looked different from a typical blonde native to the town.

"Where did you find her?" asked Lisandra.

"Now, see, that's the part I wanted your input on." Thunder replied. "I happened to notice this girl just as she was falling into the river, not too far from here. The strange part is that she doesn't seem to have sustained any injury that, you know, a person who nearly drowned would. From what I could tell, she didn't even ingest any water– and there was certainly enough time for her to, between the initial fall and when I was able to get her out of the water."

"Hm. That *is* weird." Lisandra frowned, placing a hand over the girl's chest. "Hmm... let's take a look, then."

Both Thunder and Lisandra were quiet as blue-tinged magic swirled around Lisandra's hand for about a minute, before she put her hand back down.

"An initial quick assessment shows that there isn't any hazardous water within. But even disregarding the weirdness of her not ingesting any river water... if she didn't, why is she unconscious?"

"The mysteries continue." Thunder folded his arms. "What's your expert advice, kid?"

"Eh. Just let her rest, and have someone check in every now and then. Her breathing sounds perfectly normal, those bruises are mostly healed, and there's no evidence of magical injury. I can come back and do a more comprehensive test at a later time, but she should be fine if this is the worst of it." Lisandra nodded. "Now, on to the next patient."

"Right. I'll put you on the tail end of the injured, so you can get to people that haven't been seen yet," Thunder stated, as he and Lisandra left the room.

ONE

The Mysterious Swordmistress

A few days after Lisandra's arrival to the Resistance HQ, a storm approached Compositora. The skies had marbled over with storm clouds of varying shades of dark gray in the earlier hours of the day, and they were now crackling with electricity; so much so, that the sky itself was beginning to tinge yellow. Logan watched this from the sliding doors in the back room of headquarters, the ones that led to the courtyard and training area. He stood, wondering how tonight would go, until he heard Thunder approaching; he'd lived here long enough to recognize the sound of his gait.

"I wonder if the lightning from the storm will kill any of those creepy mutant zombie... whatevers?" asked Logan, perhaps a bit too cheerfully.

"Hopefully, we should be so lucky," replied Thunder. "Be nice to have the load lessened out on the field. Less labor on the front lines helps us lighten everyone else's workload back here, in turn."

Logan nodded, but then turned, hearing more footsteps behind himself. He was surprised to see Phoenix behind him, looking noticeably more rested, but the sight made him relax a little himself. He'd been worried about her.

"Boys," she gave them a nod.

"Phoenix." Thunder returned her nod. "You look... alive."

"Thankfully. Having Lisandra around has helped much more than I could've anticipated. Seeing her again is nice of course, on a base level, but she's more capable than I was expecting. I haven't slept that well in weeks!"

"Glad to hear it." Thunder nodded again, this time with a smile accompanying.

"So, what exactly is the plan for tonight?" asked Logan. "In the two weeks we've been dealing with our little problem, we haven't had any inclement weather, but that's more than likely to change tonight. Should we approach things any differently?"

"Hm. Good question." Thunder nodded. "I gotta admit, it's been so frenzied around here that I never thought of that. Why don't we talk this over with Hunter?"

Hunter was one of the Resistance's strategists– he was the newest one, in fact, having only been promoted to the role about a month ago from the librarian role he'd held for a few years before then. He was a kind but usually soft-spoken man in his mid-twenties that kept to himself often, but was always observing behind the scenes, working hard to ensure that everything in the organization was running smoothly. Historically, he was given to holing himself up in some quiet corner as he worked on his tasks, or researched; but with this new promotion he had been more active within headquarters, speaking to more people and voicing his opinions more often.

At this moment, he sat in the conference room alone, with a stack of books near him. He seemed to be reading a newspaper, high-lighting different sections in different colors. As mild-mannered as he could be, Hunter's pale skin and vibrant red hair stood out not only within the Resistance, but in the entire town. He was very clearly not from the area, but many of the Resistance members weren't– including Logan and Phoenix– so Thunder had never pried.

"Hey, Hunter. Strange to see you in this room," Logan pointed out. "It's not one of your usual hides."

Hunter looked up from his newspaper, startled, before giving Logan a firm nod in response. "Yes, well, the library isn't quite as peaceful today. When lightning crackles in the sky– as it's do-ing now– it ends up being quite loud underground," explained Hunter. He was dressed in his usual blazer and scarf combination, this one a set of dark brown and checkered chartreuse, not unlike the chessboard on the shelf behind him.

"Oh. Well, in any case, you're just the man we're lookin' for," Thunder said then. "And it's about the weather today too. In your opinion, is there any precaution we should be taking with it in mind when we go out this evening?"

Hunter looked out of the window, and then checked the time, taking a brief moment more to think before twirling the tassels of his scarf between his fingers. This was something he often did whenever he was thinking; whenever the gears were beginning to turn inside his head. "It's late afternoon now. Reports indicate that the attacks start from outside of the town: in the opposite direction of the market, around where the forest is. I think it'd be best to try and head off the attack there as soon as possible, today. If you start early and cut off the attack at its source, then hopefully, you'll be able to get everyone home before the clouds begin their downpour. I do think, also, that it would be a good idea to keep a separate squad further within the city. You know, just in case the squad farther out has a few lapses in combat ability."

"Good stuff." Thunder nodded. "I'll get a squad together. Logan, suit up; we're going on a special trip today."

"Got it!" He saluted.

"Actually." Phoenix held up a hand, causing all the men in the room to turn to her. "Can I... come with you this time?"

Thunder frowned at her. "What?"

"I had intended to ask sooner, but then the medic work became overwhelming; I wanted a chance to observe the build, strength, and attack patterns of our current enemies. If I can see how they inflict injuries, it'll give me better insight on how to treat them most efficiently."

"I... do think that's a good point," Thunder reluctantly agreed. "And the past couple of nights *have* been pretty tame injury-wise, so I'm sure Lisandra can take care of things here, right?"

"Yes! Plus, a couple of people on the medic team have recovered enough to help her. So it's settled!" Phoenix nodded excitedly. "I'll go and change into something better suited to field work."

When she'd left the room, Thunder turned to Logan. "Well, *she's* eager."

"It's contagious. I was just as excited to be in the thick of things my first time out," pointed out Logan.

"Yes, almost three whole weeks ago," Thunder chuckled. "Now Hunter, speaking of outings, I know it's been a while–"

"Say no more." Hunter stood. "I'll arm myself. Tell me when to be ready, and I'll be present."

Some minutes later, the four had set out on the road leading away from the market, which led toward the woodlands outside of town. It was a road that was rarely traveled, so at this point, it was devoid of any semblance of human life. The silence of the road was only interrupted by the group's footsteps as they strayed farther from the town, and drew closer to the trees. Logan had a thought about how the trees looked a little strange, more gray than usual, but forced it out of his mind as he redirected his thoughts to combat readiness.

"Has this road always been so dusty?" Hunter asked as the squad made its way to the town's outskirts.

"It's slightly dustier because of the recent hot weather and lack of rain," explained Logan. "Whenever the clouds decide to empty themselves, it'll get back to the way you're used to it being– after, of course, hours of it being extremely messy."

"Ah. I missed hearing your tidbits of knowledge, Logan. The base just isn't the same, with you out on field duty," Hunter said.

"Yes, well, I'll be back whenever there's more recruits to be taught!" Logan said with a smile. "It's what I do best, after all! It's just that, for the time being, we all seem to agree that I'm more useful out here."

The walk continued. The farther out from the town's limits the group got, the more electric the air began to feel. It was as if, by drawing closer to the forest, they were getting closer to the source of the strangely static feeling; but of course, that couldn't be the case because it was coming from the sky. Even if it wasn't, no one lived in this forest. There would be nothing there to create such a sensation.

"I do wonder if such a small group of us coming out here was wise..." Hunter said then. "Where has Tornado been? I haven't seen him in quite a while now that I think of it, but we could have made good use of his brute force."

"He surely hasn't been around, so I took it to mean he resigned after our magnum opus," Thunder explained. "Many people did, after that point."

"Yeah, probably wanted to go back to normal lives, now that they can. Can't fault them, really," Logan shrugged.

The quartet continued to walk, silently.

"Actually..." Phoenix started.

It had been a chilly day in November.

The day was peaceful. It always seemed to be this way, ever since The Dictator had been eradicated. Calm. Serene. Quiet. This was overall a good thing, but it did also mean there wasn't much for the Resistance to actively do. These days, their tasks were mostly related to assisting the general populace; whether it be making them clothes and blankets, helping them hunt and gather food, restoring the local architecture as much as they could, or some other odd job. Things that were beneficial, but not exactly as exciting as the Resistance's former tasks; and, due to this, the ranks had begun to diminish. Perhaps it was also that it was now safer than ever to start a family in Compositora, without the looming threat of government-enacted malice.

On this day, Phoenix was walking around the outside of Resistance HQ, checking up on the nets she'd lain to catch fish. Just as she tightened a knot on one of them, she heard the sounds of another person nearby; she then looked up and noticed Tornado further down the bank, splashing water on his face. The large backpack on his back was impossible to miss.

Against her initial instincts, she began to walk toward him.

"Everything okay?" She asked, when she was close enough to be heard.

He glanced, clearly startled, but recognizing his new companion instantly relaxed. His gaze, though, was fixed to the horizon.

"Lovely sunset this evening. Seems to get more vibrant and colorful the further we get away from our past, huh?"

"Yeah, I noticed," agreed Phoenix. "It feels like everything is more lively these days. The more scholarly members of our ranks are speculating that the magic is returning to our world. It'd explain the newfound green of the grass, as well. Have you noticed it?"

"A sight for sore eyes. Something I never thought I'd see in my own lifetime." With a short nod, Tornado gazed out toward the river. "But I'm sure that's not why you came over."

"Perhaps not," agreed Phoenix. Why *had* she come over? She couldn't say.

"Well, as I said, the world we're experiencing now is something I never thought I'd get to see. With that came a need to re-evaluate my life, because everything has changed so drastically. The plans I'd made for myself up to this point were accustomed to fit into a world that doesn't exist anymore. Thank the goddesses for that, but my point is, Phoenix..." he adjusted the bag on his shoulder. "As I've thought about it more, I cannot ignore the voice that tells me that my story leads me away from here."

The silence between them was less shock than understanding. Phoenix knew she should say something, but she couldn't say she was torn up at this revelation. Logan would probably be happy once she told him, even.

"A favor, if you will."

Tornado stepped closer, holding out a neatly folded, creme-colored envelope, sealed closed with a blue circular stamp. "My resignation letter."

Phoenix hesitated, again. "Why... give this to me?"

"I might be a large and intimidating man, but that doesn't mean I don't get cold feet in certain situations. Would you be able to face the man who, for years, gave you knowledge, hope, and shelter– no, a *home*– and selfishly tell him you'd never see him again?"

A point that Phoenix couldn't debate. "I understand. I'll give it to him tomorrow, then?"

"Would you wait until he asks, specifically?" Tornado asked. "With so much to handle on the restoration front, I don't want to burden him with the answers to questions he didn't ask, even if I am long gone by the time he notices."

"Right." A nod from Phoenix. "Then I'll wait. May the goddesses follow you on your path, Tornado."

"I'm not a part of the Resistance anymore. Anton works." He waved as he began his departure from HQ; from Compositora as a whole. "Thank you. I can only hope that they do."

⁂

"I had no idea that Tornado's allegiance to the Resistance was so emotionally driven," Logan said after a brief silence.

Thunder nodded. "Yeah. He was with us almost from the beginning. He was one of the many people who had lost family at the hands of our former cruel dictator, this being his mother, that– as far as I recall– was the only family he'd had, that had raised him.

They had always been close, so when he lost her... I'm told she was an amazing woman, a force of nature."

"Huh." Logan nodded. "Well, despite my very obvious feelings about the guy, I hope he's found whatever it is he went looking for. Maybe that's what he needs, to not be such a grouch anymore."

"Yes. It feels good to have been a part of what makes it possible for people to go on such journeys of discovery," replied Phoenix.

"Which is why we gotta make tonight count, so they can continue to do that safely. Here we are." Thunder stopped walking, and looked up at the sky. Where the crackles of lightning had been intermittent before the quartet had left headquarters, they now were a part of the layers of yellow and gray; zipping, crackling with an intensity that could fill even some of the most level-headed people with some level of anxiety.

"Whoa. That looks bad."

"You can even feel the electricity in the air," agreed Hunter. Brushing his fingers through his vibrant hair, he added, "It's making my hair practically stand on end."

Phoenix took a look at her own hair, which was starting to frizz, and frowned.

"The sky is the most striking example of things that look bad, but I've just now noticed: look over there, in the forest," Hunter pointed. "Look at the trees in that area. Did they always give off such a sinister aura? That purple... it's almost sickly."

Thunder looked over at the trees. "Now that you mention it..."

While the two men discussed this, Logan turned to his sister. "You're going to be okay, right?" he asked her, his voice low enough that the others couldn't hear.

Phoenix summoned just enough courage to give Logan a sufficient, reassuring big sister smile. "Yes, Logan. Just because it's been a while doesn't mean I've forgotten how to fight! I'm raring to go, honestly."

Logan shrugged. "I'm just saying, if you aren't, no one would hold it against you."

"Who's the older one here, again?"

"*Taylor,*" Logan said firmly, and folded his arms. "You know how important you are to the Resistance. If something, *anything,* doesn't feel right– promise you won't keep pushing yourself, and take it easy? If for no one else, for me?"

"Fine. If it'll calm you down, I promise."

The two siblings shook hands then, the way they always did when agreeing on something; a clap of both of their right hands turned downward, a grasp, a fold so that their hands now faced upward, and a brief but firm squeeze.

"Ah! Would you look at that?" Hunter was looking out at the horizon, readying his shotgun. "It appears to be showtime."

"Oh!" Logan ran up to where his comrade and friend stood, readying his sword. "Well, then, come get some!"

The ground seemed to rumble as the horde of creatures approached. With a visage of steel, Thunder faced them, dual pistols drawn; his fingers flexed as he got ready to unleash fury on the beings that threatened the peace of his home; of *everyone's* home.

At the same time, Phoenix faltered for a moment. It really *had* been a long while since she'd last taken part in serious combat, and these... *things* had been razing the Resistance in a way the organization had never experienced before. Not even when they were being almost directly targeted by a power-crazed dictator. This was indeed beyond anything a regular human could possibly make come to pass...

She remembered then, the days of learning to fight with Logan. When they were children, their grandparents had taught them everything they knew about magic, but thought it wouldn't hurt to impart upon them some physical know-how as well. And so they had both been gifted their weapons: large double-edged swords forged by their great-grandfather at his forge, to be wielded in a similar manner as one would wield a spear. Phoenix still used that same sword today, but Logan had graduated on to a model that separated into two separate swords if need be.

Phoenix was proud of her younger brother. He was smart. Agile. Wielded his weapon with ease.

But could she? Maybe there was a reason she'd taken to medicine and healing magic, aside from her aptitude in the field. Was it because she was inept in battle?

Charging toward the horde, she set out to prove to her thoughts that they were wrong.

And, as it turned out– as Phoenix and Hunter quickly learned firsthand– it wasn't that it was difficult to dispatch whatever these things were. But they were fast; and more importantly, they were numerous. A skillful slice or shot could easily take one down, but that was of little merit when five more could take its place.

"The numbers... the sheer numbers..." Hunter panted as he spoke, after the battle had raged on for at least an hour.

"Yeah. We probably should've mentioned that," Logan replied, himself short of breath as well.

"It's... it's so much..." Phoenix said to herself near breathlessly. She was losing her strength. She meekly sliced at a couple of creatures near her...

...and so they fell, in the opposite direction, revealing a thin figure. Further observation revealed pale skin, freckles, and light green eyes, with black hair fashioned into a stylish pixie cut. They were dressed in all black as well, a strangely neat button-up shirt and skinny jeans, and some kind of bag or pouch carefully secured around their hips, also black.

"We can get them down so long as you don't lose heart," the person said to Phoenix, with a noticeable Irish accent, a small smirk adorning their face. "Let's have at it!"

"Right!" she agreed, gripping the handle of her sword tightly. "Let's do it!"

Both branched off to fight in opposite directions, Phoenix unleashing a beautiful twirl attack that left her on the outskirts of the skirmish. She was able to stop long enough to see the stranger bend back beautifully to avoid a barrage of bullets from Thunder, incapacitating a foe with a well-timed kick, before she decided to rejoin the battle.

"Excellent stuff. We can do this!" Logan cried out. "We can actually do this!"

Logan separated his sword, using it as two to supplement his fast movements. He felt himself narrowly miss a claw from one of his opponents– miraculously ducking just in time– and upon standing upright noticed a fortunate truth.

The battle was won.

"Well, how's that? We won!" Hunter cheered.

"I wouldn't celebrate just yet. It's almost certain that some of them got past us, so let's hope the squad further on in town can make fast work of those," advised Logan.

"Yes, but even so. That was... exhilarating; thanks, in part, to this gentleman here who ensured the hardest blow I took wasn't incapacitating!" Hunter smiled again, turning to the stranger. There was a dark, muddy spot about the size of an adult hand smack in the middle of his shirt, where the blow he was referring to must have occurred.

"Yeah, he's right," agreed Thunder. "You were a valuable ally in this battle; and 'round these parts, we don't go without thanking a man for his work. What can we do to show our gratitude?"

The stranger smirked. "Well, if you insist, you can start by taking note that I'm as much a man as the lass with the impressively large sword here," they replied with a laugh.

"*Oh,*" Hunter and Thunder said in unison, clearly embarrassed. Thunder added, "Well... you know... 'thanking a man' in the infinitive of course..."

Another laugh, this one much louder, accompanied by a graceful short bow. "Spencer-Lynn Cambridge, at your service; a *woman* of eighteen years, and a swordswoman for seven of those."

"Well met– and our deepest apologies," Hunter apologized.

"Ah, no apologies needed. Wouldn't be the first time someone mistook my gender. Won't be the last, I'm sure. So." Spencer-Lynn crossed her arms. "Who do I have the pleasure of meeting?"

Logan grinned then. "Oh! Well, I'm Logan. Nice to meet you! That's Hunter, this is Phoenix, big man over there is Thunder..."

"You don't recognize us." Thunder had cut Logan off.

"I don't. Should I? Don't believe we've met." Spencer-Lynn took a moment to think. "Hm. I don't recall the meeting, unless I've forgotten. Would you mind jogging my memory?"

This response gave everyone pause. How could someone in this town not recognize the Resistance, at this point? On the day of the official rebellion, it was safe to assume the entire population had been in the square. Newspapers had been published. There had to have been town gossip, at the very least. "Were you not in Compositora during the revolt?" asked Phoenix. "Haven't... read a newspaper for the past eight months or so?"

Seeing Spencer-Lynn's blank stare, Logan chimed in. "Hey, excuse us for one second?" he asked politely, putting up a finger, before pulling his friends aside into a huddle.

"Guys," he said, his voice as low as possible, "I am about 110% positive she's not from around here. If we're to consider the common demographics and appearances of this area, she's very pale, and noticeably taller than the women usually are here... and the accent, that's not familiar to me at all. But most pertinently, she's eighteen. Any fighter who's from these parts and is around that age has to have been taught by either Thunder or myself at some point, and her style..."

"...doesn't have any elements of either of yours," finished Phoenix. "I noticed that too. So, now what?"

This was certainly an interesting situation.

"Well, one thing I know we can all agree on: for a foreigner, this is the *worst* possible time to wind up here," pointed out Thunder. "Why don't we try to help her get back home before tomorrow night? That way, she'll avoid having to deal with this nastiness again."

"Sounds reasonable," Phoenix agreed.

"I have no objections to that idea," added Hunter. "Let's do that, then."

With their hasty meeting adjourned, all four members of the Resistance turned to Spencer-Lynn. Feeling a bit uneasy at all the attention, she waved awkwardly, a smile of similar awkwardness creeping onto her expression.

"Thank you kindly for waiting. So, we've been discussing the likelihood that you're not from here," explained Thunder.

Spencer-Lynn looked around. "Ahh. I hadn't given that much thought, but now that I've taken a good look, you may be right. I can't rightly say I'm very sure where 'here' is, but it sure doesn't look much like what I'm used to."

"Well, how'd you get here?" asked Logan. "Maybe that'll help us find the best way to get you back home."

"I... remember waking up underneath a tree, and walking until I saw this area. But... but what was I doing before I got to that tree..? I can't seem to remember anything preceding when I looked up and saw how *creepy* the treetops looked–"

Before she could finish, rain began to pour from the clouds overhead, kicking up dust and loose dirt from the road in the process. "Oh, goddesses, I thought we'd be back by now!" Hunter complained. "We have to go. We have to go *now!*"

Thunder turned to Spencer-Lynn. "C'mon with us, we can get you a warm meal and send you on your way back, but we need to be dry to do it!"

The sun was just beginning to rise as the group of five started to run in the direction of headquarters, Hunter leading the way as he tried to use his scarf to keep his hair dry.

Back at headquarters, Spencer-Lynn was asked to wait in the kitchen while everyone else dashed to their rooms to dry off and change clothes; she was at least given a very warm and very dry robe that she initially hesitated to accept, but then decided it was better than being wet and shivering. While she waited, she tried to understand what about this kitchen felt so odd; it had tables and chairs and cabinets and a stove like any other kitchen, but there was something that seemed to feel uncannily old-fashioned about it. She just couldn't put her finger on it. Maybe it was the lack of a dishwasher?

It wasn't too much longer before everyone returned to check on her, giving her a bowl of food and a glass of water.

"Do you think this will fit?" asked Phoenix, holding out a bundle of dark blue clothes. "Sorry if the clothes we're letting you borrow are a little baggy, but I don't think we have anyone enlisted here that's so thin. I can take your wet clothes."

"Ah– I'll be keeping that, thank you," Spencer-Lynn reached for the crocheted bag she'd had with her, black with speckles of neon colors. "And no problem. The important thing is that I'm dry and clean, and safe of course. Thank you for the bread and chili, Thunder."

"Least I could do." He smiled, proud of his cooking. "Now, not that we're kickin' you out, but you may have noticed while we were out that this town is dealing with a bit of a problem. It's been *that*, every night, for the better part of three weeks, so we understand if you wanna get."

"The good thing is that, if you got here so quickly, your home shouldn't be too far, right?" added Phoenix. "What city are you from?"

"Uh, Belfast."

Phoenix immediately turned to Thunder. "That sounds far."

"That's a–" Logan interrupted, before smiling at Spencer-Lynn and waving. "Hi. I'm so sorry. We need a... moment... again," he explained, pulling the two older adults away.

"She's gonna start thinking you're incapable of talking to her directly if you keep this up," Phoenix laughed. "What's the problem, Logan?"

Logan glanced around before whispering, "She's, she's from the other world."

"She wha–" Thunder said loudly, before Logan shushed him.

"How did she get here?!" Phoenix immediately followed up.

"That I don't know, but I've been studying as much as I can about that world with the books we have here, and I recognize the name of the city she named, it's a major city– one that most people in that world would have heard of."

"Well, ain't this something." Thunder crossed his arms. "Nothing these days is ever simple, is it? And I have a strong feeling that, if we ask, she won't be able to give us any context."

"She probably doesn't even realize that she's in a whole other world, judging by her mannerisms and what she told us outside, so it'd be useless to question her about it," replied Logan.

"Right, that makes sense. Well, then, what *should* we do?" asked Phoenix. "We can't just do nothing. We promised her we'd get her back home before tomorrow night. There's no way we can do that now."

Both siblings instinctively turned to Thunder.

"Well," he said. "I know where to start."

He walked over to where Spencer-Lynn was eating, sitting beside her. "Hey, so, about that promise to get you home. We still will make good on that, trust me; but for various reasons, it's gonna take a little longer than anticipated. I'm afraid you may be here for a few days."

"...Oh." Spencer-Lynn nodded. "You seemed sure of yourself when you first made that promise, so I'm a wee bit concerned about the sudden change; but I'm sure you'll get to explaining that, then. Where am I exactly, anyway?"

"You're..." Thunder paused. "There's someone who can explain it much better than I can. Logan!"

"Right!" Logan walked over, as sunny as usual. "What's up?"

"Our *guest* wants to know where she *is*," replied Thunder, clearly tense.

"Gotcha." Logan nodded, taking a seat opposite Spencer-Lynn. "I have no problem explaining that. It's just... how do I say this? Explaining where you are requires a bit of backstory before I can answer that, so that we don't all sound completely delusional– just as a warning."

"Ah. That weird, hm? I suppose if I'd arrived under different circumstances, I'd be less calm and understanding than I am, but so many weird things have happened since I got here. I can recall that, the moment I regained my wits, I suddenly had this sword beside me. And then there was that... that crowd of... whatever they were. *That* was not normal at all. You said they've been coming every night recently, right?"

"Yeah," replied Thunder. "For the past couple weeks or so."

"Well, then, if it's going to take a few days before I'll be able to go home, I don't suppose you'd object to me continuing to help you dispatch them whilst I'm still here?" suggested Spencer-Lynn.

This was unexpected. "You'd do that?" asked Thunder, not sure what to make of the offer.

"Why not? It's not like I've much else to do, considering I don't even know where the hell I am– oh, right, you were going to tell me that, weren't you?" she asked, turning to Logan. "Carry on, then."

"Right." He nodded, pulling up a chair so that he could make himself comfortable for this somewhat lengthy exposition. "So, as stated before, the explanation requires a bit of a brief history; please bear with me, and don't hesitate to stop me if I lose you so I can re-explain. The land you stand upon was fashioned centuries ago as an ambitious diversion..."

"As the story goes, in the days before our world existed, the goddesses were tasked with keeping watch over the universe."

A vast, sprawling network of stars, galaxies, black holes, and everything in between. To keep this complex system of being flowing in a way that allowed them all to coexist without causing too much trouble for one another meant that there had to be an authority keeping watch over all its proceedings.

"It is a job that all the goddesses take seriously, but even so, you could imagine how monotonous it would get after a while. Although all of the goddesses possess immense power, they weren't using it for their current task, except very rarely. So, that was when it was decided they would take on a... little side project, and so, this world was created, using nothing but their own magic. And that's impressive on its own, but adding another floating sphere to the universe wasn't very thrilling, so they gave this world life, in the ways they knew they could."

Logan took a drink of water before he continued; he hadn't paid attention to the fact that it had been Spencer-Lynn's glass of water, but judging by how intently she was listening to him, she probably hadn't noticed either.

"Aquatica, the goddess that presides over water, created the rivers, lakes, and oceans that decorate our world. With water, so many things can be accomplished; most notably, the cultivation of plant life. The goddess of earth is named Terra, and together the two of them were able to create some of the most stunning and diverse biomes in history. Great things happen when goddesses collaborate, such as the weather system, the next thing to be established when the two aforementioned goddesses collaborated with Vienta, the goddess of wind. There are three more goddesses, but their magic was not quite as pertinent to the creation of the world.

"Anyway, I could go on and on, but the basic gist of it is that the world the goddesses created is where you currently are now. This town is Compositora, the capital of the magic world. It doesn't look like much now, but that's... there's been a fall from grace, a lot has happened here that's not either here nor there at the moment. Do you have any questions so far?"

If Spencer-Lynn could currently see her face, she was confident that it would bear the most nondescript expression it ever had, in her eighteen years of life. "I... I think I now understand that one scene in that cooking movie where they have to tell the guy a rat made his dinner, and at first he's like, 'there's no way a rat made my dinner,' but then he's faced with undisputable evidence that the rat did, in fact, make his dinner. I'm... I'm lost *period*, but I'm especially lost when it comes to understanding what this has all got to do with me in particular."

"I do wish I could help shed some light on that part, but that's where I'm getting stuck too," Logan admitted. "I'm sorry I cannot make things more clear to you."

Spencer-Lynn stood, shaking her head. "It's quite all right. I'd probably be overwhelmed if I learnt everything at once, so I think what you've told me will do for now. Do you mind if I shower? The warm water would be helpful to shake off this dreadful chill."

Only now did Logan realize she still hadn't actually changed out of her wet clothes. "Of course! I'll show you where the nearest bathroom is," he replied, standing as well, and beginning to lead the way.

TWO

A New Frontier

"**S**ee? It looks weird, doesn't it?"

In the middle of her suburban block in the Midwest, fifteen-year-old Jaiden Winchester pointed up at the abnormal trees on her block. Currently, it was June; normally, the trees would be filled with vibrant green leaves, to the point they'd be slightly weighing the branches down with how many there were. The trunks would be their usual melange of browns, maybe with moss creeping up the bark. These trees, in contrast, were devoid of any leaves save one or two dead ones barely clinging to their branches. And where that was a normal sight in, say, December, something that was most certainly *not* a normal sight at *any* time of year was the sickly purple, almost gray color of the trunks. Jaiden almost wanted to say she'd never seen anything like it before, but she had.

Once. Once in a time and a place completely foreign to most other people, in a world composed completely of magic.

Of course, that was the kind of thing that wasn't always easy to explain. Not without making people concerned for one's mental state.

The Winchesters' block was currently throwing a block party, so luckily, it wasn't unusual to be standing around outside right now. It was even more fortunate that Jaiden wasn't alone; she was currently walking back home with her best friend, Mishaela Pagliardi, who she had known since they were both ten years old. Jaiden and Mishaela lived just far apart enough that walking from one's house to the other was uncomfortable if it was too warm outside, but luckily they'd met up at the house of the third person with them; a newer friend of theirs, Lulu Madrigal. She had moved from Michigan sometime around the start of the past school year, and to say she'd become fast friends with Jaiden and *especially* Mishaela wouldn't be exactly incorrect. Lulu's house was close enough to Jaiden's, so they had all met up there. Jaiden had invited the two to the block party, knowing her mother would be eager to cook and show off her food to the neighbors (she had always said it would be the only time they'd get to have seasoned food), but she also knew it would be the best opportunity to show the girls the weird trees on her block without inviting too much scrutiny from her neighbors, who tended to be just a little too nosy for their own good.

"It looks like something out of a video game, doesn't it?" Mishaela agreed, looking up at the dead branches. She had to place a hand just above her eyes so that the sun wouldn't bounce off of her glasses too boldly, but even so, it was clear that this tree was odd.

"Yeah. Hey, Mishaela, you wouldn't happen to have seen anything like this over by you, would you?" Jaiden asked.

"No, this is the first ti–" Mishaela paused, remembering that she, too, had seen this before. "No, I haven't."

"Do you mind if I take a picture?" Lulu asked, pulling out her phone. "One of my... I don't know if I could call her my friend, but one of the cool older girls at my old school was really into botany. Maybe she'll know something about this."

"I seriously doubt that," Jaiden muttered, averting her gaze. Louder, she replied, "Yeah, go nuts. There's no specific time we have to get back to my place. My mom probably is still cooking. For reasons I don't completely know, it apparently takes hours to cook the greens and sweet potatoes."

"Well, they're good, so she can take all the time she needs," Mishaela replied, as the three continued down the block.

It was hot today, so everyone that was outside for the block party was dressed in shorts and skirts and flowy sundresses. Jaiden hadn't bothered to dress up or anything, throwing on a purple and gray T-shirt with a swirly sun on the front, and a pair of blue denim shorts. Mishaela, on the other hand, wore a pink shirt with golden beads sewn on randomly and a cream-colored layered skirt. And then there was Lulu, never without the color black (in this case it was her oversized short-sleeved shirt with some watercolor art on it, her denim distressed skirt, and her knee-high Converse), but she at least wore a neon orange tank top under the shirt for a pop of color. Jaiden wasn't sure how she was comfortable with layers in this weather, but that just seemed to be a specific trait of the emo, scene, and goth kids at school. After all, if Chiara– Mishaela's older sister, whose wardrobe had to be at least 80% black– had been with them, she'd have probably worn a similar outfit.

When the trio finally made it to the Winchester residence, both of Jaiden's parents were outside setting up their table of food. Jaiden's older sister Violet was also in town, visiting from Canada, so she was helping with the preparations when they came into earshot. Violet usually garnered attention because she was a volleyball player, so she was very toned, and had a more muscular build than her other siblings, even the one brother. Her wavy brown hair had been past her waist the last time Jaiden had seen her, but she'd evidently had it cut to her shoulders recently, which seemed to accentuate the blue of her eyes.

"Hope you didn't eat all the cornbread, Vi," Jaiden said with a laugh.

She laughed as well in return, placing the platter on the table. "If you guys take too long to get a piece, I can't make any promises. Hi, Mishaela... and someone who I don't think is Chiara..?"

"You may be underwhelmed by her height if you actually see my sister before we leave," Mishaela laughed. "This is Lulu. She's one of our friends, one of our classmates. Lulu, this is Jaiden's sister Violet."

"Oh." Lulu nodded, visibly confused, before smiling. "Hi. It's a pleasure to meet you."

"You too." Violet gave her a nod. "Are the three of you okay with watching the table for a bit? The red beans and rice are also ready, so I wanted to go back and grab that too."

Jaiden shrugged. "What else are we here for?"

"Exactly! Be back in a jiffy."

"I was being sarcastic, but okay." Jaiden said when Violet had gone back into the house. "Lulu, are you okay? You look a little confused."

"Well, yeah, I was. She's... *white*," Lulu said hesitantly. "I've met your mom before, so it took me by surprise; but adoption exists, so I didn't want to be weird about it. I am probably *totally* being weird about it. Sorry. Can we start over?"

"No, it's fine! My family's not exactly nuclear, so I'm used to having to explain," Jaiden reassured her. "Basically, all my older siblings had a white mom, but then she passed away and my dad married my mom. That's why all my siblings are so much older than me, like Vi is the youngest of them and she's already twenty-five. I guess I was kind of an oopsie," she chuckled.

It was then that Jaiden's mother walked out with a pan of boiled corn cobs, smiling when she saw the group at the table. She was wearing a lovely yellow and green sundress, her dark hair with very few strands of gray pulled into a high ponytail puff. Mrs. Winchester had always been very good at making everything she wore look elegant, or at least, that was Mishaela's assessment of the past five years she'd known her. "Hi, Mishaela, Lucero. No Chiara today?"

"Not this time. She would have loved to come–" this was a lie, Chiara's social anxiety meant she hated events like block parties– "but she had prior obligations. There's some paperwork to file regarding our trip in a couple of weeks, so she needs to be able to translate a few things for our mother," Mishaela explained her sister's absence. "We'll be in Italy for a month, if Jaiden hasn't already mentioned it. If it's okay, may I take her a plate?"

"I didn't know your sister liked soul food," Jaiden said.

"She's partial to the ribs and macaroni," Mishaela explained. "The cornbread is too good to say no to, as well."

"Ribs and macaroni really are a match made in heaven," agreed Lulu.

Jaiden couldn't disagree. It was one of her favorite comfort meals.

"Of course it's okay, you let James and Maurizia know I said hello too. It's already time for you all to go on your trip, huh..." she trailed off as she went back inside.

"Don't mind her. She's started doing that lately," Jaiden waved it off. "Some old people habit, I guess. So anyway, now that you guys have seen those trees... I mean, it's weird, isn't it? And what strikes me as weirder is that everybody else on our block just kinda... doesn't notice it? Like, I have a few neighbors that go jogging in the morning, there's this one elderly couple who like to go on a walk together around 5 p.m. And the few times I've been by the window to see them pass, no one has looked twice. Part of the reason I asked you guys over here is so I could be sure I wasn't slowly losing it."

"Well, you aren't," Lulu reassured her. "We definitely see it. It's strange, even your sister and mom don't seem to notice. I wonder, is there something that can be done about it?"

Jaiden and Mishaela exchanged a look. If there was, it wouldn't be easy... and probably not pleasant, either. How would one even go about communicating with the magic world? Now that Jaiden was recalling the adventure, she realized something: the people of that world seemed to have their methods of reaching this world, but it didn't appear to work the other way around. *That* certainly wasn't fair. Why hadn't she dug deeper for more information about how all that worked? She probably could've nagged Logan into secretly explaining it to her. It was a youngest sibling talent; but, then again, Logan was also a youngest sibling, so he was probably immune to it. That was just how it worked, after all.

Coming back to reality, Jaiden noticed Mishaela and Lulu talking about... she couldn't hear what because they were just far enough that the words weren't reaching her, but she was able to notice the more-than-amiable body language between the two. Honestly, at this point, Jaiden was half hoping they'd just declare their undying love for one another already, but she also knew that the situation was more complicated than that. Unless something had changed in the past three years, Mishaela wasn't out to her parents; it was something that, culturally, she wasn't sure they would be accepting of, even with her still being attracted to men as well. And back when Jaiden was still trying to parse the vibes that radiated from Lulu, they'd been in gym class one day where she'd boldly said, "I know it's 2013 and all, but do you think it's that much easier to be a lesbian with immigrant parents these days?"

So now the problem wasn't whether or not they were attracted to one another, since they clearly were. All it took was one look at them interacting to see that. Now, all Jaiden had to do was come up with an idea that ensured the parents involved never found out... or find some way to make the cultural shift of accepting LGBT+ people happen faster in the Italian and Filipino communities, but the first one sounded a lot easier.

But now... now, as she noticed her mother bringing out the remainder of the block party food, Jaiden decided that dating and magic and all of that could wait a few minutes while she enjoyed her cornbread and macaroni.

On this particular day, the sun shone brightly as teenager Gavin Harplein mused to himself how funny it was that a couple of weeks had completely changed his plans for the summer. He had never really cared too much about things in the United States. He had perhaps considered visiting a few cities there, to see a few iconic landmarks and try the (notoriously trash, but in a comforting way) food. But other than that, it was never a country he'd have made a big deal about wanting to go to, let alone have made plans to go anytime soon.

Perhaps that was why the adults in his life had always warned him to never say never. After all, just eight months ago he'd experienced a literal life-changing event.

Those eight months ago, in October, Gavin had been coming home from school one day when he'd felt a strong, unfamiliar energy that had made his hair stand on end. When he had arrived home, it was empty, which was highly unusual; between his parents, the help, and his four younger siblings, there was usually always someone at home. It was when he'd opened his closet to hang his uniform that he had been whisked away into a magical world, to be sent upon a quest of rectification.

He had landed in this world with four Stateside fellow teenagers, and together they helped the native population overthrow an unjust dictator. They spent a considerable amount of time together (about half a month if he had to guess, but it had been difficult to keep track of time in this world) and grew close. Gavin had never had many friends in his day-to-day life; when he returned home, he became lonely, and started looking for ways to reunite with what were possibly the best friends he had ever known in his fifteen years.

When he got to the stage where he needed to question his parents about it, he learned that he actually had quite a few relatives that lived in the United States. One in particular– his aunt Maura– lived in New York, which was quite convenient. After much pleading with his parents, and promises that he'd be on his best behavior, Gavin's parents consulted his aunt, and conceded: if he finished year nine with good marks, he could not only visit, but stay for the whole summer.

And that was why and how, currently, Gavin was sitting in his aunt's apartment in the company of his good friend Jasiela, one of the girls who had led the rebellion with him. Unfortunately, she was the only one who lived in this particular city; but ever since the first time they'd been able to meet up, amidst their trips to the iconic parts of the city that Gavin insisted on seeing in person, they'd been putting their heads together to try and find a way to spend time with their remaining friends.

There was the day they went to Times Square, and Gavin was uncannily excited to try a hot dog from one of the nearby street vendors. His verdict was that it wasn't bad, but it was something he could live without ever eating again.

There was the day they strolled through Central Park, which had also been the day that Gavin had met Jasiela's parents. It had been an awkward meeting due to the noticeable language barrier, but there hadn't been any hostility at least. Gavin knew enough Spanish to know that Jasiela had explained to them that he was visiting from England, but that was where it had ended. This was also what had convinced him that, if he and Jasiela were going to convince someone to let them go to Chicago, it would have to be his aunt. It would be too difficult to get the message across if only one of them would be able to explain the situation.

They'd also gone to see the Statue of Liberty with all the adults and a couple of Jasiela's siblings present, but by the time both Gavin and Jasiela had worked up the nerve to begin speaking to the adults about their idea, one of the smaller Alfaro children had broken something, stealing all the attention for the remainder of the trip.

This wasn't going well, so far.

Gavin folded his hands in his lap, staring at the small red nicks from when he and his aunt had taken a weekend trip to Boston and he'd cut his hands on crab and lobster shells a few times as he tried to eat them. Worth it. He knew he'd changed since the last time everyone had seen him; he was a little taller, his brown, wavy hair was longer, and he was beginning to fill out somewhat too. *So this was what it means to mature*, he often found himself thinking. He was shocked to find out that Jasiela hadn't changed very much at all, still as small and fashionable as ever. The pearl-colored, short-sleeved peplum dress she'd worn today was more stylish than anything he'd seen back home. Then again, with going to an all-boys school, he didn't get a lot of chances to see girls' fashion choices, and of course he couldn't expect his mother and his twelve-year-old sister to be too stylish.

"I found it!" Jasiela yelled, running into the room. "The train timetables! My dad had them!"

Gavin smiled. "That's brilliant! Let's have a look."

They both eagerly scanned the list of destinations.

"It looks like a cheap ticket to Chicago is $75 per person," Jasiela said, sighing. "That means: even if only the two of us go without an adult, which is already highly unlikely, we're already at $150 before taxes. That's also before food, lodging, or any incident coverage. Gavin..." her face straight, she continued, "I have 34 dollars."

Somehow, they were both still able to find that funny, and so they laughed together.

"I don't have very much more to spend," Gavin told her. "My parents didn't trust me to not spend too much here, so they gave me a rather small allowance– one that's heavily regulated by Aunt Maura. As disheartening as this is, it needs to go in the presentation."

For the past week, the two had been working together to put together a presentation so convincing that none of the adults involved could possibly refuse to let them ride the train to Chicago. Jasiela had been researching the more logistic part of the plan, since she was more familiar with the country, and Gavin was tasked with making everything sound as convincing as possible. The very last piece of information they had needed was the price of the train ticket, which both decided they should cross-reference between the current printed prices and online prices, just in case there was a discrepancy. Luckily, there didn't seem to be. With this update, Gavin reached for his laptop, which was currently sitting on the nightstand beside his bed. The presentation would soon be complete!

Jasiela thought then, as Gavin powered on his laptop. "Speaking of Miss Harplein, have you talked this over with her yet?" she asked. "Maybe she can help us out, right? She seems really cool and understanding. Maybe she can talk to your dad..."

"No." Gavin cut her off, vigorously shaking his head. "I don't want this going back to him."

"So dramatic. Fine, be a coward. *I'll* go talk to her then." Jasiela was determined, if nothing else. She stood and turned on her heel, rather dramatically herself, her dark brown hip-length hair swishing as she walked away.

Now that Gavin was alone in what was his room for the summer, he took a good look around, focusing on the peach-tinted drapes over the window before having a thought; he placed his laptop on the bed beside him, reaching under the bed and pulling out the chess set he'd brought along. This was a set his parents had gotten him as a present for turning fifteen; the board was a typical wooden board, nothing outstanding, but the pieces had been carved from stone. Since it seemed like Jasiela would be gone for a bit, he set the board up, carefully staring at the pieces. He liked to do this, to see if he could still remember where all the pieces went.

If only I had an opponent.

As he set the board up, he felt the familiar brush of soft fur against his legs, and reached down to offer pets. "Did I disturb you? Were you under the bed this whole time, Butter?"

The black-and-orange cat purred as Gavin continued to pet her. When he'd first arrived, Butter hadn't liked him very much; perhaps he was too foreign, or too different from the usual company in this apartment. And while he wouldn't say that she particularly liked him now, they'd at least gotten to the point where their interactions didn't consist completely of her swatting at him.

Jasiela walked back into the room coolly after a while, making Butter flee from the room in the process. "Oh, sorry, Butter," she said. "Your aunt must have gone out for a sec, she's not in her room or the kitchen. Oh, you're staring at your chess set again."

Do I do it so much that she felt the need to add that "again?"

"I'll play with you, if you want," she then volunteered.

Gavin had attempted to play chess with Jasiela, once. She had a hard time remembering the rules, though, and got frustrated and quit before the game could get started. "I'd rather not," was his reply.

"Probably best for both of us," agreed Jasiela, to which Gavin nodded as well. "I just... can't get into it. Have you been practicing back home, though?"

"Yeah, my dad knows how to play. Beats me mercilessly every time." Gavin chuckled.

"Better than Mishaela?"

"I couldn't say; you know she went easy on me the whole time," replied Gavin.

Mishaela, after all, was the person who had taught Gavin how to play chess while they were planning the rebellion (actually, it was the way they'd won the rebellion– but that would be much too long a story to get into here).

"Don't start giving me the silent treatment." Jasiela folded her arms.

"I didn't intend to; I was lost in thought for a moment. It's just..." Gavin sighed. "I miss her, you know? I miss Jaiden and Madeline too. Even though it wasn't very long, the time when we were all together is very special to me. It's something I look back on fondly... something I've been striving to replicate, you know?"

"I know." Jasiela nodded. "Think of it this way: by being able to be here in New York, you've already gotten the hardest part of that ambition out of the way. You're closer now than you ever have been; now, we only need to come up with a way to travel a relatively short distance. We can do it. We're smart."

"You're right," agreed Gavin. "I think I may have the start of another idea, if our presentation falls flat. What about if we–"

They didn't have time to drive that train of thought any farther, as just then, Gavin's Aunt Maura returned home, placing some bags on the dining room table before coming into the bedroom. She was a tall woman with wild red hair, always dressed in funky colors and patterns; today it was a short-sleeved jumpsuit in assorted neons. The more boring members of Gavin's family didn't speak favorably of her odd clothes and lack of partner and/or children at the age of 39, but these things were part of why Gavin had quickly started to adore her; he admired the strength with which she dared to be different.

"I'm back; the milk went bad, so I had to go pick up some more. Jasiela, dear, it's about time for you to be setting off, isn't it?" she asked. "Unless you'll be staying for dinner."

"So soon?" asked Gavin.

"Yeah. Takes a while from here to get back to my neighborhood, and I usually wanna get home before it starts getting weird outside," Jasiela replied, standing. "Can I stay for dinner, Miss Harplein? And maybe for the night even? I do enjoy the silence of your apartment."

"You know you're always a joy to have over," replied Maura, a radiant smile on her face. "Will your parents be all right with you staying over, though? And what will you wear tomorrow, you didn't pack a change of clothing, or any pajamas."

"I did. The very specific circumstances of my life have taught me to pack extra clothes no matter where I go," Jasiela explained. "My parents probably won't even realize I'm gone. Plus, I need to be here. Me and Gavin have been working on something very important, and I think it's just about ready. Isn't it, Gavin?"

Gavin looked up abruptly, having temporarily zoned out. "Yes, absolutely! Are you busy, Aunt Maura? We've got something we'd like to share with you."

After helping Maura put the few groceries she's bought away, Gavin and Jasiela were ready to give their presentation. It took some creative maneuvering on their end because there was a lack of wall space to project the screen onto, but in the end, this was doable with the blackout curtains in the living room. And so, after a few obligatory moments of fiddling with (and subsequently, cursing) technology, and of course the popping of popcorn, the slideshow was ready to go. Jasiela turned the lights off, and pointed to signal to Gavin that it was time to begin.

"Hello and welcome to 'Get Jasiela and Gavin To Chicago For Summer 2013,' a presentation by... us, Gavin Harplein and Jasiela Alfaro. At the end of this demonstration, the two of us are fairly confident we'll have made a case that's impossible to disagree with."

Maura pointed to the screen. "It's available in English and Span-ish?"

"What?" Jasiela, now at the other side of the screen, then noticed the sticker in the corner that clearly stated, "disponible en español." "Oh. Yeah, see, about that. When we first started making this, the idea was to present it to you and my parents at the same time, but with the way that their work schedules are set up, we had to accept that it wouldn't be happening that way. Gavin added slides after that so they're not all translated, and I don't have notes for them all, so please don't expect me to do this in Spanish. It would be extremely embarrassing."

The two began their presentation then, starting with an expertly crafted story about how they'd met their friends in Chicago. This had been possibly the most difficult part of the entire thing, because it had to be believable to those who knew the two. After some debate and a lot of scrapped ideas, the explanation chosen was that, initially, Jasiela and Madeline had become friends via fashion; Jasiela being enticed to her out-there sense of style, and then being casually introduced to her friends. Gavin had actually formed a friendship with Chiara online after Mishaela had introduced them, so they were able to use that as part of the story as well. It was a tale that was cosmic enough that it fell into the realm of possibility, with how cosmic life could be sometimes.

(But as they were explaining this, Gavin wondered– was it necessary to be so secretive with his aunt? Maura was just odd enough that, if they'd explained the magic world to her, she may just believe them.)

Following the origin story was the appeal to both logic and emotion as the presentation became persuasive, as convincing as possible, laying out costs for travel, lodging, and food. It was Gavin's hope that, even though neither he nor Jasiela could currently afford any of these things, the inclusion of expenses would show a level of responsibility that relayed to his aunt that he– that both of them– could be trusted, that they weren't just two kids with crazy ideas.

The silence following the presentation seemed to have its own menacing sound, somehow.

"As I'm sure you're aware, this does bring up a few worries for me," Maura finally said as she grabbed some popcorn from the large white bowl on the couch with her. "Most of these are regarding parental permissions. I am responsible for you, Gavin, and I can't say I like the idea of Thomas berating me if something goes wrong. But... it does make me think about the fact that, before you were entrusted to me, I was going to take a little trip."

The two teens exchanged a hopeful look. "A trip?" asked Gavin, trying not to sound too oddly expectant.

"Yes; you see, during my time here in the States I've made quite a few friends in all sorts of places, but I haven't had the opportunity to travel as much as I'd like," explained Maura. "And that seems to be par for the course for many Americans as well. One friend in particular– oh, she's such a sweet young lady, I've missed her– nearing her thirties and yet hasn't ever left her hometown. And so she'd come up with an interesting idea: if I were to permit her to stay here, in my humble abode, in exchange I would get to stay a while in her charming Midwest home."

"Oh!" Gavin nodded.

"Where exactly is it located, if you don't mind me asking?" asked Jasiela.

"I can show you pictures." Maura wasted no time in pulling up some pictures on her phone. "It's in Chicago. Just look at this charming bungalow. The large windows let in a lot of natural light, I'm told, and the kitchen is just divine! So whilst it would be convenient, the deal didn't entail bringing two extra charges along. And, Jasiela, how do you know your parents would be all right with this if you've yet to ask them?"

"My parents would definitely be okay with it!" Jasiela quickly added. "That's just how it is in big families like ours, you just kinda… take off and be safe, and there's never any hard feelings about it, I insist."

"But across the country? I wouldn't object to bringing you along, but you need to be sure to actually ask your parents," Maura replied cautiously, in a very Responsible Adult way. "I can ask my friend if she's content with the idea, but I don't want either of you getting your hopes up, all right? It's very possible that she says no. Not everyone is comfortable with the idea of having unknown teenagers in their home."

Gavin and Jasiela exchanged a look before the former replied, "Of course."

"Good. Now, why don't the two of you rest for a while, and I'll start dinner?"

As Gavin trudged back to his room, he could only sigh. Had they failed, after how hard they'd worked on that presentation? How convincing he'd been as he spoke to his aunt? He thought they understood each other, but now, he was back at square one.

Jasiela turned to him, noticing his silence. "We're not giving up yet, are we?"

His response was to give her a clever, slightly mischievous smirk. "Absolutely not."

THREE

For Which We'd Move Mountains

I t had been two days since the fight at the edge of the village, and Thunder was still trying to wrap his head around why Spencer-Lynn was there. He'd have perhaps understood if the Resistance had been graced with a repeat visit from one of the kids from last time. But someone completely new to the world? There was this faint, yet very foreboding feeling in the back of his mind that this and the appearance of the vile creatures the Resistance had been facing were connected somehow... and he couldn't help but also feel that this meant there was worse yet to come.

For now, at least, things seemed to be calm. Too calm, given how the past few weeks had been, but Thunder didn't dare contest it. He'd gladly accept the time to breathe.

Spencer-Lynn had adjusted well, considering the situation, and had taken to helping the Resistance around the base whenever there weren't any battles going on. She had no problem taking on cooking sometimes; the entirety of the Resistance was rapidly falling in love with her baked goods, especially if they were sweet. She'd also been lending her sword skills, which everyone had been grateful for. Another pair of helping hands was rarely if ever discouraged in this organization. And all it cost the Resistance were plenty of questions, sometimes in rapid succession, as she tried to discern whether she *actually* believed she was in a different world.

"Hunter, are you the gentleman that I'd speak with about an... observation?" she was asking, as she walked with the taller man.

"That depends. What sort of observation?"

"I've been after trying to find out what makes those things we've been fighting feel so... off. I know, I know, their strength and their forms and their faces and their general crustiness, but there was something else that seemed strange, independent of all that. I realized what it was, last night."

"Oh?" Hunter cast a quick look at her.

"Whenever one of 'em is slain– even when it's a cut dealt with such force that it slices the bastard right in half– there has not been a speck of blood spilled. There's no type of innards that fly out at all, now that I think about it. It's just a.. a cloud of dust or something. Is that normal here?" asked Spencer-Lynn, tacking the question on at the end, realizing nothing about these circumstances was exactly *normal.*

Hunter stopped in his place, mulling over the question. "I never noticed that until now."

"Never? Really?" asked Spencer-Lynn.

"Never. You've given me a lot to think about." Hunter began to walk again, catching up to her. "The Resistance has never been in the business of killing, at least not since I've been here with the exception of that one time, so I can't say from experience whether or not that's normal. But just based on the way that a body– you know, any type of corporeal form– works, one would think there'd need to be something inside in order for it to function... I... I would need to research that to know for sure, though."

"I'm sure that– provided yousins aren't pulling my leg about this– the presence of magic complicates things," Spencer-Lynn said then.

"I... I would guess so." Hunter nodded. "You know, it's funny. Even with all your questions, you're still a lot less skeptical than someone in your position would normally be."

"Who said I wasn't skeptical, lad?" Spencer-Lynn asked, smirking. "But at the moment, we're not yet at a place where my skepticism would be resourceful or useful. Regardless of anything I ask you, the reality is that I can't get home until you're out of dire straits, aye? And I'd imagine the situation at hand would also impede your ability to give complete answers."

Hunter nodded. "Oddly reasonable. Not the level of rationality I'd expect from an eighteen-year-old."

"Eh. Well." Spencer-Lynn shrugged. "So I guess I'm not the first, then."

"The first?"

"It's just... the way you said I was less skeptical than someone in my position would normally be. It sort of implies this isn't the first time some unsuspecting person was pulled into this... wherever this is," explained Spencer-Lynn. "Is this something you have experience with?"

"Well. I, uh..." Hunter stammered a bit before replying, "It's just that... less than a year ago, we had a similar phenomenon happen, but even that... the small differences in it are what confuses me still about your arrival. You see, last time, we were more or less made aware that there would be an odd occurrence happening, because we were all but at the end of our rope, dealing with our dictator predicament."

"Right, right. Logan told me about that little excursion," agreed Spencer-Lynn, nodding. "Well, don't hurt yourself over it. We can get to it when it's more important."

"Of course. We are all very grateful for the trust you've put into us, Spencer-Lynn. I feel confident speaking for us all when I say that as soon as all our resources are not being consumed by this predicament, we will make good on our promise to get you home," Hunter said, a determination in his voice that wasn't there before. "I think I need to talk to our leader about all of this; will you excuse me?"

"Go on ahead," Spencer-Lynn waved before the two parted ways.

Hunter continued on to Thunder's room, but noticed he wasn't there, so he started to head toward one of the common areas. On the way, he was stopped by Lisandra.

"Oh! Hunt, have you seen Thunder at all?!" she asked, frantic.

"No, I was just looking for him. I can confidently say he's not in his room; I was just now there," replied Hunter. "Is something wrong, Lisandra? You look a bit frazzled."

"Well... about that," Lisandra pensively brushed her hair back. "I don't know if I should tell you. Thunder has been kinda secretive about the whole thing, so I'm not sure how many people he wanted exposed to the whole... you know what, never mind. Get over here, follow me."

Hunter stared after her before going to catch up.

"So, there was one special patient Thunder was personally keeping an eye on," Lisandra was saying as she approached the door. "We had them right over here in this room. As you'll immediately notice..."

She twisted the doorknob, pushing the door open.

"There's no one here."

Hunter nodded. "Your reaction to the situation tells me there's more to this than an overzealous patient getting up sooner than they should. What exactly... what was it that made this person 'special?'"

"Well, you see..." started Lisandra. "That's kind of a long story."

Thunder was busy walking around just outside the Resistance's base– the courtyard area, right before where Logan usually trained new recruits– when he heard the unmistakable sound of footsteps. He abruptly turned around, alert, and was confused by the absence of anything that could make such noises. Maybe the current situation was making him more jumpy than usual? He accepted that as an explanation, and turned back around.

He then motioned to continue walking, and immediately found himself tripping over something when he'd tried to continue on, falling to the ground with a surprised yelp and a thud.

"What in the fresh hell..." he muttered to himself once he sat up, shaking his head.

"Ow... hm?" he heard a voice say behind him.

Thunder turned, still confused, until he looked down and noticed a small, chubby person with fair skin and a head of long, straight blonde hair. "You!" he pointed. "You're awake?"

Sitting across from Thunder was the very girl he'd rescued from the river. The manner in which she sat was as if nothing unusual had happened in the past few days.

"Awake..? Yes, I am now..." she replied distantly, sounding disoriented if nothing else. It was easy to see that her cerulean eyes had yet to comprehend where she was, or maybe even *who* she was. "But how did I get here..."

"I can answer that. You were brought here by yours truly." Thunder turned to her, sitting in a more comfortable position. "A few days ago, I caught a glimpse of you, just as you went fallin' into the river not far from here. I'd have never been able to live with myself if I didn't do anything, so I was the one to dive in after you, fish you out, and take you to the nearest safe area. That'd be where you are right now."

"So I've been asleep for a few days..." the girl said in response. "I see. As for me being here, in this specific spot, I... remember waking up and walking down here, but I guess I needed more rest, and curled up right here for a nap. The grass here is nice and soft."

"It is," agreed Thunder. The grass had been growing back so well that this probably wouldn't be the last time someone would be napping here. He made a mental note to warn everyone to tread carefully here, from now on.

"Oh! I guess I should've said this first, but thank you for saving me. Saving me and housing me for a few days, it seems. My name is Brecken." The girl smiled nervously, not knowing how else to express her gratitude.

Thunder returned her smile. "Nice to meet ya, Brecken. You can call me Thunder. Now, help an old man out here; do you remember how you got near that river in the first place?"

"Hm..." Brecken had to think about that. "Not at the moment. I'm sorry."

"Ah. Well, you *did* just wake up. Guess we shouldn't expect everything to immediately come back. For now, why don't we get back inside? You're probably hungry, and a good meal will probably help bring it all back."

"Yes, thank you." Brecken stood, dusting off her clothes. She was quite short for a young woman, shorter than even Lisandra, although having a similar build. Thunder felt a bit sad seeing her;

a strange, familiar feeling knocked at his chest, creating pangs of longing for times long past. He wasn't sure why...

Thunder pushed the sliding glass door of the back room open, and they walked inside. "I should tell you more about where you are, shouldn't I? This is the headquarters of Compositora's Resistance. Our role has rapidly changed over the past few months, so while I can't really say exactly what it is that we do, we've lately been focusing on restoration, education, and self-defense training for residents in the general area. We also do some general protection work–"

"Thunder, there you are!" Lisandra pointed a finger at him, before she and Hunter approached. "We have a situa... oh, it looks like you've already noticed."

"This is Brecken," Thunder said, nodding toward her. "We're gonna get some food, water, and rest in her system, and hope that helps bring back the memories of the river. Either of y'all free to cook?"

"Sorry," Lisandra shrugged. "The only reason I was running around here trying to find you, was because this was part of my beat. I gotta get back to everyone else under my care."

"I'm afraid I'm on the busy side as well, but when you're free, may I have a word?" Hunter added. "Something's been brought to my attention, and I think it'll have an impact on the strategies I draft based on what we conclude from it."

"Yeah, sure. Remind me later, though," Thunder pointed a finger. "With everything going on, I've been prone to forgettin' things."

"Certainly." Hunter nodded. "Please enjoy your stay here, Brecken."

"Thank you," she replied as she followed Thunder on.

"That there's Hunter, our organization's main strategist," Thunder explained. "He's an avid reader, and he's got a keen eye for observation, so he's well suited to that kind of job. The girl with him was Lisandra, one of our medics. She's not an official member of our ranks; she's the younger cousin of our head medic, and volunteered to come help us out for the time being. Normally we wouldn't have such a young kid working here, but the circumstances are special with her."

"Oh." Brecken *had* wondered why she'd looked so much younger than everyone else.

"Kitchen's this way. If we're lucky, there'll be something delicious cooking," continued Thunder. "You usually can smell– oh, and there it is."

There it was, the enticing scent of food being cooked that often enveloped the above-ground floor of headquarters. It never failed to make heads turn and stomachs growl; it was definitely having that effect on Thunder, who couldn't remember if he'd eaten anything today.

"It smells like... bread?" guessed Brecken. "Freshly baked bread. I would recognize that anywhere; it's one of my favorite things to smell cooking."

"Yeah," agreed Thunder, picking up his pace. He'd been trying to hide it, but now he was almost voraciously hungry, and the smell of fresh bread was enticing enough to make him hurry on.

"...and so, the best way to do that is to add the rest of the seeds after the dough solidifies more. That way, you ensure that they stay at the top, on the crust; but they still adhere enough to get you that picturesque finished product."

Standing together at one of the ovens of the kitchen were Logan and Spencer-Lynn; they were doing some sort of baking tutorial, if Thunder had to hazard a guess. Hopefully, one that concluded with plenty of extra bread...

"Oh, Thunder!" Logan waved. "You're just in time for food. Who's the small one?"

"This is Brecken. She's the young lady that's been sleeping for the better part of the week," explained Thunder.

Logan turned to her, the dots immediately connecting in his mind. "Oh! In that case, welcome back to the land of the living!" he grinned. "I'm Logan; it's nice to meet you."

"Spencer-Lynn. It's a pleasure." She gave a short wave. "What happened, exactly? Thunder hasn't been too generous with re-counting that tale."

"Well, probably because I wasn't all that sure myself," he pointed out. "Why don't we, uh, help ourselves to some of that bread there, and see what we can hammer out?"

"Sounds like a plan," agreed Logan. "Have a seat. I'll prepare the accompanying bowls of soup."

When Logan placed the warm, simmering bowl of soup in front of Brecken, she inhaled deeply, the aromatic garlic, ginger, and a few other indistinguishable spices filling her senses with a sensation of warmth. Not that she was necessarily cold before, but it was like the soup was giving her what could possibly be the most warm hug of her life. There were tiny, round pasta shapes floating in the broth, along with some spinach leaves, corn, and what she was pretty sure was chicken; but, it may have been turkey as well.

Once everyone had received their food, Thunder began to speak. "So, from what I remember, I was walking one day, when I could sense the presence of somebody around me. I turned around with enough time to see this one–" he gestured toward Brecken– "near the river, looking kinda disoriented, dazed even. Just when I decided to head that way to see what was happening, she fell into the water. The funny thing about it is that I know it took me around two minutes to close the gap between where I was standing, and the depths of the river where she'd fallen. By all means, she shouldn't have survived that."

"Well, what do *you* remember?" asked Logan, turning to Brecken.

"I do remember falling," replied Brecken slowly. "I remember… everything is still so fuzzy, but I think it's because my vision itself was really hazy at the time. It was… it was the strangest feeling I'd ever felt. Like I was fading in and out of existence, almost, as dramatic as that sounds– and I know you're probably skeptical of such a claim, but that's as best as I can put it into words."

"Well, it's good you're feeling all right now," Logan said with a smile. "And now that you are, we can work on getting you back home. Being on the opposite side of the river suggests that you must be from somewhere near the City of Emerald, or Hartsaille maybe. Whereabouts should we be getting you back to?"

When Brecken was quiet for an extended amount of time, Logan followed up with, "Do you... remember where you're from?"

"No, no, it's not that– I just... it's only now sunk in that... I don't think where I am is where I was before. You see, I'm pretty sure that, before my vague memories of the river, I was vacationing in the Bay Area with my parents."

At that, Spencer-Lynn looked up. "The Bay Area. That's... San Francisco-y? That American city with the trolleys, aye?"

Brecken nodded. "Yes. Your reaction has me worried."

"Well, it's not that you should be worried. Just..." Spencer-Lynn hesitated, "it may take a wee bit before you're able to get back there."

"Logan will explain," added Thunder, nudging him.

"I will? I mean, yes! Yes, well," he started. "It requires a backstory. And it's going to take a while. You may want to finish eating first, so your soup won't be cold."

The group ate for no more than a minute before the crashing of the kitchen door against the wall caught all of their attention. "Captain!" A man who looked to be in his early 20s ran up to the table frantically, so quickly that when he finally stopped, the motion made his hat fly off of his head, revealing curly dark brown hair. "A word?"

"Uh, sure," Thunder nodded. "Carry on, y'all. I'll be back."

"Roger that," Logan waved. "Right. So, where to start? This place in which you find yourself is not, uh, any place you're probably assuming it is. It all started one day, thousands of years ago…"

Meanwhile, Thunder followed the man to a quieter area just outside the kitchen, and asked, "What's going on, and how bad is it?"

"Oh, it's bad." The man nodded. "Earlier, we received reports that the plumbing in the market area was down somehow, so Finn and Etzel took a small squad to assist with repairs. But I've just heard that halfway through, as golden hour approaches… we don't know how, but the area was swarmed by those strange mutant creatures."

"What?!" asked Thunder. "That's the complete opposite side of town from where they've been invading, and much earlier too…"

"The men we have there are holding on, with the aid of some of the villagers, but the attack worsened the plumbing situation—so that now, the battle area is flooding. We sent a few more reinforcements quickly, but we also knew we should await an official order on what to do next," the man finished. "I came over as soon as possible, and I can be ready immediately."

"Holy hell." Thunder sighed. "Good job on the reinforcements. Suit up, Handel. Tell everyone on your floor to do the same, and head for the area as soon as your preparations are complete; don't wait for me."

"Got it!" Handel nodded before running off.

With that settled, Thunder hurried back into the kitchen, where the three younger ones were eating their soup and bread, laughing at something. He sighed softly, having a distant thought about how young they all were, before steeling his gaze and drawing into earshot. "Logan, Spencer-Lynn, grab your weapons. We need to go, now."

"Oh. Whoa. Hey. What's happening?" asked Logan, noticing the shift in Thunder's mood.

"There's an attack on the plaza. Too many innocent people live in that area for us to hesitate," replied Thunder. "It's imperative that we get over there as soon as possible."

Logan immediately stood in response, and Spencer-Lynn followed his example. "Say no more. Do you need me to alert anyone else of the situation? Form some kind of brigade?"

Thunder shook his head. "Probably not necessary, because I sent Handel to do that, and I'm gonna tell Hunter to do the same on the way out; but if you know anyone else who can be ready ASAP, grab 'em."

"Right," Logan nodded, before turning to Spencer-Lynn. "Ready to kick some tail?"

She smirked confidently in response. "Is that not what I'm here for? Let's be off."

Before they could set off on the mission, though, they were stopped by a demure voice. "Wait! That's... the things you've been fighting all this time?" asked Brecken. "...Let me help, too!"

"I–" Logan started. "See, the reason we let Spencer-Lynn help us while she's here, is because she's already experienced with fighting.

Now, I don't want to make assumptions; but if you aren't, that's not a risk we feel comfortable having you take, given the severity of the situation."

"Okay, I don't really fight, you're right. But you saved my life. I have to repay you for that! I'm sure I can help somehow! Another pair of hands is always useful, right?"

"*If* those hands know what they're doing," replied Logan. "Otherwise, they turn into another pair of hands we have to help protect from peril. Plus, I mean, you've been awake, what, two hours at the absolute most. So it wouldn't be wise to assume you're firing at 100% capacity here. Are you following me?"

Clearly, Brecken wasn't satisfied with Logan's reply, even if she knew he had a point. "Well, what am I supposed to do? Just sit here and wait and wonder if the people responsible for me being alive will get to keep their own lives?"

"Yes! That's exactly what... okay, admittedly, it doesn't sound great," Logan said. "But this is how it's always been."

"We're just asking for you to trust in our ability to return in one piece," added Spencer-Lynn.

Brecken folded her arms. "Well, what if I follow you anyway?"

Thunder sighed in frustration. "Fine. We're grabbing some potions from Lisandra on the way out; you'll be in charge of administering those. Now, we can't waste any more time. Let's go!"

"Right!" Brecken nodded, quickening her pace to keep up.

"Uh–" right before leaving, Logan had hastily grabbed the first unattended weapon within his reach, and as the group ran toward the plaza, he handed it to Brecken.

"Here, this is a... spear, it's a spear," he said, once he'd gotten enough of a visual to realize what it was he was holding. "Use it to defend yourself. I'd be happy to give you a better tutorial sometime, but for now, just remember to stab with the stabby part with as much force as possible. Use two hands for more stability."

"Got it," agreed Brecken.

"You'll do great if you're as intuitive as you are stubborn." Logan gave her a big smile before hurrying further ahead.

As the plaza approached on the horizon, Thunder felt a sinking feeling in his stomach. He already knew that things were going badly based on the brief report he'd gotten from Handel, but not even that was enough to have prepared him for the sight he beheld once the squad was close enough to see exactly what was happening.

He froze in his tracks, as did everyone else in their squad.

The plaza was full of activity, full of fighting. Since the attack had begun before it was closing time for the market, there were destroyed goods all over the ground; broken glass, crushed fruits, remnants so small it was impossible to tell what they had once been. There were the pieces and remains of what mutants had been defeated. And blood... there was definitely blood.

I can't let this get any worse. We have to fight...

"All right! Listen up!" Thunder yelled, turning to face everyone. "I know that right now, this looks impossible to deal with. But these people are counting on us! There's people's livelihoods, their memories, their children in that area, and we pride ourselves on resisting, right? Well, today we resist anyone, or anything, that tries to take that away from them. From *us*! Are you with me?!"

Several passionate, affirmative yells followed.

"Good stuff, that's what I want to hear! Hunter!"

"Yes!" Hunter stood up straight.

"Direct the ranged fighters to support from a distance! Ask some villagers for access to rooftops, scale large fixtures, make sure you're safe and fire! Ranged fighters, follow Hunter!"

"Right. Everyone with crossbows, arrows, or guns, let's go!" Hunter said, running into the fray. Several members of the Resistance followed.

Next, Thunder turned to the dark-haired man that had run to give him the status report. He was, clearly, as unnerved as most of the remaining Resistance personnel that was still in the area. Handel had never been a fighter; he had pretty much been an engineer for the entire time he'd been part of the organization. Thunder could only imagine how scary this must have been for him– under less urgent circumstances, he'd have given him a reassuring, motivating speech about bravery and perseverance, but that would require time neither of them had. "Handel's team is in charge of fixin' the water issue. With less flooding, we'll be better equipped to fight– so try and make those repairs as quick as possible!" Thunder said then. "Logan! Choose four capable fighters to cover them, quickly!"

"Right!" Logan nodded, before pointing out some people to follow the maintenance crew.

"Everyone else! Fight for your lives– and the lives of our inno-cents. Charge!"

With a mighty yell, everyone did indeed charge, ready to defend the integrity of their home.

"Help! Help my baby!" A woman dressed in purple robes called out from the sidelines as the battle in the square continued on.

Spencer-Lynn was the first to hear her, and turned. "What's wrong?" she asked, hurrying over.

"My little girl got hurt," the woman said, holding a brunette girl with olive-toned skin, no more than six years old, with a brutal gash on her right leg. "She can't walk. Our house is on the other side of the plaza, the one with the gray roof, but we can't get there with all this happening. My husband is busy fighting, so he can't help…"

"We can help!" Brecken was quick to pull out one of the healing salves from her bag of potions. Frowning a bit, she said, "Cloth, I need a cloth…"

"Here!" Logan unwrapped one of the scarves from around his waist, and surrendered it before bending down to the girl's level, giving her a warm smile. "You'll be okay, all right? You're being very brave."

The little girl nodded, her brown eyes wide, although she looked terrified.

"We'll escort you to your home, okay?" Spencer-Lynn said then. "Logan, guard the back, I'll take the front."

Logan nodded, and Brecken watched as the two effectively began to carve a path to escort the mother and daughter to safety. For Spencer-Lynn to not be an actual member of the Resistance, she'd learned rather quickly to work well with them. Brecken was impressed.

Fortunately for her, handling the spear that Logan had hastily given her felt similar to handling the flags in school– she'd been a flag twirler in middle school– and so it didn't feel too foreign in her hands. However, the force thing was definitely something she'd need to work on... if she ever ended up on the battlefield again, which at this point, a part of her silently hoped this would be the last time. Of course she was grateful for everything the Resistance had done for her, but she'd overestimated her level of stamina.

When Logan and Spencer-Lynn reached their destination, the mother bowed to them in gratitude. "Thank you, thank you so so much! Is there anything I can do for you all?" she asked.

"Focus on tending to your little one before worrying about us," replied Logan. "Stay safe. We'll be making sure your husband can return to you two safely."

The battle forged on. There were a good seven or so villagers that were native to the area and trying their best to help with fighting and navigating the messy and now flooded plaza, but even so, it was difficult to keep footing– especially so for the shorter Resistance fighters. The maintenance team had made very little progress in fixing the underlying problems causing the flood. Things were looking rough.

When Logan saw Brecken again, he gave her a smile and thumbs up, although he was very clearly winded, and had a noticeable bruise on his left arm. "We can... do this!" he panted. "Long strikes, Brecken. The added momentum from them makes your strikes more powerful than if you wait until they're close to strike."

"Okay!" She nodded, holding her spear close.

"Let's get stabby!" Logan said eagerly, as he charged back into battle.

Brecken was hesitant to do much fighting because she wasn't as coordinated as the average human, and knew that if she tried to fight she'd likely trip over her feet– which in this situation could be fatal.

As the battle raged on, after some hours, there was still no clear turn to either side; it was as if the Resistance was at a stalemate, and fighting fiercely just to keep their standing in the battle. It was disheartening...

Spencer-Lynn had been all but forced back into the maintenance area; this area looked just as grim and dark. The men in here were all huddled over an assortment of blueprints and tools, working frantically to try and find a solution to the flooding. Farther back she noticed a trio of people tending to an unconscious man with sandy reddish hair and cedar-toned skin. "Have you made any progress at all on the repairs?" she asked then.

"We figured out that there's a piece missing, right here," Handel pointed to a hollow on the long pole in the middle of the alcove, "but with all the water, who knows where it's gotten to? It damn well could have floated into the river at this point."

Spencer-Lynn sighed, plopping down on the ground. "This is awful. I'm so tired... my ribs hurt..."

"Here." Handel gave her a half-empty bottle of potion. "The small blonde girl gave us this, so we've been rationing it. A couple sips should help you get right again. There's cups on your other side."

"Oh. Thanks." Spencer-Lynn picked up one such cup, which looked to be from one of the stalls in the market, based on its state; it had seen better days, for sure. As she took a sip, she noticed notes of lemon, ginger, cinnamon— and then a strong punch of something so vile she couldn't put a name to it. It was what she'd imagine it'd be like to drink kerosene; its one good point was that it went away as quickly as it had come.

"Oh! Hey!" One of the men held up a diagram, pointing. "Guys, look! I think this is what the missing piece is! You think that now that we have a shape, we can maybe make a replacement?"

"Great idea. Let's hustle, boys," Handel discarded his screwdriver to steady his hands above ground, as did two more of the men in the area. The one who'd discovered the diagram continued to hold it up so they could all see it.

Spencer-Lynn watched, amazed, as a ball of blue-tinged light appeared. The three worked together to mold the light as if it were clay, forming it to the shape of the missing piece they sought, using the diagram as reference. When it was the correct shape, the light faded, leaving the piece there; only now it looked like it was made of perhaps clay or stone.

"Here goes nothing." Handel placed the piece in its position, and then began to twist it to the right a few times.

The following few seconds were tense– until there was a notable silence.

The sounds of rushing water were gone. Only the sounds of battle remained.

"Woo!" All the maintenance men began to high-five.

"The battle isn't over yet, guys. Let's pull ourselves together and get out there. Those that can fight help the captain, and those who can't help the villagers," Handel instructed.

"Let's go kick some creature arse," agreed Spencer-Lynn gladly, and they all hurried out with the exception of the group that was still attempting to resurrect the sandy-haired man.

On the field, the water had indeed begun to drain, but it would take a while before the area was completely dry, judging by how slowly it was going down. Nevertheless, the Resistance fought on. They had no choice but to.

"I can–" Brecken had reached for a potion for an injured Resistance fighter, but was filled with a sense of dread when she felt nothing in her bag. "I... I'm out of potions..."

"W-what? What does that mean?!"

"Don't panic, please don't panic! I can still help! Um..." Brecken glanced around the area, attempting to locate any materials that may be helpful, before coming up with an idea. Hastily, she untied her hair, using the ribbon to stop the bleeding of the fighter's arm. "Come with me, this way; there are things I can use to help."

The two hustled over to an abandoned stall, and Brecken grabbed a small lemon, a bottle of water, and some aloe. "This is going to sting, all right? Brace yourself."

She then sliced the lemon in half with her spear, and used the halves to disinfect the wound. As expected, the fighter screamed a bit.

"Brecken, do you have–" started Logan, running up to her.

"Unless someone is somehow poisoned, I can't help; I'm out of everything except antivenin and... whatever the red bottle is!" she yelled quickly.

"Red bottle..?" Logan frowned, reaching into the almost-empty bag and looking for it. The bottle in question was round and was the perfect size to fit into his palm. It wasn't labeled, and had no spout. "Oh! This isn't a– I know what this is!"

"Really?! That's helpful! What is it?" asked Brecken.

"Stand back! It's a grenade! Everybody!" Logan yelled.

"A grenade?!"

Everyone frantically scrambled to clear the area. As soon as he could judge that everyone was clear, Logan threw the grenade with all the force he could muster. When it finally hit the ground, a cloud of white smoke rattled the nearby area, sending pieces of mutants flying every which way.

It was over. The market was finally reclaimed, but it was impossible to feel good about it amidst the carnage.

As soon as the battle was over, Logan fell to his knees, exhausted. He had known things would be more strenuous once he'd been allowed out on the battlefield, but this... he'd have never been able to fathom this. His younger self was a fool for wanting to leave the comfort of the Resistance headquarters. Right now, he'd do anything to have that back.

"When will it end?!" he lamented.

He heard a scream then, clearly in anguish, and turned just in time to see one of the Resistance members collapse against Thunder's chest; Flavian, he recalled, remembering his smaller stature and neat braided ponytail of the purest white. He wasn't one for many words, but Logan remembered him being an excellent wielder of magic, particularly of the earth variety. He was often seen with Etzel, one of the more headstrong and confident fighters, who Logan now realized he hadn't seen since everyone had arrived. Not only that, but he also didn't see him *now*.

Logan was sure he'd never forget how his stomach dropped in this moment.

"This can't be happening!" he heard Flavian shouting as he drew closer to the scene. "It can't! There has to be something else that can be done! We can't just give up on him like this... I can't..."

Meanwhile, although he was quiet, Thunder's face looked to be the most sullen and grief-riddled that Logan had ever seen.

"What, what's going on now?" Logan asked as he stood beside Thunder, placing a hand on his shoulder for added reassurance.

"The boys. The boys have told me that they've tried everything, but Etzel won't wake up."

If the drop of Logan's stomach had been so profound he'd never forget it, this statement had been more like a punch to it, one so strong that he was surprised he was still standing. "We... lost someone?" he asked, so in shock that he struggled to get the words out of his mouth.

"We lost more than one. Too many. Some civilians, too..." Thunder sniffled, struggling to keep his face and eyes clear of tears. "We can't keep doing this. It's past time we admit that this is a predicament that's too big for us. We need a higher power. Come over here."

He pulled Logan into a huddle with Hunter and many of the other Resistance members, and they all bowed their heads in silence.

"Our Goddesses, we beseech you..." started Thunder.

The rest of the members linked hands.

"Please... please help us keep our home safe. We can't keep fighting like this. We'll lose our home– if not our lives– in a matter of weeks if things continue to carry on this way. Please lend us your power, show us a way, anything! We just want to live! Please!"

"Please use your divine power to determine the best way to assist us. Please deem us worthy of your intervention, and save those of us that remain," added Hunter. "If there's anything that we need to do as recompense, we'll gladly do it, if you just give us a sign!"

A ball of white light formed in the middle of the circle, lingering for a few seconds, before shooting up into the clouds, into the heavens.

As one of the men began to say a prayer for the fallen, Logan found himself clenching his jaw in anxiety. If things continued this way, it wasn't farfetched to conclude that everyone here would be killed. If the goddesses refused to intervene, what would happen then? What would happen to the Resistance? To his family? To him?

There were so many questions... but when would answers come?

Four

A Whirlwind of Transportation

On a sunny, uneventful summer day in Chicago, the sounds of a group of teenage friends preparing diligently for a welcoming party for their two visiting friends could be heard throughout the neighborhood where the house was located. When the idea had been proposed– by Jaiden, of course, because Mishaela wasn't exactly a "let's throw a party!" type of person– she'd immediately ruled out both of their houses because of unpredictable parental limitations (Jaiden) and language barriers (Mishaela). Luckily, there was another trusty option that didn't require the two to completely explain the situation, and that was to host the party at their friend Madeline's house.

Although Madeline Navarro was a year older than both Jaiden and Mishaela, she'd known them both for a long time; her parents and Mishaela's parents had all been classmates back when they had been in high school themselves, so those two had grown up knowing each other in some capacity. This meant that Madeline also met Jaiden around the time that Mishaela had met her. The extra year meant their social circles were not quite the same, but it was a normal occurrence to see the brightly-colored, alien-obsessed girl wandering into either of their vicinity.

Madeline's parents had been kind enough to lend their backyard to the cause; her mother had gone to her parents' house, taking their border collie for a walk on the way. Her father was around, but promised to not be too much of a "nuisance," he'd said jokingly.

"The streamers are looking a little wimpy, Mishaela. A little higher?" asked Jaiden, gesturing upward.

"Yeah," she agreed, doing so.

"Excellent. You're the best!"

"Hey, guys. How's everything going?" Madeline walked out to the backyard then, carrying a small box. "I brought some more balloons."

Madeline probably looked the most different out of everyone compared to the last time any of them had seen their remaining two friends, because she'd cut off most of her light brown hair. She had gotten it cut into a stylish asymmetrical bob; she adored the style, saying it made her look more mature. She was known for dressing in bright colors and quirky patterns, and her skater dress with a pink and blue unicorn print was certainly living up to that expectation today.

Jaiden and Mishaela hadn't gone through any drastic appearance changes, if any at all. There was something comforting about maintaining one's look, wasn't there? Of course, during the summer, Jaiden usually wore shorts and t-shirts, like today, as she wore a galaxy print t-shirt and a pair of pink shorts; and gathered her hair into a very stylish-looking pouf of red-orange curls. When it came to hair, out of the face was always best in hot weather, after all. Meanwhile, Mishaela's long dark hair and slightly juvenile fashion sense prevailed all year long. Today, she was wearing an orange plaid sundress, one which Jaiden was at least 75% sure she'd seen a photo of her own two older sisters at some point, wearing dresses that looked almost exactly like it.

"Awesome! Everything is going great so far," replied Jaiden. "Chiara is picking up the cake for us, and I think all the food's here. Correct me if I'm wrong on that. Decor is almost done– that's what we're working on now– so all we need is our guests!"

"Good stuff. Dad and I are gonna go to pick them up soon, but Cristy and Claire will be here to help you out with any loose ends; they went to go get some extra plates and things, but should be back soon," Madeline said then. "Do you think we need to stop for anything? Need anything?"

"Hm…" Jaiden turned and called out, "Do we need anything, Mishaela?"

"Not really, but more ice would be nice," she said back.

"Ice, got it. That looks great, by the way," Madeline pointed at the streamers on the fence before turning to leave the backyard.

The back door swung open then, and arriving were Madeline's younger twin siblings, Cristina and Claire. They were fraternal, so they looked different enough to easily tell apart, but it was even easier for those who knew them to tell them apart. Cristina had a more masculine style, and her brown hair was usually unkempt; Claire was more feminine, with a more bohemian style, and had braces. The two were fifteen, and in Jaiden and Mishaela's grade level, so they were pretty good friends.

"We have snacks!" Cristina said proudly, holding up a bag of chips.

"All right!" Madeline high-fived her. "You two stick around to see if Jaiden and Mishaela need any help. I'm gonna see if Dad's ready to go. I'll see everyone in a bit, and I'll have two *very* special guests with me when I do."

As the train pulled into Chicago's Union Station, both Gavin and Jasiela felt like they were going to burst with excitement. This was it. After all of their efforts– including a second presentation and plans for a bake sale, which only didn't happen because the adults in question finally had mercy on them– they were finally *here*.

"I can't believe it. I can scarcely sit still!" Gavin whispered as the train began to slow down. Indeed, he was fidgeting in his seat, his leg bouncing at high speed.

"Well, you might wanna stay in your seat until we come to a complete stop, at least," replied Jasiela with a laugh. "If you eat shit, I'm gonna laugh, I'm warning you now."

"You're right." Gavin nodded, trying his best to stay still. He wasn't as successful as he'd have liked to be.

"Still, I know exactly what you mean. I might not look it on the outside, but trust me. On the inside, I'm bursting with excitement! So much I can hardly stand it!"

When the train finally stopped completely, Gavin reached up onto the baggage racks to retrieve his and Jasiela's suitcases. Handing hers over, they let the handles up in unison and went to exit the train. Gavin had to help Jasiela down the stairs because they were a bit steep, but they both made it off safely and began to walk toward the station exit– or what they both assumed to be the exit, if the direction of foot traffic was to be trusted.

"Oh, did we lose track of your aunt?" Jasiela asked, trying her best to catch sight of her in the crowd of people moving throughout the station. She'd believed it was hard to lose that head of red hair, and yet, here she was.

"Um." Her question caused Gavin to start looking around, nervously. "Well, I sure hope not."

"Don't worry, you won't be rid of me that easily!"

Both teenagers yelped in surprise, earning themselves a laugh from their current guardian.

"Ah, it's been a while since I've been to Chicago. All the same, I'm always filled with excitement whenever we pull into the station." Maura smiled as she led the way through the station. "You kids are

going to love it here. The lakefront, all the museums, the sights...
Portillo's. The exit is right over this way. I don't suppose you two
have a plan worked out for meeting up with your friends?"

"Madeline and her dad are going to be the ones to meet us here;
they live closest to the home we'll be staying in for the duration
of our stay, so it's most convenient for them to give us a ride,"
explained Gavin. "Perhaps I should've... thought about the fact that
that leaves you with all our luggage."

"Ah, don't concern yourself with that. There's a reason I'm able
to live alone," Maura laughed. Indeed, Gavin had noticed she was
perfectly capable of lifting boxes, crates... hell, even him, probably.
That was probably how she was able to so easily take Butter to her
vet appointments.

"Are you all right, Jasiela?" asked Gavin. "You've been quiet."

Jasiela's response was to turn in his direction as if he'd only just
now appeared there, rather than having been beside her for the
entirety of this trip. "Yeah, yeah, my bad. I'm just thinking about
how Chicago is smaller– or at least less populated– than New York,
but gee, it's still pretty big, if all the people in this station are of any
indication. I don't think I was mentally prepared for this kind of
crowd."

"It's different, isn't it?" Gavin agreed. "I was trying to put it into
words myself."

There weren't so many people that it was impossible to navigate
the corridors, but it was difficult to see what way the halls would
turn before getting to an intersection.

"Hey! Gavin, Jasiela! Over here!"

The two turned toward the sound of a yelling teenager before exchanging a confused look. How did this stranger recognize them, and know their names?

"It's me, Madeline!" She sure didn't *look* like Madeline at first glance... but a closer look was all that was needed to confirm that this was indeed their friend.

"Guys, it's me. I know, I look different," she laughed.

Jasiela laughed with her, before reaching out for a huge hug. Gavin waited until they were done to get a hug of his own.

"This is my dad." Madeline gestured to the tall man beside and somewhat behind her, who had hair the same brown as hers, and slightly more fair skin. He almost looked like a surfer. "Dad, this is Jasiela, Gavin, and his aunt."

"Maura. It's a pleasure," she extended her hand.

As the adults talked, Jasiela asked Madeline, "What did you do to your hair?"

In response, Madeline ran her fingers through the longer side of the bob. "I was going for a new look."

Gavin laughed. "It worked, the two of us didn't even recognize you at first."

All three friends laughed.

"It's nice, though." Jasiela nodded, smiling. "Fits you."

"Thanks. That means a lot, coming from you, as fashionable as you always are," Madeline replied. The pride she felt from the compliment was evident within her smile. "My dad is gonna take all your stuff to your apartment. Meanwhile, I'm gonna drive us all back to our place, so we can meet up with everyone else."

"Oh, you drive?" asked Gavin.

"Sometimes. Rarely. You don't really need to when you live here, but it's a good skill to have just in case," replied Madeline. "Dad, are we good to go?"

"Huh? Yes, I'll see you at home in a few. Drive safe, all right?" he said.

"Of course. Come on, guys, exit is this way," explained Madeline as she pointed toward a flight of stairs.

"I don't suppose we can stop to get something to eat?" asked Jasiela as they all walked. "I was so excited, I didn't eat before we left."

"We have food at home," Madeline waved it off.

"Yeah, but..."

"Will it take long to get to that food?" asked Gavin, also feeling the pull of hunger.

"Not too incredibly long... but I guess we can stop for a snack so you guys don't keel over," replied Madeline. "I'll pull over somewhere quick, and you can get a quick snack."

When Madeline pulled up in front of her house, Gavin and Jasiela looked somewhat amazed at the area surrounding them. After a moment of stunned silence, Jasiela was the first to speak. "Gavin, this must be what your aunt meant when she was talking about that midwestern charm."

"Indeed. The architecture of these houses evoke imagery of an English countryside community, but somehow still with an American feeling. It's... it feels cozy," Gavin agreed.

"Cozy. I'll take it." Madeline smiled. "All right, guys. To the backyard."

"Why the backyard?" Gavin asked.

This made Madeline pause for a moment. "Oh... no particular reason. It's a nice day to chill outside, though, isn't it? We wouldn't want to waste the nice weather on sitting inside the whole time."

"She's got a point," agreed Jasiela. "Lead the way, captain."

Madeline made sure to lead the line to the backyard, also making sure to hesitate when unlocking the gate for dramatic effect. She pushed the gate open as slowly as possible for even more of it. If nothing else, Madeline knew how to create an effective buildup.

"Surprise!" everyone chorused when they'd finally come through the gate.

In surprise (not so much shock, since they knew they'd be seeing all of their friends eventually), Jasiela and Gavin weren't sure what to do, in the typical surprise paralysis fashion. Gavin noticed all the food on the table first, of course, and Jasiela was the first to mentally evaluate everyone's outfits, also typical of her.

"Guys!" Jasiela smiled. "You did all this for us?"

"Of course we did! Now get over here and give hugs," Jaiden beckoned them over.

"Ah. So *this* is why you didn't want us to eat too much, then," realized Gavin. "I suppose I should've known something was going on when you mentioned there being food waiting for us."

"Yep, no food needed! We made sure to get all the goodies for you right here!" Madeline replied. "Now, come on; let's get settled in and dig in. We can all catch up while we're eating."

"Right, because I have *so* much to tell you guys," replied Jasiela as everyone began to pull up chairs.

Madeline was the one to pull out plates, making sure to count out the plates before distributing them to everyone. After passing them all out, when she was left with one extra, she frowned in confusion before counting them all again. After being confused once again, she realized what was wrong.

"Wait a sec. Mishaela, where's your sister? I see the cake she was bringing, but I don't see her," pointed out Madeline. "She *was* the one bringing the cake, right? I didn't hear that wrong?"

"Chiara's here?" asked Gavin. "That's great! I was hoping I'd finally get to meet her in person, after we've spoken so often online. I do believe our discussion about post-modern architecture would go over much better in real time."

"Oh, well..." Mishaela discreetly pointed to one of the windows of Madeline's house that faced the backyard.

"Wha–" Madeline squinted, and only then was able to see a tiny bit of a dark-haired head in the corner of the window.

"Chiara's very anxious in person," explained Mishaela, more to Gavin and Jasiela than anyone else, since Jaiden and Madeline would already know this. "She didn't want to intrude on our reunion. I told her it was okay– and even that you guys would welcome her– but she insisted that things would be better if she just waited inside until we needed to go home."

"Aw, no!" Jasiela shook her head. "That sounds boring as hell. Come on, let's go bring her out here!"

"That, uh..." Jaiden grabbed her arm gently. "Might not wanna do that. If you try to push her into social situations, she only gets more nervous. Could get a lot worse."

"Oh. Oh, right, you guys would have known each other a while, right?" Jasiela realized. "I trust your verdict."

With the short silence that followed, five heads turned toward the sudden sound of the screen door swinging open. There was only one other person in the house, so there was no surprise upon seeing the dark-haired, small girl in her usual black attire, today being a simple A-line dress and cardigan. She was also holding a clear, triangular instrument with a handle, almost as if it were a weapon.

"I, um... forgot the cake cutter."

"Chiara?" Gavin smiled, reaching to take the cake cutter, and then shaking her hand when he had it. "Gavin. It's a pleasure to finally meet you in person! I've been looking forward to it."

"Looking forward to meeting... me?" asked Chiara, sounding as surprised as she looked. "Well, I... I'm glad to meet you, too."

"It's a pleasure. Wait, your hair was a different color at one point, wasn't it..?" asked Gavin, looking over Chiara's hair. It had been an aqua color, last he'd remembered, but now it was black, with a small few highlights of blue, green, and purple.

"Gavin, ever the observant," Jaiden laughed. "Chiara, trust me when I say that Gavin and Jasiela are good people. Some of the best people! So they're easy to talk to, I assure you."

"Hi!" Jasiela waved. "Jasiela is me."

"Well... you wouldn't lie to me about something like that..." Chiara said, more to herself than anything.

"We have plenty of food, so come on and eat with us!" Madeline gestured to the table before holding out the extra plate she'd had. "Here's a plate. By the way, everyone is free to stay as long as you want. My parents don't mind, so at some point we should discuss today's itinerary. You guys aren't jet-lagged... uh, train-lagged or anything, right?"

"Nah, it's only an hour difference," replied Jasiela.

"I think I've gotten used to the change at this point," added Gavin.

"Excellent. So, then, what are we all doing today?" asked Madeline. "There's a mall nearby... not a terribly long drive to the beach, and I'm sure there's some other stuff we could get into! My dad also has some video games around here... somewhere."

"Going to the beach sounds like a good time, but I don't have a swimsuit on me," replied Jasiela. "As a matter of fact, I don't think I ever packed one. Do you think we could stop by that mall, and I could pick something up?"

Madeline nodded. "Yeah, I–"

Jaiden put up a hand, "I think the mall might not be in the cards, not for today at least. It's already getting late in the afternoon, so we wouldn't have much time to go both there and the beach before curfew."

"Right..." Madeline nodded. "Well, yeah, why don't we save that for another day? You guys are probably tired. Why don't we just go for a... a relaxing cruise a little later, once my dad comes back with the big car? We can go get ice cream and see some of the interesting stuff around here, and if you want I can let you borrow my telescope to look at the stars. It's a very high-tech instrument, so you'll see a lot of cool stuff!"

"That does sound nice and relaxing," agreed Gavin. "I mean, sure, I have energy now, but I bet I'll be just exhausted in a matter of minutes. I'd rather spend the energy getting reacquainted with you all. I'd love to tell you all about what's been going on since I got back home."

"Oh! Do tell." Jaiden smiled as everyone began to get up. "What's the deal over in London? Is everything cool?"

"Well, I went to school as usual. Everything felt the same, but after the whole adventure, it didn't, you know? Or perhaps it's better to say that my outlook on things had changed quite a bit. Anywho, the first day I was back..."

FIVE

In A Time of Crisis

The aftermath of the battle in the town's square was, simply put, not pretty.

Up until now the Resistance had been holding remarkably steady in terms of personnel, but this fight had been the first in years to sustain casualties. This was one of very few times that any Resistance members had lost their life in a battle at all.

Thunder wasn't taking it well.

"He's still not coming out, huh?" asked Spencer-Lynn. She stood outside of the door to Thunder's room, with Logan and Brecken.

"No. This is... going to be rough going from here on out," replied Logan. As the three began to walk, he explained further, "Thunder sees everyone in the Resistance as family, so he takes on a certain level of personal responsibility for all of our well-being. Which never had any negative repercussions in the past! It's just, uh... I mean, none of us would've expected casualties to happen *after* we defeated that dictator guy."

"Right. I understand." Spencer-Lynn nodded.

"Which, I guess, is the problem. Perhaps we were too relaxed. Personally, I'm mature enough to own that. But I'll try not to blame myself; that'll only make things worse, right?"

A short silence followed.

"Is there nothing we can do, then?" asked Brecken.

"At the moment, it's probably best to give him his space," replied Logan. "I don't think anything we say or do will make him feel any better."

"He's grieving; it's understandable," Spencer-Lynn said in reply. "It's unfortunate, but... já passou, you know."

"Da pior maneira imaginável." Logan stopped himself from speaking more when he realized what had just happened. "Did you just."

"It appears we have something else in common, hm?" Spencer-Lynn gave him a knowing smirk. "So, circling back– if Thunder is not responding for the time being, well, he's the captain of this organization, right? Where does that leave... this whole... operation?" She gestured with her hands to signify a large space.

Logan merely sighed. "A question I wish I had the answer to. I think it'll be a good idea to speak to Hunter. He's our main strategist now, so maybe he has ideas on how to... strategize."

"Does Thunder not have a second in command?" asked Brecken.

"Not really. Now that Tornado is gone, Phoenix is probably the most senior active member now, next to him– but after everything that happened last night, I wouldn't expect to get ahold of her for a long time," replied Logan.

As the trio continued to walk, there was a sudden, abrupt rumble– ending just as quickly as it had started– but powerful. Brecken fell on her butt from the sudden jolt.

"What *was* that?" she asked as Spencer-Lynn helped her up.

"That was weird. Earthquakes aren't unheard of in this area, I guess, but that didn't really feel like one does when they do happen. It was more like... as if something has shifted. I have a bad feeling," confessed Logan.

Bad feelings seemed to be quite common today. "What do you suggest we do?" asked Spencer-Lynn.

"Let's hurry to the library, and arm ourselves with knowledge!"

Logan had already started trotting toward the library once he'd finished that sentence.

"What *is* this place?"

It was quiet– *too* quiet– as Chiara looked around, utterly confused at the sandy dirt road landscape before her. It was clearly not where she had been. No, just minutes before she'd been with her sister, getting ready to take a cruise around Madeline's neighborhood in good company. She'd finally been able to quiet the insecurities in her head and progress to enjoying the company of Gavin and Jasiela. And now she was in a different place entirely.

Had she been dreaming? Was this a dream? Or had everything beforehand been the dream?

"It's so hot," she said to herself, using a hand to fan herself. "This is so strange. So strange... I'm so confused. How will I find out what this place is?"

"Chiara!" She turned around just in time to see her sister run to her.

"Mishaela. What... where..."

"I know, I know," she replied. "Well, the easiest way I can put it... do you remember the explanation behind how we met Jasiela and Gavin?"

Mishaela had entrusted the story of the magic world to Chiara, because she knew the elder Pagliardi wouldn't be a skeptic. Throughout the course of their formative years, Chiara had been the one more inclined to believe in the supernatural, now being the one who would occasionally read books about how to cast spells and perform rituals, and even try them out (on a small scale, to avoid their parents finding out about them). And as predicted, she'd believed every word Mishaela had to say; if anything, she'd been disappointed at the lack of literature regarding the subject, or tangible evidence to prove what her sister was telling her, just in case something happened that required them to mention this story to their parents. It'd be hard enough getting the story out, and then there was the issue of translating for their mother. Neither of the sisters was confident in their ability to tell this story coherently in English, before they could even think of touching it in Italian.

"We– really?" asked Chiara. "But how? I'm so confused. We didn't really go anywhere, and yet we... have arrived here. I think I need to sit down in order to process this."

"Okay, but not too long, all right? You know how the sun affects my skin," replied Mishaela.

"Mm." Chiara nodded, before plopping down on the ground, making sure her long, dark purple and black striped skirt shielded her legs from the hot ground as much as possible. Wait, wasn't she wearing something different before..?

None of this was *impossible*, she supposed. After all, wasn't this how Mishaela had said it happened before? One unassuming step through a door was all that was needed to find themselves in another world, right? The difference being that last time, it was an *unfamiliar* door. Chiara was fairly sure she knew what was behind the door to the Navarro family's bathroom.

"There you are! Hey!" Jaiden was in the distance, waving.

"Oh!" Mishaela waved back. "Over here!"

The rest of the group approached quickly. "We were wondering where you... Chiara." Jaiden was clearly surprised to see her.

"Yes?" Chiara asked, looking up at everyone.

"Nothing. It's just kinda weird, you being here, since you weren't before." Seeing her expression Jaiden quickly added, "I didn't mean it to say we don't want you here! It's just interesting that there's more of us, when I've personally always gotten the vibe that the magic world is supposed to be a secret. The more people you let in on a secret, the harder it is to keep it, right?"

"Well, that may be true, but–" started Madeline.

"Guys? Sorry to interrupt, but I can feel my skin starting to burn," Mishaela interjected. "Can we hash this out in the comfort of some type of shade?"

"Yeah. Let's go that way." Madeline gestured to a building to the west, on the horizon. "If I remember right, that's where we stayed before? An empty house, with room to spare."

"Let's get going, then," agreed Gavin.

It took a walk of about fifteen minutes before the quintet arrived at the building– but to Chiara's surprise, when they entered it was clear that people already lived here.

"I guess we need to go somewhere else, then," she said.

Madeline giggled a little. "Not at all, Chiara. I was a little off, but this is good, too. It's a place full of people we can trust; the Resistance HQ."

"Oh..." Chiara said softly. This was the second time in less than an hour that she felt as though maybe things would be better if she wasn't around. She kept drawing attention to herself in the most awkward ways.

The group was then passed by a familiar curly-haired woman, who didn't seem to recognize them as she walked, her sky blue sundress with spaghetti straps hugging her figure in a way that looked very comfortable.. "Please keep the entrance clear, guys, everything will flow easier that way," she said in almost a dazed way.

"Hey, Phoenix," Jasiela said. "Busy these days, huh?"

"You *know* I am." Phoenix replied exasperatedly, before gasping and stopping in her tracks. Once she realized who had been speaking, and who she was looking at, she hurried over to the group. "Oh, my goddesses. I can't believe it. You're back! Or at least I hope you are, and I'm not just hallucinating from lack of sleep."

"Yeah, not really believing it myself," replied Jasiela. "I don't think any of us were just yet, until we saw you."

Madeline then turned to Chiara and explained, "This is Phoenix– she helped us out a lot with our mission last time. As a matter of fact, she was the one who took care of all the medicinal stuff when your sister had an allergic reaction."

Mishaela nodded, confirming everything that Madeline had said.

"Oh." Chiara nodded.

"That is all correct," Phoenix agreed. "Although I'm a little intrigued as to why you're back, you certainly came at a good time, so I won't dispute it."

"A good time? Is something amiss, then?" asked Gavin.

Phoenix had a troubled look on her face. "Not to grossly understate the situation, but I think there's something that you all can help us with again. Come with me. I need to find someone who isn't so pressed for time that they can explain in detail."

"Logan! Logan, get over here! Phoenix said frantically, grabbing at her brother's arm.

It was natural for Logan to be surprised at this; he hadn't even seen her. "Whoa! Hey, hey, what's the matter?" he asked, concerned.

"Can you... we... listen, we have guests," Phoenix finally settled on saying, gesturing to the six still somewhat confused teenagers behind her. "Do you think you can explain what's happening to them? I need to get back to my rounds."

"I... guess..?" replied Logan, staring at his sister's retreating back. It was then that he recognized who the guests were; and it would not be incorrect to liken his expression of happiness to a puppy who had just been promised their favorite treat.

"Hey, Logan!" Jaiden waved.

"Hi!" Logan grinned at the group that was now entrusted to him, determined to not let his usual upbeat demeanor falter. "It's great to see you all again! I always knew we'd be reunited! Um... so I guess I'm explaining to you the situation we now find ourselves in. Fortunately, I've been doing a lot of research on the matter, and have very recently gotten to the point where I was able to put together a slideshow in the conference room. At this point, I've gathered enough information that it should be sufficient for a decent synopsis now. Follow me, and it will be my pleasure to catch you all up."

Upon arrival at the conference room, everyone took seats at the large, oval table in the middle of the room. This was when Logan noticed that there was one more person in this crew than he was acquainted with. "Oh. My apologies, but I've just now noticed that there are now six where there were once five. I don't believe we've met?" he asked, holding a hand out in Chiara's direction.

A few seconds of awkward silence ensued.

"This is Chiara!" Mishaela said happily, grasping her arm. "She's my sister! My older sister, even though she's littler. She knows the basics of what happened here last time, because if there's anyone we can trust with supernatural knowledge, it's her!"

"Ah? Then it is a pleasure to meet you," Logan said, bowing to Chiara. She blushed, not used to being thanked, or bowed to. "I'm Logan, and I try my best to prepare the Resistance for the perils that may await us; whether that be through combat training, the sharing of knowledge, or whatever other space I can be of some use in. Most of the time, it's the first one. If there's ever anything about our world that confuses you, I encourage you to bring your questions to me. Now, shall we begin?"

Logan turned to the table in the middle of the room. In the center of the table was a spherical device, which displayed holographic images. It was initially projecting the image of the sky, with the fluffiest of clouds and a few birds occasionally flying past. After Logan consulted some notes in front of him on the table, he punched in a few keys and pulled up a projection of the market and abandoned palace in Compositora.

"This place is unindustrialized, but futuristic at the same time," Chiara whispered to Mishaela, who nodded. "It's fascinating."

"If you'll all take a look at this," Logan said, gesturing up at the display.

The first slide consisted of a video. It was dark, and was still at first, but then a lot of human-shaped creatures began appearing, one by one, until there was a sizable crowd of them. They were moving sluggishly at first, as if attempting to find their way around the area where they were- which, at this time, seemed to be lush and full of trees. As they continued on, the trees began to thin and give way to buildings and beaten dirt paths; a sign that they had arrived at a town, and found humans. The increased activity seemed to invigorate the creatures, and they quickly gained speed. Before long they began to run, beginning to attack people and destroy as many fixtures as they could with their strength.

"Aliens?!" asked Madeline. "They *do* exist! I knew it!"

"Not.. quite. These are things that aren't quite human; mutants of some kind," Logan explained. "From what little research we've been able to conduct, it would seem that they are created when there's some sort of magical interference that occurs within the bodies of the undead spirits that sometimes roam the graveyards at night. They seem to only awaken in the evenings, and they come into the village and attack everyone and everything, from either dusk until dawn, or until extinction of that specific horde."

"Wait. This sounds new. How come they didn't do it when we were here last time, then?" asked Jasiela.

"It is indeed a fairly new problem. In our experiences, this isn't something that was ever an issue, back when The Dictator was our most pressing disaster," pointed out Logan. "So that fact alone is a little worrying, as if there was perhaps some unknown reason we shouldn't have completely done away with the guy. It's interesting to note, by the way, that there is mention of these things in a really old history book I found, but so little of it is legible that the only things I got out of it was the vague explanation of how they're formed, and how to get rid of them. I saw an unfamiliar word in the passages, 'holzomen,' which based on the context, is probably what they were called in those days. But I wasn't able to learn anything else about them."

"So, that means there was a time they existed... just so long ago that no one alive remembers, I assume?" asked Mishaela.

"That's what I assumed, as well," agreed Logan. "It leaves us in quite a difficult situation; and to make things even more compli-cated, last night we had a battle with them so dire we sustained casualties– rest their souls– and Thunder is taking it *very* hard. He's not responding to anyone when we go to his room."

"Oh, no..." Jaiden said softly. Indeed, this resonated with every-one in the room, even Chiara; she'd never met Thunder, but was familiar with the type of funk that rendered a person unable to respond to a knock at their door.

"So, that's where we're at now," Logan finished, as he turned off the projection. "The situation doesn't look very promising at this point, I know. All the same, we'd greatly appreciate any help you all are willing to offer."

"In other words, we'd have to help you stop those strange creatures?" asked Gavin. "I mean this in the most amicable way possible, but don't you think you're asking a lot from us? How would we ever be able to fight something that's creating this much of a problem?"

"Yes, I realize that. I was hoping we'd have more information after all this time..." Logan admitted. "We'd never ask you all to run into the face of danger alone, for our sakes. Hmm... I'll have to take some time and think about where you all can fit into this operation, if you're willing."

"My dude, you guys are our friends," replied Madeline. "As long as we're inexplicably here, it wouldn't make any sense to not help!"

"I agree," added Jaiden. "Why not? I'm sure we can do something, right?"

Logan sighed a sigh of relief. "I'm so glad you feel that way."

"So, since everything seems so uncertain right now," asked Mishaela, "where do we even start?"

"Well... I do have a bit of an idea about that," replied Logan. "If you'll all follow me?"

Everyone got up from their chairs, following Logan out of the conference room and down a flight of stairs, like when they'd gone down to explore the building all those months ago. Instead of going further down, though, they turned down a hallway and continued on that level.

New to this, Chiara looked around in awe. From the outside, the size of this building had seemed close to that of the bungalows of Chicago that she was familiar with, but now that they were on a basement level, it almost felt as if there were endless hallways and rooms underneath ground level. This must be what it was like to be a life form that established a tunnel system underground, like meerkats... or ants.

After some time, a short, brown-skinned girl passed them, but then abruptly turned back. "Oh! Logan, wait."

He turned, his hair neatly falling over his shoulder. "What?" he asked.

"Do you think we can... wait a second, who are all of these people?"

With all of the Resistance's recent activity, Logan hadn't realized that, at some point, someone may need to explain to his cousin how exactly the revolution had happened here. Of course something that monumental had been reported on worldwide, but the details would likely have been fuzzy– or even not reported on at all– in other parts of the world. That was simply what happened when information had to travel large distances.

This now being top of mind, Logan knew they'd all probably be seeing a lot of each other, if they'd be working together again. "Let me introduce you to some special friends of the Resistance. This is Jaiden, Mishaela, Madeline, Jasiela, and Gavin; oh, and Chiara! Everyone, this is Lisandra."

"You..." Jaiden looked from Lisandra to Logan.

"You guys look similar," Jasiela said, pointing a finger, completing Jaiden's thought.

"Well, yeah, I guess we would. Logan and Phoenix are my cousins," replied Lisandra.

Mishaela frowned. "Really? Then... why are we just now meeting you?"

"To keep a long and annoying story short, I don't live here; my parents wanted to keep me out of the Resistance's affairs. It's too bad, though. I wanted a piece of that action." Lisandra laughed a little. "But when they heard how stressed out Phoenix has been over all the medic work she's had to do, they let up on being so protective. As they should, I mean, I'm practically an adult."

"You are *fifteen*," Logan said exasperatedly.

"Oh, hey! We're the same age," Jasiela said.

"What was it you wanted to ask me, Lisandra?" asked Logan.

"I wanted to know if anyone has time to pick up some materials for potions and stuff. We're clean out, pretty much," replied Lisandra. "I'd like to try to start rebuilding stock as soon as possible, for obvious reasons."

"Yeah. Uh..." Logan looked around. "Come along with us. Let's all go to the cafeteria and discuss this."

In the kitchen, there were two young women behind the door, looking like they were getting ready to prepare a meal. The first girl was noticeably short, with blue eyes and blonde, almost platinum hair in a braid. The second girl had her black hair cut into a pixie cut, and her eyes were a light green; she was quite skinny, and had a light dusting of freckles around her nose. Both were dressed in relatively simple black pants and blouses.

"Oh! How fortunate it is that we came here at this time," Logan said then. "Everyone, I have more people for you to meet."

Jaiden was the one to start everything off. "So, hey, we're the people that helped overthrow The Dictator. I'm Jaiden, and this is Mishaela, Madeline, Gavin, and Jasiela. Nice to meet you all."

She forgot about me, Chiara noticed immediately.

"Nice to meet you. I'm Brecken," the blonde said with a reserved smile.

Lisandra then gestured to the short-haired girl, "And this is Spencer-Lynn, the requisite swordswoman. We just met her recently; she's from your world."

"Really? Where are you from?" asked Jaiden.

"I'm from Belfast. But I also lived in Tokyo for a few years, where I learned the whole sword thing."

Hearing her accent, Gavin smiled, seemingly pleased to have met someone from his general area of the world.

"Dude, don't take this the wrong way," said Jasiela, "but your voice just shocked the hell out of me. Until Lisandra said 'she' I genuinely thought you were a guy."

Madeline gasped. "You can't just *say* things like that!" she scolded her.

Spencer-Lynn laughed. "It's fine, I get it all the time. I'm taller than a lot of girls tend to be, and my hair is really short. A reasonable conclusion, really."

There was an uncomfortable silence after that, during which Brecken looked at Chiara. "What about her?" she asked.

Everyone looked confused, so she explained, "You didn't introduce her when you introduced everyone else." She stepped closer, and offered her hand for Chiara to shake. "Hi. I'm Brecken. Pleased to meet you. What's your name?"

Now, everyone was staring at Chiara, and she hated it.

I was fine with not being known...

Mishaela walked next to her. "This is my older sister, Chiara. She's a bit shy." She nudged her hand then, practically making her shake hands with Brecken.

I usually don't like to shake people's hands because it's always like they're trying to crush my hand, but Brecken's grip is just as weak as mine. We do seem to pretty much be the same size, anyway.

She smiled a little, then. *It's nice having someone a little bit like me around.*

"Nice to meet you, Chiara," Lisandra said. "Yeah, now that I think about it, you two do look alike. Well, welcome to the team."

"Thank you," she replied, her gaze downcast.

"How old are all of you, by the way?" asked Gavin. "You seem as though you're our contemporaries, rather than the adult–" Gavin quickly changed his sentence when he remembered Lisandra– "*mostly* adult members of the Resistance. Whereas, all of us except Madeline and Chiara are fifteen. Madeline is sixteen. Chiara is seventeen."

"Like Logan said a few minutes ago, I'm also fifteen," replied Lisandra. "Brecken is seventeen. Spencer-Lynn is eighteen. Speaking of common age groups, I assume you'll all be here for a few days, right? With the exception of Gavin's room, which he most likely will get all to himself–"

"Lucky," interrupted Jaiden.

"–it's probably for the best if we reserve rooms for you all that don't require you to share with any of the adults, you know? Each bedroom has three beds, so we need to decide who is going to shack up with who. Are there any preferences?"

A silence followed. "Uh, not really," replied Jaiden. "It would be nice if me and Mishaela get to share again, though."

There were a few minutes dedicated to the logistics of bedroom sorting, and when that was done, it was decided that the older group should share a room, and the younger group would share another. This meant that Mishaela would be with Jaiden and Lisandra, and Madeline and Jasiela would take a third room.

In the bedroom with the older girls, Spencer-Lynn was the first to use the bathroom, so Brecken went over to talk to Chiara. "By the way," she said, "I'm from Portland. Oregon, not Maine. I don't think Lisandra knows that yet; she wasn't around when we had that conversation."

"Oh! How did you end up here, then?" Chiara asked.

Brecken's fair skin reddened a little. "If you mean 'here' as in with the Resistance, when I ended up in this world, I somehow fell into the river that flows behind this base. Thunder, the captain of this organization, found me, and brought me here. I'm still not sure why or how I'm here, but... here I am. So, where are you from?"

Chiara smiled a little. "Harwood Heights," she said. "Suburb of Chicago, one of the more quiet ones."

"Then, the marketplace must terrify you," Brecken said sympathetically. "If you've seen it, that is."

"No, I don't think so.. but I think, based on your reaction, I'd remember if I had seen it."

The door to the bathroom opened then, and Spencer-Lynn walked out, drying her hair with a dark blue towel. "Has everyone gotten settled in?" she asked. "I suppose that we'll be hearing about some type of plan of action tomorrow, as long as Thunder is himself again. I do worry about the fact that there's no second in command, though. I mean, it's probably something that no one worried about until now, but."

"Yes, I worry about that too," agreed Brecken. "I haven't outright asked, but this village is in dire straits without the protection of the Resistance, isn't it?"

"That's the impression that I get, aye. I do wonder if Logan has spoken to Hunter yet," replied Spencer-Lynn. "They're both intelligent men. I'm confident in their ability to come up with something; my worry is the timeliness of them doing that."

There was a knock on the door then, and all three girls turned toward it. "Come in," Spencer-Lynn said.

Their visitor was Phoenix, peeking her head in. "Hi, girls. Have any of you seen Logan at all recently?"

"What do you mean? He was just with us, not very long ago," replied Spencer-Lynn. "I do believe the last time I saw him was when we were deciding who would be in what room, which was right before I took a shower, which I just got back from. I couldn't have been gone *that* long. Have you asked Lisandra, then?"

"He's not with me." Lisandra also poked her head in.

Spencer-Lynn looked at Brecken and Chiara, then back to the cousins. "Wonder where he got off to so fast. Should we be worried?"

"Nah. He wouldn't do anything too drastic at a time like this," replied Phoenix. "Besides, he may not have gone anywhere. He might have just disappeared within the aisles of the library; it wouldn't be the first time. No worries at all."

"I'm inclined to believe you, you being his sister and all." Spencer-Lynn nodded. "That's still really strange that he disappeared so fast, though. Will you let us know when you find him, if you aren't too busy at the time?"

"Sure." Phoenix left then, with Lisandra following close behind with a wave.

"It's risky for him to have disappeared at this time of day," Brecken noted.

"It is." Spencer-Lynn agreed, turning to Chiara. "You see, throughout my time here I've gotten the impression that Logan is one of the more important members of the Resistance when it comes to brute force, which is why he's been working so hard to fight against the invasion himself instead of just sending his charges off to do the same. But one does have to wonder what will happen if he doesn't make it back in time to help fight off anything that comes here. And that's before we even start considering what may happen to his ability to get back into town, if he's gone that far."

"Yeah." Brecken nodded. "But if Phoenix and Lisandra trust that he won't come to any harm, they'd know best. All we can do is prepare for the next task."

"Which means finding dinner." Spencer-Lynn turned to the girls. "I'd be honored if you wonderful lasses would scavenge for food with me."

Chiara felt a wave of comfort wash over her as she followed the other two girls out of the room. She was still feeling nervous about being dumped into a strange world in dire straits, but so far, at least Brecken and Spencer-Lynn were making her feel welcome.

Atop the hill, Logan was still panting for air when he arrived at the cave on top. The reduction in sunlight felt good on his skin, because it definitely was a scorcher today, and the stone interior progressing to sand felt good under his feet. Taking his shoes off, he set them aside as he all but collapsed into a sitting position.

"Whew... it's been a long time since I made this trip..." he said to himself, looking ahead at the pond inside this cave. There was a poignant moment where he wondered if the water was safe to drink, but he ultimately decided against it. He had no doubt it was clean, but drinking it might be frowned upon for other, mainly mythical and religious, reasons.

Louder, Logan's voice resonated within the walls of the cave. "Hello, our all-powerful goddesses! My name is Logan Oliveira. I beseech you! ...even though I kinda already did that with the guys a few days ago. Maybe I should've thought about this plan a little more before I came up here. I'm sorry if I'm bothering you, goddesses! Should I go..?" he added, hitching a thumb toward the cave's exit.

When he only received silence in return, Logan couldn't help but let out a small sigh. Even now, after spending the past hour or so traversing this hill, reaching out to the goddesses didn't seem to help. Why were they being ignored? Had they not suffered enough? All he could think of was how distraught Flavian was to hear his partner had died, and he was far from being the only one who had. How were the circumstances not dire enough?

I hope you don't think so lowly of us, Logan. The voice echoed in his mind as if it was his own train of thought, but he was familiar enough with this sensation to know that it wasn't.

"Of course not!" was his reply, punctuated with a nervous chuckle. "But of course, I think we can all agree that the way things have been happening doesn't exactly instill a lot of confidence in a person. I mean, this is the first time in all of my nineteen years that I've had to bury people I've called friends. And maybe it's my fault for being naive, but I never thought things would get this bad–" he stopped himself. He knew how foolish it would be to add, "before the goddesses did anything," while he was sitting here in their domain. Gods didn't usually take such bold criticism kindly.

This is why you've come here then, correct? To ask us for assistance with your plight? Different voice in his head this time, but still familiar.

"If it's not too much trouble, that'd be great," he replied.

There is a natural order to things. Our assistance requires more than just you here. The first voice had returned. *Return here with those not of this world, and then we will be able to aid in your plight.*

"Hold on. So what you're saying is, I have to go all the way back *down* that hill, and then come *up* it again?" Logan knew the goddesses didn't really do joking, but boy, was he hoping they were giving it a try today.

Is there a problem with that?

He could only sigh– as softly as possible, of course. "Not at all," he replied in a very resigned way, rising to his feet. "Off I go, then. I just hope my legs don't give out halfway down the hill."

Logan put down his shoes and started the trip back down the hill, almost feeling as though he could hear a faint laugh in the distance as he did so.

SIX

Aquatica, The Goddess of Water

Early the next morning, after an eerily quiet night, Logan trudged into the Resistance headquarters, tired from the long trip he'd taken. He had been gone for at least two hours– he'd lost count– but all the same, hoped that all of his efforts weren't for naught.

As tired as he was, he was tempted to get a hold of someone to ask if Thunder had left his room at all the previous night. It had been the main thing on his mind the entire time he'd been gone, and he wasn't sure if he'd be able to rest until he knew. Thunder was the Resistance's leader, but to think of him as just a leader would be an understatement. To many resistance members– even more so to Logan– he was like a father. He was the entire reason Logan was even able to join the Resistance; he owed him so much that he worried he'd never be able to repay him someday.

But for now, he would try to not dwell on that. If he didn't get any sleep, he wouldn't be of any use to anyone. This was what he repeatedly reminded himself of, not even taking the time to remove any of his clothing as he flopped into his bed.

"I have news for everyone," Logan said, after everyone had congregated in the conference room, after breakfast.

"Whoa, what in the world happened to you overnight? You look like you've barely slept," Spencer-Lynn noted. "Are you going to be all right?"

"Yeah, yeah, I'm fine," Logan nodded. "Don't worry about me. As it happens, my lack of rest is because of the news I have for everyone; but I think that first I'll have to give you guys a bit of a history lesson in order for it to make sense. That is, unless someone here already taught you about Deity Hill."

"Uh... the name's not ringing a bell," replied Jasiela. Everyone else looked just as unfamiliar.

"Okay. Got it. So, explanation."

Logan sat in front of the control panel at the conference table, fiddling with a few buttons and knobs until he found what he was looking for; smiling in satisfaction as a projection of a tall, grassy hill with a cave at its summit appeared.

"This is Deity Hill. Those of you who have been here before may recall seeing this hill in the distance whenever you'd go to the market. Years ago, when this world was first formed, the goddesses created certain... um, I guess you could call them havens? Places where people could call upon them in times of need. To ensure that they don't do so frivolously, each of these is placed in a location that takes a certain amount of perseverance to get to. For example, Deity Hill is- as the name suggests- a hill, one that takes some effort getting to the top of."

"Is that where you disappeared to last night?" asked Lisandra. "I hope it was worth it."

Logan wanted to give an equally snarky response back, but decided he didn't have enough energy for that. "Well, the response I got was to return with all of you," he replied. "I wasn't told why, or given any further detail, so I can only assume whatever's to happen requires all of us to be around for it."

"I see. Since this seems to be the only lead we have, I guess we're heading out soon, then?" guessed Lisandra.

"You got it." Logan nodded. "As much as my body is clamoring for some more rest right now, there are more important things than my prospective nap. Although... matters would be made a lot easier if we had some type of transport up the hill."

"Are there cars here? I've never seen one," pointed out Gavin. "We noticed that last time."

"They're rare. There's only three or four in this village," replied Logan. "Thunder has one, but I wouldn't feel right taking it without his permission, and well... I doubt we'd be able to get that from him anytime soon. But there's also plenty of wagons, so, if you guys could give me a bit while I go try and procure one, I think all of our feet, ankles, and calves will thank us."

"Work your magic then, Logan," Jaiden replied. "We can sit tight here until you get back."

When everyone went outside to wait for the wagon, trying their best to conceal themselves within the minimal shade that the head-quarters building created, they were surprised to see Logan seated on a stagecoach, headed their way.

"Look, when he said 'wagon,' I don't know what I expected, but it wasn't *that*. I feel like I'm in a period drama," Madeline said softly, to Jasiela beside her, who nodded. It made sense, but it was still shocking to see for people accustomed to the advancements of the 21st century.

"I don't suppose any of you know anything about horses?" asked Logan, when he was close enough to be heard. "Not that I don't know what I'm doing, but with the assistance of another driver, we'd get there and back a lot faster."

"I gotcha," Jasiela volunteered. "My family has something like this on my grandparents' ranch in Mexico. I'm sure I can remember enough about horses to help us *not die*."

The rest of the group got settled into the back, and with that, they were off.

"Lisandra, you're a native to this world, right?" asked Jaiden. "What can we expect when we get to the top of this hill? I mean... goddesses aren't exactly a thing we deal with in our world. At least not directly."

"Can't say. I've never had face-to-face interaction with one myself, but from what we're taught in school, basic formality is all you need," replied Lisandra. "You know, like how you talk to an old person that you respect. All the same... hey! Logan!"

"Yo!"

"Is there anything special we need to do in preparation?!"

"Uh." Logan thought for a moment. "I wasn't advised as such when I came up here last night, but just knowing what the cave on the hill is like, I'd bear in mind that at some point we may be entering holy waters."

"Holy waters? What does that mean?" asked Mishaela, straining to shout over the noises of the moving wagon.

"Whenever the waters that someone enters are holy, it means that we should pay extra attention to the clothes we wear while within it, so as to not pollute it," replied Logan. "There's reasons for that, but it requires more knowledge than I have time to give at the moment, considering we're already about halfway there. I guess the best way to summarize is: no shoes, clean bright cotton. Lisandra, there's a box back there. I made sure to grab you guys some stuff you can borrow; it's in there."

"Oh." Lisandra stood up, wobbling over toward the back of the wagon, lifting the top of the box. "What's in here... oh, ceremonial robes. This'll do." She turned to the rest of the squad, as she held up a white robe with embroidered detailing. "No special way to wear them, just cover up your privates and such."

Everyone reached out for a robe as Lisandra distributed them; she paused once to be sure there were enough for everyone, but there were. "So if we're to go into the water, it's kinda like a baptism?" asked Jaiden.

"I guess you could say that?" replied Lisandra. "Of course, I think our baptisms may be different from what you have in mind."

As the wagon rolled on, small pieces of the conversation between Logan and Jasiela drifted out into the back part of the wagon and further on, seeming to be mostly about food. This was not a smooth ride– the vibrations of the wagon could especially be felt above the wheels, and it was impossible to ignore when they'd hit a larger rock. The good thing was that everyone seemed to be faring well despite this, although Gavin definitely seemed like he'd seen better days.

"I can see the statue of the goddesses!" Logan called to the passengers on board, pointing farther up the hill. "We're about ten minutes away!"

"Whoa! The wagon really does make a difference," Lisandra noted.

"I know, right? If we had an automobile, we would already be there, if you can believe it!" replied Logan.

Meanwhile, more than one of the group looked horrified at the idea. "How... long does it take to walk..?" asked Mishaela.

"Hours, from what I hear," replied Lisandra. "It's not just the distance– which definitely is a factor, don't get me wrong– but, well, it's like Logan said. It's meant to be a difficult trip, so that people won't be trying to bother the goddesses for every single little issue. The paths are difficult to walk, the incline is uncomfortable. Not impossible; just inconvenient."

"Logan, are you doing all right?" asked Spencer-Lynn. "Will you have enough energy to bring us back, do you think?"

"Yeah, I'll be fine! I'll probably collapse the moment we're back, but my priority is making this trip safely," replied Logan. "Thanks for asking!"

When the wagon arrived, slowing into a halt in front of the large goddess statue, everyone hopped out. A few more minutes were dedicated to changing into the clean white ceremonial robes. They were surprisingly plush and comfortable.

"Ow, my butt," Madeline lamented. "Wood is *not* comfortable."

Logan chuckled. "Is everyone ready?"

Everyone took a moment to survey themselves and their surroundings.

"By the way... um, you said this is a statue of the goddesses, right?" asked Chiara.

The statue they were parked by, made of marble, depicted six human, feminine forms in an almost half-spherical formation. Even with the lack of color, it was easy to tell that the form with flowers and leaves covering most of her body was the earth goddess, and that the one standing amidst the waves, perched on top of a small geyser, was the water goddess. The other four were more difficult to place, but that didn't mean the piece was any less stunning for it. It was the type of art that commanded attention from anyone who came near it.

"You are correct! They are the six goddesses who created the very world you find yourself in now. I can give you some history on our way back, if you want."

"Oh! If it's not too much trouble, I mean..." replied Chiara.

"No trouble at all. I'll need the conversation to keep me alert. You can be my assistant driver for the return." Logan smiled. "Well, here we go, then. Inside the cave, everyone!" he said, beckoning everyone to follow as he led the path inside.

The cave on top of Deity Hill was nice and cool, and was somehow naturally lit as well– most likely owing to the supernatural signifi-cance of the place. The ground was noticeably devoid of any grass, feeling stonelike at first, and then becoming sandy as it progressed to the pond of water on the far end. It wasn't a huge cave, but was still large enough to feel like one had walked into a completely new biome.

"Hello?" Logan called. "Hello?! Good afternoon, most esteemed goddesses! It's me, Logan. Are you around? I've brought everyone here, just like you said to!"

The area remained silent.

Logan was beginning to wonder what the people of Compositora had done to afford such cruel treatment from the goddesses. The portion of the group from Earth was, likely, collectively beginning to feel a little concerned for Logan's sanity– but before anyone could say anything to that effect, a small, trembling rumble began under all their feet. The water began to move, creating waves, and it housed the same type of lively energy as the light, as the ground began to resonate with it. Then, the area began to grow brighter. So bright, no one could see, and they all promptly shielded their eyes.

When the light died down, it left a woman who appeared to be made of water. Everything, from her cascading long hair to her presumed feet, rippled with the flow of water. She was such a sight to behold that, for a few moments, everyone remained silent, not so much as batting an eye. And then, of course, Logan spoke.

"It is a pleasure to behold you, as always, Lady Goddess," he said with a bow. Quickly, everyone else followed behind with bows of their own.

She spoke, and there was a surprising amount of bass in her voice; every word she spoke resonated in the group's bodies, as if the sounds of her voice could easily touch their hearts. "A pleasure indeed, Logan. May you all come closer, that I may behold you?"

"No shoes, remember? Now you just step into the water," instructed Lisandra. "It'll be cold, but don't be too alarmed. We shouldn't have to stay in there for long."

Madeline nodded, and was the first to step in. She almost stepped right back out when she felt the temperature of this water, but somehow muscled past that to keep her foot there, and continue on.

"'Cold' is an understatement of the temperature of this water," Jasiela whispered. "My legs feel numb!"

"Same, but don't complain too loudly," replied Mishaela. "I wouldn't want anyone to think we're being disrespectful."

"Oh. Right. Sorry." Jasiela nodded quickly.

"Greetings, young ones. I am the goddess Aquatica, who presides over the element of water."

Everyone remained quiet, in respectful reverence.

"You asked for divine intervention?"

"Yes! Begged, practically. You see, we're currently... we... well, everything's going so wrong that I'm not even really sure where to start," admitted Logan.

Aquatica hummed, the entirety of the cave feeling more alive with the sound. "I see... and, indeed, this corner of the world has been plagued with evil for quite a while, hasn't it?"

"Unfortunately so." Logan nodded. "When you think about it, it's like we can't get past one catastrophe here without getting body-slammed by another. Is there anything you can do to help us? We don't expect you to make all of our problems go away in the blink of an eye, of course. We just... don't want to see any more of our people die, you know?"

"Indeed. As you may know, there are certain reasons I cannot divulge everything I know about your current situation."

"Oh..." Logan said. He did *not* know that, and he couldn't stop the traces of his disappointment from slipping through his words.

"However, there *is* something that can be done to assist you in your plight. Something that *must* be done, one could argue: I bestow upon you gifts from the other goddesses as well as myself."

The ground began to vibrate then, and soon came a particular type of energy underfoot, bringing with it a feeling of serenity. Streams of light coursed through the floor of the pond, swirling around before bursting through the water, surrounding everyone with their luminance.

Then, the goddess spread her arms, and small, ball-like orbs of light, of all colors, appeared. They fell from the ceiling of the cave over the group, creating a fantastical display of light and color. Various smiles were formed in the group, amazed at what they were now beholding, and feeling a special kind of calmness from the vibrations of the ground.

When the colors and lights dimmed, the water formed a throne, which Aquatica the goddess then sat on. She lifted her hand and a staff, which was surprisingly not made of water, appeared. The handle seemed to be carved from a dark wood, and the jewel on top was made of sapphire, with a spiral of silver encapsulating it.

"As assistance with the perils that now plague the land, we have bestowed upon you the powers of the elements. Use these as you see fit to battle your opponents."

"Magical powers?! Cool!" Jasiela said.

"However!"

The word resonated strongly throughout the cave, instilling a type of caution, even fear, within all present.

"Understand that these are special circumstances. These are powers that you have been permitted to use by our good graces. If we ascertain that you are misusing them in any way, they *will* be taken away."

"We understand," Logan agreed quickly.

"Very well. I shall now explain to you the extent of your power. Listen carefully.

"Gavin, you have been given the power of the winds and air. You may control them, and use them as a weapon against adversaries in ways such as creating cyclones and sharp gusts.

"Jaiden, you can control plants and other greenery. You may use them as an extension of yourself, instantly causing vines and produce to grow. Madeline, your powers are similar, but you can also create powerful tremors with which you can overthrow opponents.

"Jasiela, you have the power of fire; self-explanatory, you can create fireballs and fire walls.

"Mishaela, you have the powers of my own element, water; and with this comes control over ice, steam, and snow. Use them to create geysers, icicles, vapors, and many more forms. This is a power that you share with Brecken; may you both use them well.

"Spencer-Lynn, you have the powers of lightning. With these powers, you gain command of bolts of lightning, and can use them at will."

"Um–" she said softly, before Logan placed a hand on her arm, silencing her; a swift, silent gesture to remain quiet.

"–and, Chiara, you have the powers of controlled darkness; these include dark lightning, dark energy, and spirits. The most abstract of powers, but we are quite confident you will be able to master their mechanics."

There was a short silence then, so Logan was the one to break it. "Thank you, to you as well as to the other five goddesses, for entrusting these powers to us."

Everyone bowed respectfully to the goddess.

"So, then, how exactly do we use the power we've been given?" asked Jaiden. "Will you teach us?"

"I cannot, because the manner in which a human wields magic is vastly different to the way a goddess does. But not to worry; you have friends knowledgeable in these matters. They will be more than willing to assist you."

"Understood," both Logan and Lisandra agreed.

"We goddesses trust that you will use these powers for good, so you would do well to not disappoint us. Until the day where we meet again, so long."

The goddess stood again, and with a grand wave of her arm, her body began to decompose into water. The waves became violent as they fell, splashing everyone in the vicinity. Slowly, the room began to become as it had before the goddess had appeared.

Jasiela was the first to speak. "Oh man, this goddess totally gets me! Getting magical powers? This is awesome!"

"Congratulations to all of you," Lisandra says, making a sign of prayer with her hands. "This is a very rare occurrence, as I'm sure you guys have already determined. A shame we had to get drenched in water for it, but this should be really helpful!"

"It should. With this, I am more confident than ever for our future," Logan said, trotting a bit forward. "Well, if there are no qualms, then let's head back. Chiara, you're riding up front with me this time, right?"

"Oh! I-I... if that's okay," she agreed.

"The trip back is quicker, if only by a little bit, because we're going down instead of up," explained Logan. He then pointed forward. "Em diante!"

Everyone fell in line behind Logan once again, walking out of the cave and back to the wagon, parked right beside the statue of the goddesses. They all climbed into the wagon then, ready to set off for home. As they began to set off, Logan turned to Chiara. "So, you wanted to know more about the history of this world?"

"U-um, as long as that's not a bother..." replied Chiara.

"Gaining more knowledge can never be a bother," replied Logan, with a smile. "I am not sure how much you know already, so to be sure, I'll just start from the beginning. This world– its inhabitants, its structure, the atmosphere itself– was all created via the power of the goddesses. Because of this, everything that is living in this world is imbued with such magic, even its people. That's an interesting story too, by the way."

"Really? How so?" Chiara was intrigued now.

"Well, the initial population of this world is nothing short of amazing. When the goddesses finished constructing this world, one of the ways they populated it was by grasping the souls of the recently deceased from your own world. Once here, they were reborn, given a chance at life anew. Because of the nature of their transportation here, they acquired magical prowess themselves."

"I see." Chiara nodded. "And so, is it safe to assume that the particular element mastery one received was based on which goddess grasped their soul?"

"Precisely." Logan nodded. "I'm impressed. You catch on quickly."

Chiara just smiled.

"And from then on, element mastery has been passed on hereditarily. Phoenix and I both inherited our mother's light-aligned power, for example, although it manifested in different ways in both of us; she's a healer, and I'm more of an attacker. Elements do that, you know. The simplest example I can think of is water. One gains power over all its forms, but one will also almost always be more proficient in a specific form than the others."

"You're so wise," Chiara said in awe. "You must have spent a lot of time studying this."

"Most of my life." Logan chuckled. "I'm very fascinated by our world's history, so I take pride in sharing what I know. It's why, even though I'm only nineteen, I spend a lot of time educating the other, older members of the Resistance. It's as I said before: the gaining of knowledge is never a detriment," he wagged a finger. "Ah, but as we get closer to headquarters, I just grow more tired. I'm missing my bed more than I thought…"

"I'm sure." Chiara nodded. "How long were you awake?"

Logan paused. "I'm not entirely sure; I just know that, by the time I got back to headquarters, the sun was beginning to rise.

I cannot possibly overstate how happy I am that this second, subsequent trip was more fruitful than the first. I'm not sure how well I'd have been able to hold my tongue if I was told again that there was nothing that could be done about our lot in life."

At this, Chiara had a thought about this being the first time Logan actually sounded his age. She'd accepted that being the consequence of fighting with the Resistance, but it was comforting, in a way, to see he hadn't been so hardened that he was serious about everything, all the time.

"Yeah, well, I knew that I'd be tired on the way back. Even so, thank you for keeping me company." Logan smiled as he steered the wagon to the side of the HQ building, looking for a safe place to park it. If he was lucky, someone would agree to return it to the rental place while he took a much-needed nap...

SEVEN

A Magical Tutorial

When everyone re-entered the house, Logan immediately waved before retreating to his room, mumbling a short farewell.

"I have *never* seen him that worn out," Lisandra said in awe. "He's usually such a ball of energy; he must be utterly exhausted."

That was the assessment that most of, if not all, of the group had of him, so no one dissented. "Since Logan's probably out of commission for a few hours, what should we do from here, Lisandra?" asked Gavin.

Lisandra stretched, a yawn escaping her lips. "Well, *I* am completely famished. Our breakfast wasn't very big, and the sun is heading toward the west, so lunchtime is well over. I guess, if anything, I'd be eating an early dinner. Or something to tide me over... but none of this is helpful. Look, today was a lot, especially so for you guys. Why don't we just call it? Besides, I can't train you without Logan, and I don't think we'll be seeing him much until tomorrow."

"Reasonable." Madeline nodded. "I'm gonna go see what's going on in the kitchen."

When everyone dispersed, Chiara accompanied Brecken back to their room. "How are you feeling?" asked Chiara, noticing that Brecken seemed a little more sluggish than she had been earlier.

"Okay. I try not to think about it too much, but I am still a little uncomfortable around so many people," replied Brecken. "They're all very nice! It's just that I'm not used to people being nice to me, or even knowing I exist, for that matter. I'd love to become closer to them, though, and be able to communicate with them effectively. I'll keep trying. I know I have it in me!"

"That's good." Chiara nodded. "You seem passionate about this."

The two had arrived to their room, each sitting on their bed. "Maybe. I'd more so say stubbornness than anything else. My father always says he's never heard of anyone changing my mind once I've made it up," Brecken laughed. "That's to my detriment sometimes, but at least I'm not that much of a pushover because of it, I guess."

If only I could say the same, Chiara thought to herself.

"You've been relatively quiet the entire time we've been here, so I'm assuming you feel the same way as I do, or at least similarly," Brecken said then.

"You can say that, yes. Although I guess the situation is a little different for me, since I have my sister with me. And even more so than that, Madeline's parents have been friends with my and Mishaela's parents since they were our age, so we've known her for a long time. Oh, and Jaiden has been friends with Mishaela for so long now that they're like a sibling to me as well. A-and over the summer I had a few opportunities to speak with Gavin online. We have a lot of common interests, like food and certain artistic movements. I suppose I... know this group better than I give myself credit for," Chiara realized.

"You're very fortunate for that," Brecken replied. "Well, even though everyone here started out as strangers to me, it's like I said before: they're all very kind. I know it'll take some time, but if my judgment could possibly mean anything to you, I believe they're people you can trust."

Chiara nodded silently. She'd seen their kindness firsthand, and it was also pretty evident in the way that everyone had worked to be sure her sister hadn't come to (too much) harm.

"Dinner is ready, girls," Spencer-Lynn called to Chiara and Brecken then, from outside the room. "We're eating in the conference room."

"Okay," the two answered in unison.

With this, Brecken turned to Chiara. "Do you wanna sit together?"

"Oh! Um... re-really?" she stuttered. "I... I guess that would be okay, yes." She nodded, and the two got ready to leave, and then walked down to the conference room, where everyone was gathering.

"What kind of grub is on the table tonight?" asked Jasiela.

"I've heard we're having sushi for dinner," replied Spencer-Lynn. "One of the members of the Resistance was kind enough to make a bunch of different rolls. Don't worry, that would include some specially deep-fried ones, for those present who may flinch at the thought of raw fish."

"Plus, the guy said he'd bring us some more stuff to eat with it," added Lisandra.

With that, everyone took seats, ready to eat; once dinner was served, Brecken was the first to speak. "Sushi is nice. I've only had it once before I came here, when my family lived in New York. It was okay, but here, it tastes a lot better. Fresher. Are there fish in that river nearby?"

There was a small pause in the room. "There should be, right?" asked Mishaela. "I remember Phoenix mentioning that it was illegal to fish in them while their dictator was around."

"What a dick of a tator, know what I mean?" added Madeline—causing groans en masse at the table. "Ah, yes, the markings of an excellently executed pun. Anyway, so what are we doing about training? It's tomorrow, right?"

"Yeah, it is, actually," replied Jaiden. "I heard we might be out in the field at midnight to help with the fight."

"We're going to be out there with those... *things*? Tomorrow night?!" Brecken asked, horrified.

"Having a few jitters, Brecken?" asked Lisandra.

Brecken wasn't sure if there was a better word to describe how she felt at the thought of being face-to-face with those vile creatures. She'd be perfectly fine if she never had to see them again. Of course she knew that wasn't an option, especially now that the goddess they'd visited had lent her power, but that didn't stop her from having the thought. She wasn't sure why, but she also felt an extra duty to not fail the goddess who had herself given her power. Being in that cave and being told that Aquatica had given her a piece of her own power felt like she'd personally been given a gift that one she (and Mishaela) could be trusted to have. How could she break that level of trust, just because she was a little scared?

"Well, these things do terrorize villages and eat people," Spencer-Lynn defended her. "I think she'd be daft to not be at least a little afraid, but she's also been out with us before you all got here, and I needn't remind you of how horrendously that wee skirmish went. You'd have to admit that would be scary to behold for someone with no fighting experience like her."

Brecken smiled at her, glad to see that someone was on her side.

"Are you certain that they *eat* people, Spencer-Lynn?" Gavin asked, turning his head slightly and squinting.

Her response was to shrug. "Not entirely. But, I mean, in that slideshow that Logan was preparing, some of the footage that the Resistance has gotten of them is really gory, and why would they just let their victims rot? Might as well eat them then, right?"

The room was silent, apart from the sounds of a few chairs scooting away.

"I'd be lying if I said that didn't disturb me a little," Mishaela whispered to Jaiden, who nodded in agreement.

"At... any rate," continued Lisandra, "if we're expecting to conquer the mastermind, who or whatever that may be, we have to be able to get the minions too."

That's true, but I still don't feel any more confident about the situation... Brecken pushed it to the back of her mind, though, as she continued to eat.

"Besides, as of now, this is all just hearsay," Jaiden reminded her. "Best not to get too worked up until we know what we'll be doing, and have seen what we're dealing with."

"That's a good point," agreed Gavin. "Until then, let's just... take everything as it comes to us. That's all we really *can* do, right?"

And so, everyone continued to eat.

The next day, Logan was up early due to sleeping most of the day yesterday, and decided to get going by making breakfast for everyone. It was the least he could do, as he was feeling a bit guilty for having held training up for a day. Thinking back, there was probably a more logical way he could've gone about going up the hill... but arranging his ideas in practical ways wasn't always his strong suit. Many members of the Resistance would agree that he always had plenty of ideas, but organizing them, well, that was another story.

His thoughts then went to training, attempting to form effective ways to guide everyone through exercises without expending all his energy. After all, he'd also still need to help defend the town that evening. He would have to find a way to do both. Hunter had been kind enough to take over the fight last night, but Logan didn't feel comfortable with the idea of continuing to ask him to do that. That wasn't his job.

"Ah, so he lives."

Just as Logan looked up from the oven, he noticed Spencer-Lynn; she looked to be getting a cup of tea.

"So it seems." He nodded. "How do you feel?"

"Still a little tired, but nothing so drastic that I'd want for more sleep. Why do you ask?" She tilted her head a bit.

"That's interesting. From what I've read, borrowing power from the goddesses usually takes heavy tolls on human bodies– and by you not being from this world, I thought for sure it'd affect you even more," explained Logan. "Peculiar indeed."

The kitchen became silent then.

"On the subject of peculiarities, I've been wondering something, by the way," Logan said then.

Spencer-Lynn had found a tea flavor she wanted, and with a small "ah," began to dip the bag into her hot water. "Yeah? Don't suppose it's something to do with me."

"It is, actually. I was just... kinda shocked to learn you speak Portuguese. It's something I wasn't expecting to have in common with the very specific subset of people who are brought here from your world, because it isn't a common language here. The question I guess I'm trying to ask is, is it a common language in your world, is that why you know it?"

"Wouldn't say that, really." Spencer-Lynn shook her head. "When I was still a wein– not possibly older than seven– this lovely Portuguese couple opened up a bakery near our house, so I went one day with my father and older sister. They had so many beautiful pastries... and when one of the women began telling me all the names of their products in Portuguese, I can't explain it, but... it was like the sound of the language tickled my ears in the most satisfying way. So, I continued to come round. After so long, her wife ended up giving me one of their recipe books from Portugal, so as you may have inferred, I got my motivation to learn to bake and to learn Portuguese at the same time, and they've both remained with me ever since."

"Yeah." Logan nodded. "It's always so interesting, the way that there's no way to tell which childhood experiences end up following us for the rest of our lives, and which we forget by the end of the day. By the way, I used your recipe for the muffins I put into the oven just now, and they already smell amazing."

Spencer-Lynn smiled. "Oh! I'm glad it was of some use to you! I look forward to tasting them. What did you add to them?"

"Cranberries and walnuts. It's going to be delicious," Logan grinned, clapping his hands together. "I can't wait."

With a nod and another smile, Spencer-Lynn continued to stir her tea before lifting the mug to her face. She took a moment to inhale the aromas of lemon and lavender, savoring the calming effects, and then took a sip. The mornings here were always a very specific type of calm. Not quiet– that would be impossible with the number of people that called this place home– but definitely more calm than the cacophony she was accustomed to, back at home.

When everyone had gathered to eat, Lisandra sat beside Logan and asked, "So what's the agenda for today?"

"I was really hoping we'd have heard from Thunder by now, but..." Logan thought. "That seems unlikely still, at this point. I'd ask you to help me, but healing magic is so complex; and last I heard, there's no weapon you've practiced with."

"Yeah..." agreed Lisandra. "I wanna help, but I can't help but think I should be on the trainee side of things, if anything. What I *don't* wanna do is be in the way."

"I understand completely." Logan nodded.

"Hey, no worries. Don't you usually train the new recruits anyway?" Jaiden asked. "I remember that."

"Yes, but those are usually people with at least some sort of battle experience. People who are familiar with magic, and the lay of these lands..." Logan sighed. "But I suppose we all start somewhere. We'll start from the beginning, then."

"What *is* the beginning?" asked Gavin, finally noticing an opening.

"The beginning is when we all go and select weapons for you guys and start training with them," replied Logan.

"Weapons?" asked Madeline. "I'm a little confused. The whole point of going up that big hill is so we could gain the ability to use magical powers and such, right? So if that's the case, why would we need weapons?"

Logan's eyes lit up at that question; he'd have a chance to explain his approach to combat training. It was what he did for a living, after all, so it made sense that he got excited whenever he had an opportunity to talk about his methods. "You see," he began, "the situation as we know it so far, is just that we're protecting our town. We still haven't deduced the cause of this, and it's possible that this cause will be something that completely negates magic. This is the approach that I make when I train new members of the Resistance: that we cannot assume any adversary we may face is susceptible to every attack."

"That was a lot of words, just to say 'something might be immune to magic,'" Lisandra teased him.

"I guess it was," admitted Logan. "I'll admit that. Anyhow, if you could all meet me in the back by the river in about an hour? We'll be starting then. Wear comfortable clothes that allow as much movement as possible. Keep a minimum on extra fabric if possible."

"Will do!" agreed Jaiden. "This is kinda exciting."

When the group convened in the back area to begin training, Logan was waiting beside a crate full of weapons, which seemed to be able to wheel around. He was dressed in a manner that was a little more familiar: an open button-down shirt in a very vibrant light yellow, and loose gray pants, although they weren't as loose as his usual parachute pants.

When he noticed everyone approaching, he waved. "Oh! Hello again, and welcome to the training grounds! Are we ready to get started?"

He was faced with eight faces, which were very clearly *not* ready.

"As ready as we'll ever be. What is all this?" Mishaela asked then, pointing to the crate.

"You'll need to choose a weapon to use, right?" asked Logan. "I put together the most diverse assortment of them I could find, to account for whatever your needs may be. It is important to choose something that complements your physical abilities. No rush on that. I am here for advice and support, of course. Once you've all chosen, we can move on to the next stage."

One by one, everyone began to grab weapons to practice with, before heading farther out to test them out.

Chiara nervously approached the crate, the last person to do so. "I think I'll need your counsel, Logan."

Logan smiled, trying to make both his face and posture as welcoming as possible. He'd been conscious of Chiara's timidness ever since yesterday, and wanted to be as easily approachable as possible. It would make training a lot easier for them both. "Of course, Chiara. Where do we start... well, would you say you're agile?"

"Not particularly."

"Okay, noted. Are you physically strong?"

"Not at all." *How will I be of any help if I'm not strong in any aspects? Will Logan decide I'm not good enough to fight with everyone? Will I be a burden to them?* The questions poured through Chiara's mind like a river at high speed. *Would it be better if I just waited until everyone else is done?*

Before she could voice any of those concerns, though, Logan was asking her another question. "If you were to choose, would you say that any strength you do have is stored within your upper body, or lower body?"

"Upper, I guess..." replied Chiara. These weren't difficult questions, but they were things she'd never thought about, which made it difficult to give answers.

"Ah. In that case, I believe I may have something for you. Please give me a moment." As Logan searched the crate, he noticed Brecken practicing swipes with the same spear he'd lent to her during the battle in the market. "Have you taken a liking to that, Brecken?" he asked her.

She turned toward him. "It makes sense, I think," she replied. "All of the stabby, with a nice, long barrier I can put between myself and any adversary."

Logan nodded. "I'll have to teach you some useful maneuvers with it; the techniques will surely help. Hey, Jaiden, watch it with that hammer, that's heavy– oh! Here it is!" He smiled upon pulling out a small crossbow, holding it out to her.

"I think your strengths will shine as a ranged fighter; someone who largely stays away from the thick of things, while still contributing to the fight. The crossbow is probably the most beginner-friendly weapon I have on hand that fits the idea; it doesn't require as many particulars as a bow and arrow, and it's not as hazardous as a gun would be. Today, we can set up some targets and check out your aim. I just wish I was able to give you more hands-on advice. I'm not a ranged fighter, so I can't give any specific tutorials."

"Oh…" Chiara nodded.

"Then, why don't we leave that tutorial to someone who knows about all kinds of shooting?"

Logan gasped; he recognized that voice. Both he and Chiara turned, simultaneously, to see Thunder; holding both of his pistols, with a smirk on his face.

"Thunder!" Logan grinned. "It's so good to see you again!"

The older man could only smile as his mind began to register who all the people in the area were; as they congregated, hearing Logan's sentence. "You too, Logan, and all the kids here," replied Thunder. "Sorry it took so long for me to pull myself together."

"Oh, no, you shouldn't apologize," Spencer-Lynn said in a soft tone. "You were grieving, after all. We shan't fault you for this."

"Of course. Still, before we get into any more situations, I think it's important that I have a talk with you kids, all of you. Come over here."

Thunder sat at a table not very far from the area the group had been practicing at, and everyone abandoned their weapons to follow him. "Is everything all right, big guy?" asked Lisandra. "You aren't telling us you're resigning or anything, are you?"

"No– no, not that," Thunder laughed a little. "I wouldn't dream of that, especially not at a time like this. But if we're to go on as a force– if we want to move forward as a cohesive unit, if I want you all to trust me, and if I want to feel worthy of receiving that trust–

I have to be open with you about things. In particular, I want to talk to you all about why it was so difficult for me to regroup after sustaining casualties in our last large battle."

"Oh, we were assuming it was because we hadn't sustained any casualties before," replied Logan. "Unless I remembered wrong?"

"Somewhat. Since you've joined the Resistance, we haven't had anyone die on us– at least, not as a direct result of our actions– and we were fortunate for that. It's my fault for never telling you this story, but I'm fixing that now: a story that goes back even farther than the origins of the Resistance, way back before you were even born, Logan.

"Before I started the Resistance, I was somewhat of a privileged man, I guess you could say. As privileged as someone could be in that kind of society. You see, I was the administrator for the Dictator's official produce garden, which was a pretty prestigious position. And for years, I never questioned it, because it's what my father did, and what his father did, as well. It was a good life. Not without its stressful times, but peaceful enough. Paid well. Everything went as was expected; I married fairly young, my wife and I were happy. We had three beautiful daughters. But there was a day when all of that changed.

"One interesting thing about being a glorified private servant was that, even though I ultimately was the person in charge of determining what fed some very important people, I still was never given too much insight on the goings-on of the palace, so to this day I'm still not sure *why* this all happened. But it did coincide with the time I started really wondering about The Dictator and his motives, so I always wonder if that's what prompted everything. I'd always heard whispers that your thoughts were never really private, if you lived on the castle grounds, but like many of the youth, I guess I made the mistake of thinking myself untouchable. One day, I was out driving my truck around the field to check on the people who handled the harvest– you know, normal work day. Nothing seemed amiss then, but when I got back home, I knew something was wrong judging by the eerie silence. Everyone should have been home at that hour, but to my horror, I found out they were all gone... my wife and daughters had all been slain by a witch's hand."

There was silence, even from Logan for a moment, but he felt that he had to explain the last part to their guests. "If you're wondering," he said softly, "in our world, most notably within the past generations, there would be women who dedicated themselves wholly to the art of magic. These women were called witches. In those days, a witch was specifically a woman who sought to free herself from the limitations of a completely human practitioner, but in more recent times, the term is applied to people who similarly devote their lives to magic, regardless of intent. But..."

Logan turned to Thunder. "How did you know this was by a witch's hand, if you aren't certain on why it all happened?"

Thunder sighed again, the longest and weariest sigh that anyone in the area had ever heard him heave.

"Should I... not have asked?" Logan added nervously.

"It ain't that. It's just..." Thunder paused. "The witch was there when I got back into the house. Good for finding the direct reason, but bad for... just about anything else. You see, witches pretty much follow their own societal and moral codes, and no one bothers 'em because some of them *do* have the type of power to level a mountain, and it's not always easy to tell whether they do or not. The Dictator was never so dumb as to take that as a challenge, so it didn't make any sense for one to be on the palace grounds. They had a mutual level of disdain for each other. To this day I still don't understand... even though it coincided with my doubts, a witch would've never done The Dictator's bidding, is what I'm trying to say. So I still don't understand why one would be at my house.

"Though I will say, I used to have a passing knowledge of the witches' society, because my wife's mother was a retired witch. And the witch that I saw in my house that day... well... has always been known to be a piece of work, to the point that they were excommunicated from their coven. That's a long story, but when a witch is excommunicated, that means the rest of the witches want nothing to do with 'em. So if they weren't beholden to the judgment of witches anymore... but even then, I don't know. I'll never forget that taunting expression, their words of relishing the hurt flowing through me. In one day– in a matter of hours– I went from having a whole family, to having nothing. No one. I don't remember falling asleep that day. It's more likely that I passed out after hours of bawling my eyes out, but when I woke up the next day, I knew what needed to be done."

"That's when the Resistance was founded?" asked Jaiden.

"Yes. It was when I was expected to continue my work the next day, when the official order from The Dictator was to 'get over it and start a new family if that mattered so much to me,' that my decision was solidified. I quit immediately, and founded this organization."

"Oh, my goddesses," Lisandra said softly. "I had no idea at all. I'm so sorry you went through that, Thunder. I think I can understand, now…"

"That was the worst day of my life, and after that, I worked endlessly to make sure I didn't lose anyone else; that no more lives would be lost because of my absence, and complacency. And I was making good on that premise, until a few days ago."

A silence passed.

"Thunder, I… I think you're being unfair to yourself by saying any of these deaths were caused by your complacency," Spencer-Lynn said, in a noticeably soft, shaky tone. "I don't… think it's fair to yourself to have such certainty that you were the cause of such tragedy."

"Sounds like you're speaking from experience there."

"Well." She looked away.

"Some truth in there, though." Thunder nodded. "And I pretty much came to a similar conclusion myself, which is why I dragged my sorry ass out of bed and out here. I can't be spending too much time dwelling on the past while our future is bein' threatened, now can I?"

"They say that those who don't know history are doomed to repeat it. With this in mind, thank you for baring your soul to us, Thunder." Logan gave him a polite bow.

"Right. There's actually another reason I wanted to tell y'all this story. Lately, I've been giving a lot of thought to the current situation, which has led me to wonderin' if our current dilemma has been brought upon us by a witch."

"Oh? What brought you there?" asked Lisandra.

"When Logan first explained to me how these things are formed, he mentioned magical interference making those creatures behave the way they do," replied Thunder. "I do wonder... what is it that would cause that kind of interference? Now, this is also something that could happen should the balance of the elements be thrown out of whack, but we'd know if that would be the case; this world would be affected in many other ways. And the act of animating a spirit– correct me if I'm wrong here, Lisandra– that would take way more magic potency than the average citizen would be able to conjure up on their own."

"You're right." Lisandra nodded. "I follow. So then, I guess it makes sense for us to start training with weapons. If we end up having to fight a witch, magic is good for defense, but I don't think it would give us much offensive power."

"Right," agreed Thunder. "So then, let's get back to work trainin' you kids."

"Isn't a crossbow... weak?" Chiara timidly asked Thunder as he began to set up some targets on the far end of the training area. "Especially compared to your guns. Is there a point in learning one?"

"Ah, the youth. Always assuming more advanced means more effective." Thunder laughed. "And while it's true that a gun does have more power, don't take that to mean a crossbow is powerless. Did you know," he held his hand out for the crossbow, and Chiara relinquished it.

"The crossbow," Thunder aimed at one of the targets, "when utilized correctly and at a suitable range, the arrow has the potential to pierce a human heart?"

The arrow shot, whipping through the air and landing right in the middle of the target.

"And I guess maybe you could say that that's the part of crossbows that make them a little less effective than guns– that precision is key, but then again..." Thunder said, "I don't think you're aiming to kill anyone. Just incapacitate."

"Oh, I didn't realize that," confessed Chiara.

"Yep. The nice thing about fighting the creatures we've been headin' up against is that you don't have to go to the effort you would to kill a human. You just have to get 'em where it counts– and Logan will be teaching y'all all about that later."

"But what about the witch?" asked Chiara. "That's a human, right? Will we have to kill them?"

"If it has to come to that, I'd never put that responsibility on you. That I promise you." Thunder gave her shoulder a pat, startling her at first. "Let's start by working on your posture while you're aiming. The correct stance is extremely important to effective aiming."

Meanwhile, as Logan bent over to search through the weapons, he noticed Lisandra also looking through them, before pulling something out. "Hmm. What is this..?" she said softly, meaning to keep it to herself; but of course, Logan heard her due to their proximity.

"Oh!" Logan stood up straight when he realized what she had grabbed. "I can definitely impart some knowledge on that, and it'll be knowledge that will directly benefit you. Have you ever read the tales of mages who fight with ribbons?"

"Is that what this is?" asked Lisandra, as the red fabric unfurled to her feet. It was embroidered with golden organic patterns, evoking imagery of the leaves that would fall from the trees when the weather got colder, in certain parts of this world. When the trees were normal.

"Indeed. The magic ribbons are made by those who have studied magic for–"

"I know the rest!" Lisandra quickly cut him off, not in the mood to hear one of Logan's endless rambles about the history of weaponry. "Wow. I don't think I've ever seen one in person. Logan, do you mind if I take this little baby for a spin?"

"Please do! Take it for many spins!" He grinned. "You never know when you'll need it."

Logan had thought he was alone, and finally able to try and think up some type of training itinerary, but he jumped in fright upon realizing Spencer-Lynn was behind him. "Whoa! Could you not do that? Scared the life out of me."

"I'm sorry. I suppose I'm just too accustomed to walking quietly."

"Ah, nothing of value was harmed. Can I assist you with something?" asked Logan.

"Actually..." Spencer-Lynn shifted her weight from one foot to the other. "I wanted to ask your assistance with something. I'm not sure if it's a something you could do anything about, but... I think it's something I'd at least like to go over with you, before the plan goes very much farther."

"Of course. Why don't we go somewhere that's currently less populated, then? I'm personally partial to the river," suggested Logan, gesturing away from the practice field. "Oh, wait. Thunder!"

"Yo." He looked up from teaching Chiara how to reload the crossbow she'd been given.

"Could you take over here, maybe start teaching everyone about magic? I have to speak with Spencer-Lynn about something really quick–" he looked back at her, "quick, right?"

"No more than ten minutes," she promised Thunder.

"Y'all don't be gone too long." With a wave, Thunder turned to everyone training. "Yo!" He yelled, to get everyone's attention. "Gather 'round. It's about time I explained magic to y'all."

He waited until everyone had come close to begin his explanation.

"Just so that you understand: everyone who's born in this world, everyone who inhabits this world is born with the ability to use magic in some form. For some, like myself, their natural ability is low. And so they train with weapons or work to improve their magical strength, whichever they prefer. Some, like Lisandra here, are gifted with an immense amount of power. Even so, it's important to study best practices so that you don't hurt anyone.

"The process for summoning magic is the same, regardless of element. What you want to do is gather your energy into your core. The solar plexus is the greatest source of the magic that lies within one's form. And once that's all gathered, you're gonna wanna project that energy from your chest, outward. Think of it like a chest pass, if any of you are familiar with that technique. But don't just take my word for it– this is something ya learn by doin'. Uh, preferably facing away from headquarters?"

As everyone took a chance to turn over toward the river and practiced concentrating their energy, Thunder noticed Logan in the distance, approaching him. "Hey," he waved. "Where's Spencer-Lynn? She needs to know this stuff too."

"Uh, yeah, about that," Logan said, once he'd gotten closer. "She's, uh... look, if we need light and thunder magic for anything, I'll take care of it, all right? Let's have her stick with using her sword. That's what she's good at, after all."

Thunder squinted a little, confused. "But why?"

"Well." Logan exhaled sharply. "It's–"

"Thunder!" Both turned to see Hunter running toward the training area. "I need to speak with you about something– hi, Logan– if you're not busy?"

"What's going on?" asked Thunder.

"As you know, a few of the men and I have been investigating the origin point of our current nemeses," explained Hunter. "It's reasonable to conclude that it's somewhere within the forest to the northwest. I wanted to ask– would it be possible for us to take the fight closer to that area? We'd have to leave earlier than usual, but I thought it might be beneficial for, you know, the new recruits, for practice?"

"Oh! That's not a bad idea!" Logan agreed. "It'd be easier to send them packing!"

"*If* they're right about the origin point," pointed out Thunder. "If they're not, it could be disastrous. I think... we'll leave some of the guys here just in case, have them stationed at the usual area."

"I'll stay with them, if you want," volunteered Logan.

"Good deal. Now then, Hunter– let's round everyone up and explain how tonight's gonna go."

EIGHT

Optimistic Trials, Near-Fatal Errors

"This evening's plan requires us to divide our forces. Most of you will be stationed at the usual spot of defense, here."

In the conference room, Thunder was reviewing the night's itinerary with everyone. He was making use of the large map that was spread out on the conference table, making note of where everyone would be. This was, most likely, a formality– or a courtesy for the non-natives in the meeting.

"Everyone who is not part of the special group I was helping train today: Logan will be overseeing your operations tonight, so bring any specific questions about this evening to him. As for the rest of you, you'll be with myself. We're gonna venture closer to the forest that's to the northwest, so that we can try and observe any evidence that would indicate it's where the holzomen, those nuisances, are coming from."

"Those of you with me will be departing at the usual time," added Logan. "However, those of you venturing farther on will have to leave about an hour earlier, just to be on the safe side."

"Which means y'all should be fixing to go soon," Thunder finished. "Suit up. We'll be leaving in ten."

The meeting adjourned then, the Resistance members going to ready their weapons and equipment. "Is there any particular... suiting we should do?" asked Brecken, her question aimed at Logan.

"No, no. Don't worry about that. All we need from all of you is to remember the things you were taught," he replied. "I know it's only been a day, but that's why Thunder is bringing reinforcements, plus you'll have Hunter and Lisandra. They usually stay here, but having them with you means that you will all be protected– and that we won't run out of healing capacity again."

"Not if I can help it!" agreed Lisandra.

"We feel ever more safe with you around, Lisandra," Gavin told her, earnestly. "But even so, we're going to try and make it so that you don't worry about us too terribly much."

"Yeah! Just point us at those dumb things and we'll knock 'em into next week!" agreed Jasiela.

"You guys' optimism is reassuring." Lisandra closed her eyes, smiling. "But please make sure you're taking this seriously too."

Jasiela's expression fell, and she turned to Lisandra. "Well, yeah, sure. Didn't mean to give off the impression that I wasn't."

"We shan't forget, although she's a teenager like us, that this is Lisandra's home," pointed out Gavin. "She's probably under an unimaginable level of stress."

"Oh!" Logan sat up straight then, a thought occurring to him. "Speaking of stress, I should let Spencer-Lynn know that you're heading out soon."

"No need. I'm right here." She waved, signifying her arrival. "I've been told we're to depart for the woods soon?"

"That's right." Gavin nodded.

"Ah, nice. I wonder if that'll give us any insight as to how and why I ended up here, since that's where my earliest memories here are."

"That's a good question!" Logan nodded. "And now that I think about it, Brecken, didn't you say something similar?"

"Hm? Oh, yes, actually, I think I did wake up in a forest when I first arrived here," she suddenly remembered. "I can't say if it's the same forest, but."

"Yeah, I forgot about that until just now. Hmm, I do wonder... and my curiosity is kinda making me wish I was on you guys' team now. I wonder if Hunter would be up for switching with–"

"No, because we're leaving right now," Hunter said as he entered the room. "Everyone, let's head out."

"Right now? Like right now, right now?" asked Jasiela.

"Come on, dude, we have to knock these things into next week, remember?" Jaiden said supportively. "The sooner we do that, the better."

Everyone stood up then, getting ready to leave headquarters. A preliminary check for weapons and other materials that it was wise to have along. A second check to make sure everyone was present. A third and final check, just in case something may have been missed the first two times around.

"Logan." Thunder re-entered the room.

"Don't mess this up. I know." He nodded. "I've got this all under control, I promise."

"No promises you can't keep, youngin." Thunder chuckled as he pushed the door open. "I'm looking forward to a complete and thorough briefing when we get back."

"And you'll have it!" Logan grinned eagerly as he waved.

With that, everyone began to trudge out to the woods. It wasn't a horribly long trek, and thankfully, the weather had been on the pleasant side after that thunderstorm a little while ago. Still, the tenseness was definitely in the air, as it always was whenever one of these battles was to take place. There was always that chance of mortality, and given how the last big battle had turned out, it weighed much more heavily on everyone's mind that had been present for that.

"So, the plan is to have me near the back, right?" asked Lisandra. "Nice and protected? Just checking."

"Yes. Protected, but not too far behind," replied Thunder.

Lisandra nodded. "Good to hear it." If either of her cousins had been there, they may have been able to hear the tiny tremble in her voice.

Thunder's guns were in their holsters, fully loaded. "This is important, girls and boys," he said. "I know we've been kind of cryptic about the situation so far, but think of it this way. Every mutant you kill means potentially one more life that can be saved in the villages."

"So, go nuts?" asked Jaiden.

"Show no mercy."

She nodded, and turned to everyone else. "No mercy. I think I can manage that. I'd be lying if I said I didn't have first-time jitters, though."

"Yeah, definitely," agreed Mishaela.

A brief silence ensued.

"I can hear something to the west!" Gavin whispered hurriedly.

"West?" Hunter turned in a completely different direction than Gavin had intended.

"Er, north I suppose," he corrected himself. To ensure he wouldn't be misunderstood again he pointed as he added, "That way."

"Time to rock and roll!" Madeline yelled.

Using magic, for the portion of the group that was unfamiliar with doing so, was an experience that was difficult to put into words; first there was the building pressure in one's chest, and then there was always a tingly feeling upon one's fingertips that pro-gressed to the palm, before the power that they were summoning materialized in their hands. The resulting resistance to the element (such as not being burned by fire, or the hands not becoming dirty when handling the earth) was an interesting effect, but not one that anyone had been able to contemplate for long due to the current situation. There would, hopefully, be other times to marvel at the ability to hold fire or lightning in one's hands.

Before now, Lisandra, Brecken, and the members of the Resistance had been the only people to see Spencer-Lynn with her sword; now, everyone was seeing it, and it was easy to tell that they were impressed. She would charge toward the mutants and slice them in whatever area her momentum felt comfortable with. It was usually their middles; she'd explained to Chiara and Brecken previously that if one was cut in half, it would be *pretty hard* for it to get back up.

It was difficult for Brecken to adjust to her first battle that was solely based on combat. She struggled to keep her footing, especially when she was progressively pushed toward an area where the ground she was on was muddy because the river was nearby. It was only a matter of time– when the area began to get crowded, she slipped; she panicked, and screamed. At this point there was only one of the holzomen in her immediate vicinity, but she was finding it hard to get back on her feet due to the mud. It raised its foot, ready to start attacking, when suddenly a shard of ice impaled it, and it fell to the ground.

Brecken was certain that not only had her heart never beat this hard before, but that it would possibly never beat this hard again. She hoped it wouldn't, even, but the most important part was that– despite what had just transpired– she was alive.

"Need some help?" Mishaela was suddenly standing above her, and she extended her hand.

"Yes, thanks," Brecken replied as she took Mishaela's hand, and she pulled her up. "I promise, I wasn't this hopeless in the last battle. It's just that the ground is really slippery in this area and... I'm *really* glad you came in time."

"It's what we're all here for: to keep each other safe." Mishaela nodded. "That's the important part. Are you okay? Can you walk?"

"I think so," Brecken answered, testing her legs. "Yeah, I can stand. I'm just a bit rattled, that's all."

Mishaela smiled. "Stay with me, then. You managed to get awfully far away from everyone else."

The two of them returned to their group, where Thunder had taken out his pistols and had started to give out backup. It was impressive to behold him keeping his aim so precise as he darted through both the crowd of holzomen, and the trees in the forest. He was impressively nimble for an old man; and, nearby, Hunter was handling the nuisances in a similar way. Even Lisandra was now working to fight off some of the forces with her newly acquired ribbon.

"That's not backup," Brecken realized, as she watched. "There are too many."

Everyone was working hard to keep their ground. Jaiden was using all the vegetation in the area as weaponry, particularly the vines. They were used as whips as well as ropes that tore apart their enemies. Jasiela was throwing fireballs at as many mutants as she could, creating walls of fire for protection, and Gavin was with her; when there was enough time he'd blow a twister through one of Jasiela's fire walls and create a fiery cyclone. These were very good at clearing out large areas, so they had been working together on synchronizing their magic to do it as often as necessary without getting tired.

Meanwhile, Madeline was busy with her tremors, which were very useful for the smaller mutants; they were rendered immobile from the impact against the ground when they fell.

Mishaela pointed to one of the fire walls Jasiela had created. "Can you do that, Brecken?" she asked. "Just with water?"

"I think so!" They'd had to start yelling at this point; it was getting loud.

"Good! We'll work together; catch as many as you can within the wall and I'll freeze it in the process!"

Brecken took a deep breath and began to summon the magic energy to her core. The tingling sensation, which was beginning to become more familiar to her the more she had to use magic, quickly began to simmer throughout her entire body. There was a moment, always a very potent and obvious moment, in which the magic sensation would almost begin to hurt; and that was when she would release it, working to summon the largest quantity of water she could muster, to make the waterwall as big as she could.

Before Mishaela was ready, though, electricity surged through the wall, leaving them with about a dozen fried holzomen.

"You're welcome, ladies." Spencer-Lynn gave them both pats on the back, rather confidently, but Mishaela noticed her flinch when the wall crackled particularly loudly.

The amount of holzomen were starting to dwindle at this point, so everyone was finally able to breathe. With the new calm, though, it became rather obvious that something wasn't quite right. Almost instantly, Mishaela realized what it was, and gasped.

"Spencer-Lynn, have you seen my sister?" she asked then.

That's when she and Brecken both realized: they hadn't seen Chiara since they first arrived in this area. "Not to alarm you, but I don't believe I have," replied Spencer-Lynn. "*But,* that could just be because I was too concentrated on fighting, and helping you two just now. It doesn't necessarily mean anything is wrong. I'm sure she's fine."

"Who's fine?" Gavin asked, walking into earshot. He looked about as dirty as everyone else, but there was a large, round hole in the side of his shirt, as if he'd gotten a little too close to one of Jasiela's fireballs. Knowing that the two of them had been working together for most of the fight, it was likely that that had indeed happened. "Where's Chiara? I thought she was with you."

This, clearly, didn't make Mishaela feel any better.

"So I see. We'll find her," Gavin comforted her, placing a hand on one of her shoulders. "Don't worry."

"Aye, Chiara's a bit hard to miss with her dark aesthetic," agreed Spencer-Lynn. "I'll go tell the captain that we're having a spat of trouble finding her, and I'm sure he'll be able to help. You just keep searching in this particular area."

Everyone searched for about fifteen minutes before Gavin called, "You guys! Over here!" He waved his arms over his head in an attempt to be more visible.

When they'd finally found her, Chiara was worse off than all of the group combined; she had a nasty bruise under her left eye, and the stomach of her long black dress was covered in blood. Lisandra ran to her and scooped her head into her lap, immediately beginning her healing spells.

It was quiet enough that one could hear muffled sobs escaping Mishaela's throat as she cried into Gavin's shoulder. Impulsively, Brecken grabbed her hand. "She'll be okay, I'm sure of it. Lisandra and Phoenix are really good healers, and they know how important she is to you."

"To all of us," added Jaiden. "There's no way we're letting anything bad happen to her."

Mishaela nodded, her tears still flowing, but slowing enough that she would be able to begin the walk back to headquarters.

Once Chiara's bleeding had stopped and Lisandra had gotten her cleaned up a little, Thunder picked her up and put her over his shoulder, and everyone started on the walk back to base. No one said a word for the entire trip.

NINE

The Trouble With Particularly Large Parties

The air was tense when everyone returned to headquarters.

Logan had wanted to express his pride over a successful defense on his end, but he could tell the minute the group got back that this wasn't the time. It was difficult to decide what he would say at all, even, because everyone had gone so somber. Was it right to ask what had happened? He wasn't sure the question wouldn't cause more tension than was already present in the air. But he also didn't want to stand around doing nothing. What was a man to do? Although he stood still, his body trembled with the desire to move. To speak. To do *anything*.

"Logan." He was gently grabbed by his sister to get his attention. "Hey, hey, what happened?"

He shrugged. "I wish I knew. The teams split this evening, remember?"

"Oh, right, right," she nodded, remembering the conversation about it. "That must be why you're out here looking like a lost puppy."

"I do *not*." But Logan's pout was certainly not unlike a puppy.

"In any case, it looks like the group you weren't in took on more than they were equipped to handle. I was going to assist Lisandra with Chiara's treatment, but she insisted–"

"Is Chiara okay?" Logan cut her off, clearly concerned.

"At the moment, it's hard to say. There's evidence of at least one really bad cut, but as I was saying– *before you cut me off*– Lisandra's very adamant about handling her treatment herself. I don't know why, but I at least made sure she could realistically handle it without my help before I left her to her devices." Phoenix sighed, running her hands into her dark curls. "This is such a mess."

"Everything is a mess. Everything has *been* a mess for the past three weeks!" Logan complained. "Can– can I lose my mind yet? I'm really close to losing my mind here."

"Logan," Phoenix said, in a warning way. "Não faça isso. You know, even with as much grief as we give you, as... I... give you, nobody can dispute that you're important to us. Without you, we'd be in a worse way than we are now, and that's not something I want to think about. Maybe later, when everyone is asleep, we can go out back and scream, but try to keep it together just a little longer, all right? You've got a bunch of kids here that look up to you for some odd reason."

"Yeah." Logan's face couldn't hide the fact that he was very happy over hearing his sister encourage him. "As for now, we should probably call some type of meeting. To find out what happened, but also to determine how that'll shape our future operations."

Phoenix nodded. "There's the Logan I know. Let's go find everyone."

When everyone was shepherded into the conference room, noticeably one person down, the room was still tense as everyone grabbed a chair, sitting around in a circle to prepare for the impending discussion.

A discussion that no one appeared ready to start.

"From the top, then?" Phoenix was the first to speak. "Logan and I weren't with you, so we don't know what landed us here, but a lot seems to have happened since the last time we were all in this room together. Would someone be so kind as to catch us up?"

There was another silence before Hunter spoke. "Apologies, Phoenix. The reason none of us are beginning the conversation is probably because it all happened so fast that it's difficult to know *where* to start, but I can certainly try. We went out further from the town than we have in the past, as you may be aware. Our foray into the forest was mostly successful, but at the end of it, we noticed that Chiara not only wasn't within the immediate vicinity, but that many of us hadn't seen her in a while. This made us all very worried, naturally. After a few minutes of searching, we found her, unconscious and–" he glanced around the room, locating Mishaela to see if it was a good time to go into detail or not, and deciding not was the better idea– "injured. With that, we rushed here. I believe you know the rest."

"Right." Phoenix nodded. "Lisandra, how is the prognosis on that, then?"

Lisandra shrugged. "Standard fare. Expect her on her feet by tomorrow morning, but probably not at a hundred percent until the evening. Probably should miss a day or two of training."

"Good to hear. So now I guess we should be discussing how to make sure this never happens again," Phoenix finished.

Another short hush fell over the room. "I guess I should start by sayin' you were right," Thunder said first. "It was much too soon to send them out there with those things. I should have listened... now look at what's happened."

If there was a specific feeling to match the idea of a record scratching, it would likely be similar to the current shift in mood that had just happened.

"Hold on. I know you are *not* trying to shoulder all the blame for this. In no way is this your fault," Phoenix reprimanded him. "Unless you tried to reach incredibly far with your reasoning, were you really expecting this to happen? Of course not. No one would have."

"We need to do a lot of things from here on, but one of them is certainly not beating you up about an informed decision you made with the knowledge you had at the time," agreed Logan. "What would be the point? Who would that serve? To do so would be to betray all the other times you've guided us to prosperity."

"That's exactly the kinda thing I got in mind when I apologize to y'all, Logan. As the leader of this organization, I'm responsible for all of you, which means I can't be out here making decisions that endanger anyone; and yet, that seems to be all I'm doing these days. It's completely on me. I've been a fool. Especially after what happened in the square, it's downright stupid of me to go and put y'all in danger again so soon. What was I thinking?"

"Thunder, are we gonna have to go through you beating yourself up every time we have any kind of misstep?" asked Lisandra. "Look, I get it, everything sucks right now. Nobody's disputing that at all, but getting hung up on that keeps us from moving forward, which is something we need to do if we ever want our lives back. Plus, it's not your fault that Chiara is so weak."

A stunned silence fell over the room– but it wasn't a long one.

"You don't understand a damn thing, do you, you petulant child. Who in the hell do you think you are?" Spencer-Lynn addressed Lisandra directly.

"Who do I think I am? Who do you think *you* are?! You've been here a week and now you think you can talk to me like I'm a kid?"

"You *are* a kid!" Logan pointed out. "And this is why Tio didn't want you to be part of the Resistance until you were an adult. If this is how you regard your comrades outside of the battlefield, you don't have the maturity to do what we do in any capacity!"

"You can complain about me speaking to you like you're a child all you want, but that pales in comparison to you speaking to the leader of the organization you've been begging to be a part of since you were a wee lass like he's been mildly inconvenienced. Blood was spilled less than a week ago. We just almost lost someone that's not even from this world. How would we explain that when we're all back on the other side? Have you even started to think of the repercussions that might have had on both of the worlds involved, not to mention how that would have derailed any plans to fix things here? Do you... do you even understand what it's like to have a duty to protect anyone? Or did you just want to be here to serve that inflated sense of superiority you've got?"

"You..." Lisandra stood, facing Spencer-Lynn. "What do you think gives you the right? You don't know anything about me!"

"And you know even less about me, or else you'd know I'd never be intimidated by some child who's just roleplaying the part of a rebel." Spencer-Lynn stood as well, but then turned to head back toward the bedrooms. "You're pathetic."

Before Lisandra could speak, Phoenix held her hands up. "That is enough, everybody go to bed! Everyone's emotions are running high right about now, and the last thing we need is anyone saying things they can't take back. To bed. Or at least to your rooms. *Now.*"

"But shouldn't we..." started Hunter.

"Bed, Hunter! I mean it!" Phoenix pointed toward the hallway where his bedroom was. He hurried in that direction, afraid of what would happen if he didn't.

If there was one thing Phoenix was good at, outside of her Resistance duties, it was having the last word.

The bedroom was quiet when Jaiden and Mishaela returned to it. Chiara had joined them for the past two nights, but because she was still recovering, she was going to spend the night in another room. For tonight (and for possibly a few more nights, depending on her recovery) it was just the two of them.

"Well, this sucks." Jaiden was the first to speak.

After a brief pause, Mishaela finally spoke. "Everything was so much easier last time," she said quietly. "All I did was play a game of chess and everything was okay. We got along fine and stuff. Now everything is just..."

"Yeah." Jaiden nodded, folding her hands over her stomach.

"It really does *suck*," Mishaela said then, getting a laugh from Jaiden. It wasn't often that Mishaela said that things sucked, and especially not with such emphasis.

"Yeah. For real. But don't forget things sucked last time too. Obviously not at this level of general suckiness, but we were in an unfamiliar situation then too, and despite how much it sucked, we got through it somehow. Even with things sucking at near-catastrophic levels at this point, I still don't think we're so far gone that it's hopeless. I refuse to believe that, because if it's game over here, I doubt we'll just get to go home. And I think we can both agree that we are way too busy back home to be prevented from getting back there. I still have to visit my sister in Seattle... and you and Chiara have to go visit your family– *and* say goodbye to Lulu before you go."

"Jaiden." The room was dark, but it was easy to tell Mishaela was moderately flustered.

"What's going on with you two, anyway?" Jaiden asked then. "Are my 'they're definitely more than friends' instincts right this time?"

There was another silence. "I'll tell you if we get through this in one piece. Would that be all right?"

"Absolutely." Jaiden laughed. "We can face that tomorrow. Let's just try and get some rest tonight."

Mishaela nodded, but she also could feel she wouldn't be sleeping anytime soon, so she pushed her blanket aside and stood. "I'll be back. I'd like to get a cold glass of water and maybe check up on Chiara before I go to sleep. You don't have to wait up for me."

"Okay. But make sure you get some sleep tonight," Jaiden said then, much in the manner of an older sibling, before turning over, pulling the blanket over herself.

It took getting turned around a couple of times, but eventually, Mishaela remembered the way to the kitchen. She wasn't very confident in her ability to remember which room Chiara was resting in, but as she drank her glass of water– savoring the coldness as it rushed down her throat– she tried to convince herself that she could remember. There couldn't be *that* many rooms here. Could there be?

The door opened then, interrupting her thoughts. Spencer-Lynn, in her pajamas as well, entered. "Oh. Wasn't expecting anyone to be here."

"I'm sorry. I'll leave," Mishaela apologized, but Spencer-Lynn shook her head.

"No need." She hoisted an empty glass. "I'm only after a glass of water. Feeling a touch dehydrated, after everything that's transpired today. Er– sorry."

Mishaela waved it off. "Don't worry about it."

"You've been quiet since we got back," Spencer-Lynn said as she poured herself some water. "You've probably spoken to your friends about everything already, but there's something to be said about the type of honesty you can achieve with a stranger. Or someone who's pretty close to one. I won't be sleeping anytime soon, so if you need to get some things off your chest... I'll be here."

Mishaela nodded, pausing before gesturing toward the water, wordlessly asking Spencer-Lynn to pass it. "Everything is... horrible. It's all horrible. It's horrible to the point where I'm not sure if us being here is even helping at all. I'm almost certain you and Lisandra and Brecken could've handled everything without us getting in the way."

"Hmm, I'm not so sure about that. Maybe we could've. But you were the one who saved Brecken this evening, aye?" Spencer-Lynn asked her. "Things would have been very bad for her if you hadn't found her, and as bad as it is that Chiara's currently out of commission, I shudder to think of what things would be like if two of us had been hurt as badly. So I can't agree that you're getting in the way."

Mishaela's spectacled eyes were stuck on Spencer-Lynn, so she continued, "I've noticed that Brecken and Chiara are already becoming friends. She hasn't come outright and said it but... your sister, she doesn't make friends easily, does she?"

"People tend to make her anxious," Mishaela confirmed. "We're not too unlike each other in that way, sometimes."

Spencer-Lynn nodded. "When you pay attention to her mannerisms, it's easy to tell. It's not entirely foreign to me; it reminds me of one of my younger brothers."

"Oh, you have siblings," Mishaela noted.

"Too damn many," Spencer-Lynn laughed. "Two sisters. Four brothers. I suppose the young ones are a bit too young to discern a defining personality about them so far, but I will say that Vincent– that's the third youngest one, the fifth child overall– is probably heading toward an emo phase any day now. If I were ever asked about the sibling I'm closest to, though, that would be a tie between one of my younger brothers, and my older sister. My brother, Mumford– he's the middle child, and you certainly can tell. He's about as timid and unassuming as you'd expect a middle child to be. Even so, I've never questioned his love for me. It's a quiet love, but it's always present in subtle ways, and I'm grateful for it; it's like the feeling you get when coming home. My sister, Maceida, she's... definitely a unique one. Her love for me is always present too, but it's always a more loud, obvious, in-your-face thing. That's pretty much how you could describe her as a person, too, actually; rooms don't stay quiet for long when she's about. Even so, I miss her. Haven't seen her in about three years. She's in Canada for her studies."

"Oh. Jaiden's sister is doing the same thing. What a coincidence," Mishaela said then. "Toronto?"

"Montreal. Fluent French speaker."

"Ah." Mishaela nodded. "I can't imagine having so many siblings. It's always been just Chiara and I. I suppose that's why I'm always so worried about her, and probably vice versa as well. I just don't want to lose the one sister I have."

"It's understandable." Spencer-Lynn finished off her glass of water, hesitating to decide if she'd pour another before deciding not to, and placing her cup in the sink. "This was a good talk, but I think we'd both be better off trying to get some sleep now so that we can face tomorrow with fresh heads, aye?"

Mishaela nodded. "Yes, of course. Thank you, Spencer-Lynn."

"It was nothing. I should be thanking you as well."

"Thanking me? For?" Mishaela asked.

Spencer-Lynn hesitated again, before shutting her mouth in a line of discontent. "Sorry. It's not that I don't want to tell you–but it's too much to get into right this moment. You probably understand."

"Yeah." Mishaela nodded. After all, everything felt like a lot at this point in time.

The room was silent, with the exception of the sound that the chrome, heavy ball made as it rolled over the table every time Lisandra pushed it from one side to the other, her chin resting on the table. Occasionally, she'd blow her bangs out of her eyes. Her cousins sat across the table from her, but other than Logan asking if she wanted any water, it had been quiet for at least the past three minutes.

The ball continued to roll. Left to right. To one side, and then back again.

"I mean, it's not like I was *trying* to be mean!" Lisandra suddenly blurted out, holding the ball in one of her hands. This, of course, earned confused looks from both of her cousins. "What was I supposed to say? Why is it that every time I try to say something, it's always wrong?"

Phoenix was the first to speak, probably because she was more familiar with Lisandra's home life. "Your lack of tact is something that, while I certainly don't like it, I can't... really blame you for it. Your parents are both, with all due respect, some of the most tactless people I know when it comes to how they speak to people, *especially* your mom. I've felt it when they speak to me. When they speak to Logan. I've seen it when they speak to you too, Lisandra."

Lisandra nodded slightly.

"And you– you're a kid who's had so much responsibility thrown onto them from a young age, the type of responsibility that makes you be a little colder than you want to be, just so that you can survive. It's because I know this, that I know your intentions are never bad. But, Lisandra– and I hope you know by now that I would only say this with love– you have *got* to start doing better. Knowing why you're the way you are isn't enough. There will be situations like now, when you're working with people who don't know you. You'll work with people who won't be able to be convinced to forgive you when you've disrespected them. What will you do then?"

The silence of thought fell over the room.

"I don't know..." Lisandra mumbled. "I feel bad. Awful, even. But you're right; what do I say to a bunch of strangers so they know I wasn't trying to be mean?"

"Hm, I suppose we can never be too sure about that kind of thing. That's the part that's unfortunate; that we will never know how someone will respond to our words until we've already said them out loud." Phoenix turned to her brother. "What do you think, Logan? You've been uncharacteristically quiet."

Logan remained silent for a moment longer before looking up, sliding closer to the edge of the chair he was sitting in. "I have, haven't I? I don't have a lot to say. You know me and Lisandra used to get into arguments all the time because she's like this."

Oh *boy*, did Phoenix know. She wished she wasn't as familiar with the phenomenon as she was.

"But I will say this: as much as the Pagliardi sisters obviously deserve a sincere apology from you, I think you should apologize to Spencer-Lynn as well," Logan continued. "Don't forget that she's done a lot for a bunch of people she barely knows, and was never obligated to help. Plus, I mean, she wasn't wrong in anything she said."

When Lisandra opened her mouth, Phoenix put up a hand. "And with that, I'd ask you to think about that for a moment. We *did* just have a horrible loss happen recently, and you *did* speak as if you were minimizing the situation. You *are* a child, Lisandra. You're fifteen! Logan wasn't even allowed outside of headquarters at your age!"

Lisandra sighed. "Yeah, but I don't have an inflated sense of... superiority... I don't, okay?! But I guess I can see why it would look that way to somebody who doesn't live here."

"Exactly." Logan pointed a finger. "See, what you just did is the type of self-consciousness you need in more conversations. You're clearly capable of doing it, so now you just need to put it into practice more often."

"We believe in you," added Phoenix. "Now, before you get to work on your apologies, why don't you get some rest? We've all been working hard today."

"Yeah." Lisandra stood. "Thanks, guys. You've always been my favorite cousins."

When she'd gone, the door shutting behind her, Logan turned to his sister with a smile on his face. "I believe we had an engagement after everyone went to bed?"

"Today was probably the worst way a day could've gone," Phoenix said to Logan with a short exhale, as she sat beside him on the bank of the river.

"Yeah. Yeah, you're not wrong," he agreed. "This is all such a doozy. But, hey: the day is now at its end, we're out here, and since most of the people inside have gone to bed, I don't think we'll be interrupted. You can vent to me, if you want."

Phoenix turned to him and opened her mouth to speak, but then hesitated, before standing up with a small grunt of effort.

Logan was confused until she let out the loudest scream she'd screamed in at *least* five years.

It was the loudest that he– that anyone, probably– had ever heard her voice get. Not only that, but this scream was also long; impressive for her to have not warmed up or taken a breath before- hand. Where was it all coming from? As she graduated to shouting in Portuguese, Logan could only stare. He wasn't sure he'd *ever* seen his sister this way.

When she was done shouting, Phoenix took a few deep breaths. "Whew. Wow. You know something, Logan? I didn't think about it until just now, but I don't think I've taken a moment to unload like that ever since I joined the Resistance. I've been so busy being responsible and upstanding that I guess I never noticed how much of a toll it's been taking on me. Guess that happens when you run away from home at 14."

"By the way, speaking of your departure, you reminded me just now that when Mom noticed you were gone, she sounded exactly like you just did." Logan laughed. "Why did she do that? Did she...

did she think yelling would bring you back? It was so stupid!" He continued to laugh.

"Part of growing up is realizing that your parents aren't infallible," Phoenix replied. "They're regular people who make mistakes."

"You think it took me until I was an adult to notice that?"

"All right! Your turn!" Phoenix rose to her feet again, before placing her hands under Logan's arms in an attempt to get him to stand up as well. "I got my frustration out, now it's your turn!"

"But I vent my frustration all the time when I'm fighting," Logan reluctantly stood. "That's the benefit of being in a combat position. I don't have to worry about taking my frustrations out on an unsuspecting citizen; or worse, a friend. I don't... really..."

Logan mimed a punch first, then another, then he motioned for a third, but stopped his fist halfway through the motion. His movements gradually became more graceful– a sweep of the arm over his head, a sweep of his leg– until Phoenix realized what he was doing. He was *dancing*.

"...six, seven, eight... all these dreams of mine..." he said to himself under his breath.

"What in the world are you doing, Logan?"

"What does it look like? I'm dancing." He smiled. "I never get time to dance anymore. Everything's so busy these days with all the fighting and the planning and the... threats to our way of life." He spun, ending in a pose so graceful that Phoenix was sure he'd have accompanied it with a few stars if he'd have thought of it. "I've still got it! Glad I got that out of my system. Now what?"

"I don't think we'll know the answer to that until tomorrow, unfortunately," replied Phoenix. "Let's go back inside. Might as well face that mess with a good night's sleep."

"Yeah." Logan nodded as the siblings began their walk back to headquarters. "Maybe... we could do this again sometime. You know, when the world isn't on fire somehow."

Phoenix smiled up at him, earning herself a smile back. "It's difficult to imagine the world calming down at this point, but I'd like that. I'd like that a lot."

TEN

Reconnaissance...

The next morning, everyone gathered in the kitchen to eat. Usually, when congregating for a meeting, Thunder would already be dressed and have an itinerary in hand, but today he was still in his pajamas, empty-handed. The meeting would also usually take place before breakfast, but by the time everyone had arrived, there was already a simple spread of toast and scrambled eggs on the table, with various flavors of jam in mason jars on the table as well.

"This is certainly different," Phoenix noted as she sat beside Hunter.

"Different is good, ain't it," Thunder said, as a statement and not a question, as he walked closer to the table to sit at the head. "I wanted this meeting to be different from all the other ones we've had, because today is gonna be the start of handling things differently than we have up to this point. Help yourselves to the food."

"Don't mind if I do." Madeline was already grabbing a piece of toast.

Thunder smiled, amused. "Before I get into today's plans, I need to share something else with you that'll ultimately be helpful when it comes to rollin' those plans out. Hunter will do a better job at explaining that, though. Why don't you take the reins?"

"Right, er..." Hunter nodded. "Ever since the first creature invasion, I've been working with some of the engineers here to see if there's anything we could come up with to keep our town safe. There's been considerable slowdown at multiple points due to the gravity of the situation, not to mention all the failed prototypes we've gone through– but late last night, I received exciting news. It would seem that we finally have a functional mechanism for defense of Compositora!"

Scattered, uncertain applause sounded within the group.

"What this means is that we won't have to put as much manpower behind defending the town for a little while," Thunder explained. "With that out of the way, we can dedicate more of our time and effort into researching how to stop this mess at the source."

"I want to be happy about that, but..." Jasiela hesitated. "There's a catch, isn't there? There's always a catch."

"Indeed." Hunter nodded again. "There is. As the mechanism is now, it can only hold enough energy and power for a finite amount of time. This means that, after... three or four days at the maximum, it needs another one or two days to recharge. Those will be days that we have to approach the situation in the way we've been doing; by going out and defending the town ourselves."

"Still, it gives us a few days to try to get ahead of this whole thing, and I can't complain about that," Phoenix noted. "This is amazing. So, what's the plan now, then? Where are we going to search for intel?"

"Actually, I was thinkin' we could hold off on that for the first half of the day."

Thunder stood, stepping a few paces away from the table.

"While I know that all of our minds and hearts are aligned when it comes to taking our home back and finally making it peaceful for longer than a few months, I realized last night that simply wantin' the same thing ain't enough, especially now that so many of us are involved. Everybody's on different wavelengths, and while that ain't necessarily a bad thing, it won't cut it against something this big. We gotta get in harmony with one another. Move as a unit; as one. And with that in mind, I want us to take on a project."

"A project?" Logan asked. It was easy to see that he was intrigued.

"A project." Thunder opened one of the cabinets nearby, shuffling through its contents until he found what he was looking for. "Here we go. On each of these cards is a vague explanation of a pivotal point of history here in our world. I assigned pairs to each of these. For the next couple of hours I want y'all to go and find an ingredient that represents the event. Bring 'em here, and I'll taste test them. Winning team gets to decide how we go about gathering intel for the rest of the day."

"Well, this is an interesting way to go about things," Phoenix noted. "It sounds fun, though, and considering how scarce fun has been lately..."

"Right," Logan agreed quickly. "I'm in! Let's hear those assignments!"

"Of course. I'm gonna try my best to pair ones from this world with ones from the non-magical world, which means a few of y'all will be staying here. I just need a few moments to consider the assignments."

This was probably the chilliest day that Mishaela had ever experienced in this world, but considering how hot it usually was... that didn't mean a lot. Still, the cool breeze was refreshing, as she walked down toward the river with Logan. Before, she'd been filled with the desire to pick his brain; that still existed, but at a lower level than before, since most of her brain power was currently devoted to worrying about her sister. Logan would understand, right? He had an older sister too, that he clearly cared about.

"So..." Logan said as he sat at the bank of the river. "The creation of our world."

"Is that what we got?" Mishaela asked, sitting beside him.

"Fortunately for you. I remember how badly you and the other kids wanted to know everything about our home. And it pained me just as much to not be able to depart that wisdom, but fortunately, we are no longer bound by the restrictions that we were last time."

"Really? Why not?" Mishaela asked, curiously.

"Well, while I'm sure there's a part of Phoenix that would still like to forbid me from talking too much, we've been given a missive by our commander in chief. You've also been literally entrusted with a fragment of the goddesses' power. My sister would never be as foolish as to try to reach over that kind of authority," Logan laughed. "But with Spencer-Lynn and Brecken being here, I've already had to give this explanation twice recently, so do you mind if I give you the summarized version?"

This made Mishaela laugh this time. "Sure."

"Right. So, as the story goes... this world, it was more or less only created because the goddesses got bored. They created this world to test the extent of their abilities. So came the world, but then, an entire world is boring if it doesn't have anything in it, so they began to add things to it. Mountains, hills, trees, flowers, oceans. This river." Logan gazed across it then, at the trees, some of them bearing those sickly purple-gray colors.

"Why are the trees doing that, by the way?" Mishaela asked. "Do you know?"

"I don't, unfortunately." Logan shrugged. "If I had to guess, I think this is the kind of reaction that signifies there's some seriously bad auras around– that must be why Hunter's sources have con- cluded there's something sinister happening there. The good thing is that most of the trees are untouched, so it'll be a wonderful place for us to forage today."

"We're foraging?" Mishaela asked. "Is there a reason we're not just going to the market?"

"The *market*?" Logan repeated, sounding as if his entire family line had been insulted. "You have to expand your horizons, Mishaela. Everybody is going to go to the market for food. We have to do something that will differentiate us from everyone else. And what will that be? Freshly picked foods; what better to signify the birth of the world than things that we harvest directly from it? I'm not familiar with the fruits that grow here, so I'm not sure if they're edible, but I think we'll be able to find some vibrant herbs here. Maybe some tree nuts."

"Oh, I love peanuts!" Mishaela nodded.

"Ah!" Logan all but screamed. "Not those. Those are bad. Last time I tried to eat a peanut, I couldn't breathe for two hours."

"Oh, you're allergic?" Mishaela asked. "That... kind of sucks. Peanuts are great, but don't worry. Just steer me toward things that won't make your throat close again."

"Yeah." Logan nodded, as he and Mishaela began to walk. "By the way, did you know that peanuts are actually legumes?"

"The Great Population. Good thing this is something I know a lot about already," Lisandra said confidently as she held her card. She then turned to her assigned partner. "Hey, Madeline! Wanna know why people live here?"

"Oh! Yeah, didn't Logan tell us about that?" Madeline asked. "Something about reanimating the recently deceased? Very metal, I gotta say."

"Right, but if you'll recall, he mentioned that it was *one of* the ways the world was populated. There's more than that," Lisandra replied as the two girls began to walk. They were headed to the market; since it was only recently that Lisandra had moved here, she wasn't aware of any other places to potentially shop; and of course, Madeline wouldn't know either. "There was also the Great Population. This is a phenomenon where the goddesses, rather than grabbing the souls of those who had recently died, grabbed those of people who were currently living. To summarize what happened after that: they pulled them through to this world, and jumbled their memories of their past– making them effectively new people with new lives here."

Madeline frowned. "Whoa, hold on, stop the car; something about that seems *crazy* immoral to me. I mean, those were people with dreams. Ambitions. Families. And they just yanked them away like that?"

"Rarely will you find a god that adheres to the morals of humans." Lisandra shrugged. "Besides, from what I've been told, the vast majority were taken because they were already in dire straits in their past lives. Think of your homeless, alone, chronically depressed, despairing in some other way. Why not give them a new lease on life?"

This, admittedly, made a lot of sense. "Yeah..." Madeline agreed. She still wasn't sure how she felt about the whole situation, but also knew she'd probably need some time to sit on the idea. "So then, is there any specific reason they didn't wipe their memories completely, rather than just scrambling them up like the eggs we had for breakfast?"

"I don't know. There are conflicting scriptures about the reason, but the most reasonable one to me is that they still wanted them to retain distinct personalities. And of course, a goddess would never spend time reteaching people to walk and go to the bathroom. Considering how much time that would take, I can't blame them."

"Yeah. So I'm assuming that's why everybody here speaks English."

"Not everybody does," Lisandra corrected her. "Most people do, but something I've learned ever since I've been living with the Resistance that really fascinates me is... so, you know how sometimes you build something, or maybe even in the case of having a pet, you just... come up with a name for them? The belief has always been that the goddesses did the same with languages, just called them something so we'd have a name for them. But I'm learning that they're apparently named after places or cultures in your world. That's so interesting."

"Yeah. Yeah, and then there's different dialects and stuff. Linguistics are neat; but they make my head hurt if I study them too long."

They reached the market then. It still wasn't as lively as it had been in the past, likely due to the plumbing situation about a week ago now. Somewhere around the fountain was a makeshift memorial to the people who had died in the battle. Lisandra abruptly stopped here, placing a few coins in the jar at the front of the memorial site before kneeling on one knee, and softly saying what Madeline assumed to be a prayer. Madeline didn't remember any prayers from when her grandparents would take her to Easter service, and she also didn't know if Earth currency meant anything here, but she decided the least she could do was put the nickel, dime, and quarter from her pocket into the jar as well.

"So now that you know about all this, we need to find a food that's somehow related to that," Lisandra reminded her as she stood back up. "Something to signify... new beginnings? A sort of birth, or rebirth? Places with people? Hmm... oh, I think I have an idea! This way! One of these stalls is always crowded, so it must have something that people generally love!"

"Yeah, right behind you!" Madeline replied, nodding and hurrying ahead so the two wouldn't get separated.

When Hunter had been given his card, he stared at it for a while, as if he was unable to read it. Once he'd finally moved, he turned to Brecken with a very resigned look on his face. "I'm terribly sorry, Brecken. I believe we've gotten the worst of the bunch, when it comes to attempting to relate the topic to food."

"Well... 'worst' doesn't automatically mean 'impossible,' right?" she asked optimistically. "What does it say?"

"This card details the migration of this world's people that eventually led to establishing the cities and towns we live in today. It may require some knowledge of what happened before, if you are not yet familiar with those occurrences. Shall we discuss over tea? It's a lovely day outside."

"Oh! Yes, let's do that," Brecken agreed.

"Wonderful. Thunder, we'll be in the backyard so that you can continue to discuss things with your group."

"'Course." Thunder nodded. "Need a tea flavor suggestion? I'm partial to the orange blossom white tea myself."

Hunter carefully arranged the necessary cutlery onto a tray: two opalescent white teacups with saucers that shone with rainbow hues when the light touched them. Golden spoons that made the most delicate tinkling sound when they touched the cups. A teapot with water, the tea leaves, a strainer, a small bowl of sugar, and a small cream jug, which he poured milk into. When it was all assembled, he carefully carried it all out of the room with Brecken following behind.

The duo set up in the backyard, at a table that was very similar to the one at which Gavin and Mishaela had first played chess, an event that felt so long ago now. This area felt very similar to that courtyard in general; how fitting it was, that the makings of a plan may form in such a place.

Hunter took a few minutes to remind Brecken of the origins of this world; something that, as a person who was not only very new to it, but had spent her first few days here unconscious, took her some time to comprehend. Fortunately, Hunter was capable of explaining things in a way that was easy to digest for an ordinary Earth dweller. Whenever Brecken had a question, she found that before she could ask it, Hunter got around to giving her the answer.

"So, now we find ourselves in the era from which we have to provide an ingredient: the departure into cities and towns. This is something that was bound to happen, due to people and their individual sensitivities. Some sought the mountains for their cold air and beautiful views, some craved the lingering salt of the seas, and some preferred the desert-like climates much like the weather here. There is, I believe, an innate human desire to build community, so those searching for similar things banded together. Built towns. Some of those towns remained small. Some of them became bigger cities."

"And all of these towns and cities are as varied and diverse as they are on Earth?" Brecken asked.

"Yes. Ah, I– so I've been told," Hunter replied. "I've also been told that this used to be a city too. A beautiful one. But I'm sure you've been informed why it is no longer what it once was."

"I have." Brecken nodded. "It's unfortunate that another problem has arisen so soon after you guys finally got through that."

"It is unfortunate, but I believe in the Resistance's ability to persevere," replied Hunter. "And I can only hope that you do as well. Now, how will we be relating this phenomenon back to food?"

Brecken sipped her tea, savoring the notes of rose and cinnamon, before replying. "I have an idea. We should look for a food that separates naturally; maybe something oil-based."

"Ah! Very clever!" Hunter nodded. "Let's begin our search as soon as we've finished drinking our tea."

"Oh. This is an interesting phenomenon."

When Phoenix said this, she successfully grabbed Gavin's attention. "What is?"

"The Second Great Population. It requires knowledge of the first one, as well as The Dictator's rise to power. Fortunately, you're already pretty familiar with one of those."

"More than any of us would like to be, I'm sure," Gavin agreed. "But I'm afraid my knowledge of that first subject is scant, if not completely nonexistent. If it isn't too much trouble, a summary would be appreciated."

"Of course. The first Great Population, as implied by the name, occurred when our world was first populated by humans. Logan or Thunder may have mentioned this a few days ago, if I'm not mistaken. People were brought over to this world from your own, and given new lives here. Those are all our ancestors."

"Right. Easy enough to follow," Gavin replied.

"Good. So now you know that there was a Second Great Population. It... how do I say this?" Phoenix sat down on one of the satisfyingly soft cushions in the conference room. "I know that you and most of our visitors faced The Dictator– and ultimately defeated him– but it is necessary to understand that the man that you faced was not the man he always was, and that alone was a mercy on you all. Especially at the beginning of his reign, we were faced with a much more heartless and vicious man. This is why there was no Resistance back then; everyone was too afraid to even think of opposing him.

"I wasn't yet born at the beginning of his reign, but I'm told it wasn't unheard of for people to be killed just because they crossed his path the wrong way, or he didn't like the way they looked. These were the days in which Compositora was much more large and populated than it is today. Most people of this world lived here. As time went on, the amount of deaths... you obviously can't just murder people left and right, and expect to have much of a population left. So, the Second Great Population happened, in which more people from your world were brought into this one. This is when my own great-great-grandparents began to live here."

"Wait, I'm sorry. Hold a tick. There's something about this that confuses me," Gavin held a hand up. "If the death toll was so high that your goddesses noticed and had to resort to bringing more people into the world... wouldn't it have made sense to have intervened in at least some type of way, however small it may be? To this to have been three or four generations ago... if my maths are correct, that means there were roughly two generations before the Resistance was formed, and maybe even another before we were brought along. It sounds really cruel, to have you all suffer here this way in the meantime."

Gavin could tell that Phoenix wasn't exactly equipped to respond to this, not immediately anyway. He could see a look of resignation overcome her before she could speak. "It does really make a person wonder if there's any meaning to their life... doesn't it."

It was then that Gavin sat beside her. "Does it?"

Phoenix sighed. "It wouldn't be entirely incorrect if you were to interpret the teachings of the goddesses as us all being their playthings. I did, a long time ago, and my family... well, you've met Logan and Lisandra. You've probably noticed how strongly they believe in our goddesses. I didn't want to believe this was what I was here for, and my parents did *not* like that. It's part of what led to me running away and coming here, when I think about it. If this is what the goddesses think of our lives, there was no point in sitting around and waiting for things to get better. Our prayers would always fall on ears that couldn't care less. If I wanted to see the world get better, I had to take matters into my own hands; and I hope what I do here with the Resistance is enough to do that."

"I think so. You clearly care about everyone here," Gavin reassured her. "Your bedside manner is better than any I've experienced in all of England, for one."

"Is it? I'm glad to hear that; I do try my best." Phoenix smiled. "Sorry for getting a little sentimental there. It's past time for us to do a little shopping, if we want to win this friendly competition."

"And I do enjoy winning friendly competitions," Gavin smiled back, before standing with a small grunt, and holding his hand out to Phoenix to help her up as well.

"May I ask you something whilst we wait, Thunder?"

Meanwhile, in the kitchen, Thunder was waiting for everyone to return, in the company of Jasiela, Spencer-Lynn, and Jaiden. It was mostly quiet, but every now and then, the younger charges would talk about fashion or food. Spencer-Lynn had been the one to speak, for the first time since everyone else had left.

"Not like I'm doin' much else at the moment," he replied. "What's on your mind, Spencer-Lynn?"

"The other day, I was speaking to Logan, and he mentioned... 'the decline of magic,' I think were his exact words," she explained. "It confuses me a wee bit, because as far as I've been told, magic is... it's what this entire world is made of, right? Does this mean that there was a period of time where this world was dying?"

Thunder rested his hands under his chin, his elbows on the table, unsure on how exactly to answer this question. "It's... complicated. The short answer would be yes, but the situation is a lot more nuanced than that."

This got the attention of Jaiden and Jasiela. "Whoa, dude, the world is dying?! You could've told us that! Why are you so calm?" Jasiela asked.

A heavy sigh from Thunder; this was the exact type of reaction he'd wanted to avoid. "No, but also yes. If you'll let me explain without losing your composure, you'll be able to draw your own conclusions about that."

"Yeah man, keep your cool," Jaiden nudged her. "What's going on, Thunder? And is there anything we can do to help?"

"I'd like to say yes, but this is something that was set into motion long before any of y'all were born, so you shouldn't fret too much over it," Thunder explained. "This, like many of our resulting problems, can be traced back to our unfortunate Dictator problem. The simplest way to put it is that his existence was a drain on the magic that surrounded him."

Jaiden remembered then, the way that the cruel and unsettling man had met his end. There was all that black smoke. The earthquake. The pile of ashes. Certainly not a way in which a human would pass away. Did that mean that he had never been human? She remembered having similar thoughts at the time, too.

"To sustain his palace and his state of being, it meant he had to drain magic from other sources. That's part of why the Resistance attracted members from all over our world. He knew what he was doin' when he set up shop in this town– knowing that, in order to keep this place from dying, the magic would slowly pour in from other areas to here. To protect the longevity of this town is to protect the world, in a sense."

"Is that why everything has more color now than last time we were here?" Jaiden asked.

"Smart girl. Now that the drain is gone, the magic can continue to reaccumulate; and so it has."

"I'm not a–" Jaiden sighed, again realizing that now was probably not the best time for this. "Okay. So, that points toward everything being okay, but the way you were talking, it sounds like there's more to it than that. Does it have anything to do with those eerie creatures we've been fighting?"

"Yes. As you've noticed, we've had a lot of improvement in the last eight months, but for reasons I don't yet know, the presence of those things we've been fighting... it's like them being around halts any further regeneration. So you see, it's not just the immediate threat that they pose with how numerous and destructive they are. If we don't send them packing, we risk them spreading to the point that the magic begins to drain again."

"So that's why the atmosphere has been so dire since I've been here." Spencer-Lynn nodded. "In that case, I suppose we're doing all we can whenever we help you kick creature arse, but I really wish there was more."

"That'd require us to know more than we currently do, so the fault's not on y'all completely," Thunder replied. "For now, just being here, willing, and cooperative is invaluable."

The door to the kitchen opened then, Madeline and Lisandra returning first to share their findings. "Are we early?" the former asked.

"You're the first duo back, as far as I know," Thunder replied. "Hand your submission over and feel free to relax until the others get back.

Lisandra stood at the table, feeling a little anxious. Resting was something she didn't think she'd be able to do at the moment. "While we're waiting for that to happen, do you think we could have a little talk, Spencer-Lynn?"

"Hm?" She looked up from the book she had been reading. "Are you certain?"

I wouldn't be asking you if I wasn't certain. Lisandra had the thought, but knew it would only make things worse if she said it out loud. After a moment she was able to settle on a neutral, affirmative, "Yeah."

"I see. Let's be off, then. We'll be back in a few, everyone."

Walking through the residential halls of the Resistance headquarters always felt equal amounts of intriguing and confining. Of course, there were no windows because this part of the building was underground, but at the same time, the network was so advanced and intricate that neither of the girls had lived here long enough to have completely memorized the layout, and that made it interesting to walk around.

"So..." Lisandra started. After the pause had gone on long enough, she expected Spencer-Lynn to make some sarcastic remark– and was surprised when she didn't.

"What is this about, Lisandra?" she instead asked.

It was a question that Lisandra knew she'd have to answer very carefully. She didn't want to risk having Spencer-Lynn blow up at her again– and, by extension, her cousins agreeing with her again– and, even more so, she didn't want to endanger the team-building vibes that Thunder was working so hard to establish. How could she put into words what she was feeling in a safe way?

As it turned out, the easiest way was just to come out and say it. "Look, my ability to communicate with people sucks, all right? It's a defining feature of mine at this point, but that doesn't mean I want it to be. And, like, it... I don't want you to think I don't appreciate everything you've been doing for us. You're good at fighting, and your desserts are five stars, top-tier. We're all really glad you're here! I... I can't... I'm sorry, okay?!"

Spencer-Lynn was quiet at first, stopping to carefully observe Lisandra. There was something familiar in the way she'd just spoken, but familiar in a way that wasn't exactly positive. As she placed a hand under her chin she asked slowly, "What is it exactly that you're sorry for?"

"Oh, come on!" Lisandra complained. "Are you really gonna make me drag this out?"

"Dragging it out isn't my intent," Spencer-Lynn replied. "How do I explain it... there are few feelings worse than accepting an apology that was only used as a manipulation tactic. I'm just trying to protect myself from that."

Lisandra quickly shook her head. "Oh, no, no! This is definitely not that. Logan would kill me if I– darn it."

It was impossible to miss what she was implying; or so it felt to Spencer-Lynn, who couldn't help but laugh upon hearing this. "Is that so? I had a feeling he may have been behind this somehow."

"Really? How?" Lisandra asked. "If he said anything to you, I will *end* him."

Spencer-Lynn laughed again. "No, it's not that. Something I've been able to easily notice during my time here is the efforts that Logan will go to if it means he will be able to ensure that everyone feels welcome in this organization; even those like you and I, and our friends in the kitchen as well, that are technically not a part of the Resistance. I admire that about him."

The two began to walk again.

"That being said, I may have been a little too harsh on you," Spencer-Lynn said then. "I made some assumptions. I didn't really think a lot about whether or not they could actually be true. I was just really pissed off at how tactless you were being."

"Is this a really long apology?" Lisandra asked.

"It's not an apology," Spencer-Lynn quickly corrected her. "At least, I don't think it is. I'm not sorry for calling you out. I'm regretful about the manner in which it was done."

There was a part of Lisandra that wanted to lash out– but the more that she let Spencer-Lynn's words settle down within her, the more she found herself agreeing with her. Not only that, but she was a little stunned at how articulate she had been. It was far preferable to the non-apologies she'd often receive from her parents. And there had been no screaming involved.

Hallways often had dead ends, and by the time the two arrived at theirs, the dynamic between them felt much more different.

"Lisandra, I do still think– on some level– that you are a horribly precocious child. But I also feel as though I can trust you. That, if I was ever to fall in battle, or if I needed some knowledge about magic, I could approach you about it. And I think that's enough to get us through this excursion in a much more fluid manner than the way things have been going so far."

"Yeah. That's something I could agree with," Lisandra nodded, as the two started on their way back to the kitchen. "Could you let me know if you find Logan before I do? I have another stop on this apology tour."

Spencer-Lynn almost immediately agreed, but then paused. "Now hold on a minute there, why do you think I might see him before you do? You know this place better than I do."

Lisandra just smirked. "Oh, no reason. Just... covering bases and such. Besides, it's his partner I need to talk to," she clarified, as she tried to think of a more tactful way to apologize to Mishaela. She had a feeling she wouldn't be able to be as direct with her as she was just now.

ELEVEN

...and Re-Education

I n the kitchen, after dinner, Thunder asked everyone to hang out a little longer so he could let them know what the next course of action was.

"Thanks. And thank y'all once again for cooperating to complete your tasks," he said. "Aren't we all just a bunch of friendly comrades now?"

"As if there was ever any doubt," Jaiden replied confidently. "What do you have for us now, chief? Got a plan?"

"I do, actually. That's why I wanted y'all to hold back," Thunder replied. "Now that we're all confident in our ability to work together as a team, amiably, we can continue with trying to get our heads around our current situation. I came to a fairly obvious realization: the most potent blow we can deal at once is to stop our enemies at their source, right? So, we need to be putting much more effort into findin' that source than we have thus far, or else it'll be months before we have peace again."

"Right. If I recall correctly, we still don't have a precise location on that," replied Mishaela.

"Not just the location," Logan pointed out. "The circumstances, as well: the magic that was used to create those fiends is just as important, if not more; we need to be sure that it hasn't been executed in a way that will regenerate itself when we do away with it. We need to learn more about that whole situation, but what's been stopping me here is, how?"

"That's up to Phoenix and Gavin. They won the challenge," Thunder replied. "You two have the floor. How will we be approaching this, findin' more information about the current pain in our collective asses?"

Phoenix and Gavin exchanged a look, before Gavin was the one to speak. "Well, I can think of one method that worked astonishingly well the last time we had to gather intel: to the library!"

"The *library*?" Lisandra asked. "I guess it makes sense, but this late?"

"Late? The night is still young!" Logan replied, hopping to his feet. "Even the best scholars would agree that every hour is a good hour to acquire knowledge. I'll lead the way!"

"Does he always get that excited about the library?" Brecken asked.

"Yeah," at least three people immediately replied. Mishaela added, "It's part of his charm."

Logan waited for everyone to get back on their feet before leading a line down to the library. It was a marvelous room, encompassing the entirety of the lowest level of the basement. While the walls were made of stone, intermittent stained glass windows dotted the walls. Elaborate chandeliers that hung over the bookshelves set the mood, casting everything in a warm and inviting light. There was a cluster of file cabinets in one of the corners of the room, but judging by all of the dents and rust on them, they had not been opened in a long time.

"This looks so similar to the library in the basement of the home we stayed in last time," Jaiden noted. "Is this the same library, somehow?"

"It can't be. The orientation of the room is different somehow, I think it's rotated just a tad," Gavin replied, surveying the room. "There's also a different tint to the walls, it's more blue. This one is also better kept, as can be expected by there being a considerable amount of people living here."

Jaiden hummed, agreeing, as they continued to walk.

"You know, now that I see this type of setting again, knowing what I know now, it feels really obvious that this world is a magical place," Mishaela said as everyone arrived at the base of the stairs.

"Really?" Jasiela asked. "I don't disagree, but what exactly makes you say that?"

"To start, we're at, what, level B3 at the highest?" Mishaela asked. "It's not visible now because it's nighttime, but when we were in a place like this before, sunlight came through those stained glass windows. That... shouldn't be possible. I have similar thoughts about those chandeliers and how they're perpetually lit."

Everyone took a moment to look up at the chandeliers. They had that air of mysticism about them, but even so, they looked nicely tended to; the candles placed in the holders were a stunningly dark black, and weren't caked in melted wax.

"Huh. I never noticed, but you're right," Jaiden nodded. "By the way, Resistance. What's in those file cabinets? We noticed some like them last time and assumed they were records– but they were so old we couldn't open them."

"You're right," Hunter nodded. "Those are the records of people that are born here, married here... this became the safest place to keep them after, you know, corrupt dictator and all. We wanted to be sure that our existences were never wiped from record. There's not much purpose to them other than record keeping, though, so that's why the cabinets are so disused aside from the one that keeps the most recent records."

Mishaela took another look at the forsaken cabinets, and then back at Hunter. "How do you know that?"

"For most of my Resistance years, I was a librarian," Hunter explained. "It was required of me to familiarize myself with these walls, that they may become a second home to me."

Jaiden then had a thought about how being a librarian suited Hunter's personality extremely well– and glancing at Mishaela, she could tell that she'd also had the thought– but neither said anything, deciding that it was a thought that didn't necessarily need to be voiced.

"Right, then. So what exactly should we be looking for down here?" Gavin asked then. "We know that we're looking for location and process pieces to the puzzle that is our current predicament, but how exactly does that translate when it comes to books or other resources to look for?"

This was a good point, especially so for the members of the party not from this world; how would they know which books were the ones they needed? With all the bookshelves that were here, it could be hours before they found anything even remotely relevant. Not only that, but what if the book they needed was in a different library?

"I have an idea. Remember when I was saying that this kind of thing never happened back when The Dictator was around?" Logan asked. "Since the library is sorted chronologically, that gives us a start; it means we can disregard a whole section of the catalogue based on that. From there, any books or research material about magic spells and locations that are particularly mystic should help. Let's take a few minutes to look for things like that, and then bring any books back to the table right there," he pointed to an oak wood table that was bare, just a little dusty.

"I knew the kids would come up with some good ideas," Thunder said, smiling. "All right. Y'all heard the man. Back here in thirty."

"Hold on. How will we know when thirty minutes have passed?" Madeline asked. "I don't know about you guys, but if I get sucked into an interesting book, there's no way I'm gonna be able to tell time."

Thunder hummed to himself, looking around for something; his face morphing to a positive expression when he'd caught sight of it. It was an hourglass, one he had been given for his birthday once, long ago. He quickly went to retrieve it, before placing it in the middle of the table where everyone could see it.

"Come back to the table periodically to check how much time you have left," he instructed, flipping the hourglass over so that it could begin to count down the minutes. And, almost immediately, everyone dispersed in the pursuit of knowledge.

After thirty minutes had passed, everyone gathered back at the table Logan had singled out, placing stacks of books on top of it with every new arrival back to the area. By the time everyone had returned, there were enough books on the table to create a border around its perimeter, but there was also still enough space in the middle that one would be able to open a book up, in case anyone would need to share a specific tidbit.

"Okay, okay, this is all looking extremely promising," Thunder said. It was easy to tell that there was hope in his voice. "Who wants to go first?"

"If you all don't mind, I'd love to," Hunter replied, grabbing a book off of the top of the pile he had brought to the table, opening it and flipping through the pages. "If the phenomenon we're experiencing is truly something that strictly did not exist during the times of The Dictator, then as we discussed before our departure, there must be documentation of it occurring before those times. I devoted most of our search time to attempting to find anything to support that kind of hypothesis, and just in time, I found this."

Hunter placed his book back on the table, open to a spread of art that bore a striking resemblance to the same creatures that had been plaguing the Resistance. The art was quite similar to the slides that Logan had shared with everyone, back when he had been explaining the situation to everyone visiting; they were walking around the town, a foreboding presence that made everything else in the area appear just a bit more gray.

"It is stated that this, a folktale usually told to children to teach them to behave, has its roots in history– from a week in which a bunch of strange creatures plagued the greater Compositora area. Sadly, what I was not able to find is what happened to ensure the problem only went on for a week; as you're all aware, we're well over that at this point," Hunter added.

"Oh. I think I may have accidentally found the answer to that," Jasiela said. "I mean, maybe not *exactly*. But one of these books I read mentioned that the longest any single-use conjuration– that being any type of spell that creates something that wasn't there before– can continue producing results is a week. If the caster intends to make it stick around any longer than that, they need to do the spell again."

Jasiela pulled out one of the books from her stack, and placed it on the table. It was called, "The Basics of Casting," and was a strictly typographical cover, dark blue letters contrasting the pristine white of the rest of the cover.

"That's right," agreed Lisandra. "That's because the average human body only holds enough energy to sustain a spell for a week. And even then we're talking maximum potency, to the point where holding it together that long would drain you to exhaustion, so it's more normal for something like that to only last for about three or four days."

"Right," Jasiela nodded, now holding the book open. "And this book also says that this is a conscious effort, which means the caster has to remain alive in order to keep it going that long; there's no future stores of energy or power."

"So that means that the individual who brought all of this on is not only still alive and kicking, but that they're actively and probably intentionally causing mayhem," Logan noted. "Okay. I guess we need to figure out who that is. Or, at least, a way to figure out how to... figure out who that is."

"Circling back to the spell to conjure the holzomen and its longevity..." Brecken said. "It brings me back to Logan's explanation of witches."

This clearly surprised Logan, judging by the way his eyebrows rose as he turned to Brecken. "You think a witch is behind this?" he asked.

"I think it's possible, yes," she replied.

"Then I think we should hear her out," Thunder replied. "You have the floor, Brecken."

And it was easy to see that this frightened Brecken, if one just paid close attention to her hands nervously gripping the one book she'd picked up, or the way her eyes refused to focus on any one area. "I-if the typical longevity of the creation spell is one week..." Brecken paused, determined to steady her voice. "Not to mention the numbers and power they have whenever we face them. It would be excellent if we could have something to compare it to; something that lets us know what the standard output of that spell is, to compare it to what's been happening."

There was silence in the room then.

"If we continue on with the idea that a witch is behind this..." Mishaela said then. "Would there be a way for us to be able to track them down? How does one even tell a witch apart from a regular member of society? Is that even possible?"

"It is. There's a few ways you can. This first one doesn't apply to most of y'all, but since witches are so attuned to magic and are able to wield such a great quantity of it, people who possess a level of magic in their body are able to sense them," Thunder replied. "Of course that could all change since y'all were given some magic as a gift... but receiving magic in that way is such a rare occurrence that I wouldn't be able to know for sure."

And there wasn't enough time to confirm that with the goddesses. The last thing they needed was taking almost an entire day to traverse that hill again, and potentially losing another day depending on how tired everyone was after the fact.

"There's also... I think it's better if I show you guys."

Lisandra reached for one of the books in her pile. She then sat it down on the table with a thud, almost instantly landing on the page she needed: a picture of a feminine figure donning a purple, velvety cape adorned with roses and thorns in dark, foreboding tones of burgundy, mauve, mulberry, and black. She wore a circlet of silver with obsidian adorning the front, and her red dress had an elegant train, as well as a split decorated with an assortment of silver rhinestones in varying sizes. "The way witches dress is always *a lot*, you know? This is actually one of the more minimally dressed ones, even. Of course, this alone doesn't account for people who are naturally inclined to maximalism, but since those types of people generally live in the bigger cities, I don't think we'll need to suspend our disbelief that much in a small town like this."

"So, what? A weird feeling in our tummies plus a person nearby that's dressed like a museum exhibit equals a witch?" Jasiela asked.

"In so many words," Lisandra nodded. "But that does still leave us with the question of where to start."

This would be another more challenging part of this adventure. This onslaught had been going on for the better part of a month at this point, and there had been no signs or sightings of a witch during all that time. Clearly, they were dealing with an adversary that not only didn't want to be seen, but was rather good at it. What could be done to change that?

"Hunter, you said that the town's records are here, right?" Mishaela asked. "Would something like a person becoming a witch be worthy of record keeping?"

"It wouldn't, but..." Thunder replied, placing a hand under his chin. "The rest of y'all are too young to remember this, but there was a time during The Dictator's reign that his administration kept records on all the witches who lived in the greater area of Compositora. Most likely it was to keep tabs on them, just in case one of them got powerful enough that they could end him. The data there would be a bit outdated because many of the witches all either gradually moved away or went into hiding by pulling stunts like faking their deaths, but it might be a good starting point."

More thought progressed through the group.

"But at a base level... it would be nice if we could learn a little more about the process of the creation of holzomen," Phoenix added. "Remember, the idea that they're being spawned by a witch this time, while feeling incredibly likely at this time, is still just a hypothesis for now."

This was also a good point. If it was true that a witch was the perpetrator of everything that was currently wrong in this corner of the world, there would need to be a strategy formed to deal with them– but as long as this was still an "if," it would be more beneficial to concentrate more on the definites: which meant, first and foremost, dealing with the holzomen.

"Aside from here, would there be any other place that would have more information about magical conjurations and things?" Madeline asked. "I mean... if witches are that powerful it would've been nice if we could have asked one, and they'd probably have some more information about holzomen, but then Thunder *did* just say most of them have left this area by now. Hmm."

Taking a moment to think a little more before finally speaking, Spencer-Lynn asked, "Would it be reasonable to assume books of more detail would have fallen into the hands of your former government?"

"Wait, that would make a lot of sense," Mishaela added. "Especially knowing that there was a time The Dictator kept records on witches, it wouldn't be too farfetched to think he'd put some effort into making it harder for even more of them to come to be. If he were to seize as many magical resources as he could, that would be one heck of a preventative measure."

"We can only hope they weren't destroyed somehow," Jaiden said then. "But if we're gonna go on assuming they weren't, where would we begin looking?"

Thunder shrugged. "Considering how the guy met his end, I don't see any reason they wouldn't still be in the palace. We can go there tomorrow– with a full party," he nodded toward Mishaela with a small smile.

TWELVE

In An Abandoned Palace

Arriving in front of the former Dictator's palace, after everything that had transpired, brought about a feeling of unease. Perhaps it was because of how different it was in the present day. Whether one considered the chaos of the rebellion, which felt so long ago now, or the more recent battle in the square, one commonality between the two events is that the area had been noisy. Discordant. Filled with the essence of life, be it determination, celebration, or desperation; but this was something that was very obviously not present today. The stands in the market were empty. There were no people out and about. There was a certain air of understandable desolation surrounding the general area, and that was before one acknowledged the palace it-

self.

Where the palace had been a dark but brilliant red during The Dictator's reign, the structure that stood in front of the troupe today was more of a faded burgundy. It was reminiscent of a once grand shop– not unlike those that could commonly be found around the cities in which the party from Earth usually lived– that had once drawn the intrigue of people the world over, but had long since closed its doors, and withered. Its color bleached by the sun, the cracks chipping away at the structure itself... it was a shell of its former being.

"Certainly didn't age well," Gavin noted softly.

"No kidding," agreed Madeline. "Well, I guess there's no other way in but up. Let's get going!"

And so, everyone began to ascend the long flight of stairs.

"I can't believe it's this easy to get into this palace," Jaiden said as everyone walked through the main corridor.

This was... was it right to call it nostalgia? There certainly was a feeling of fleeting familiarity, recalling the last time they had been through these halls. Or would it be more of a vague familiarity? Vague both because of the amount of time that had passed since then, but also because without any residents, the environment had sunk into decay. The checkered floors were cracked in a manner that resembled strikes of lightning, and the paint on the walls was peeling; curling into little circles reminiscent of chocolate shavings, or maybe even rolled ice cream.

"No one's living in it anymore," Logan reminded her. "With that in mind, it seems about right."

"Can I ask a question?" Madeline asked then, raising her hand.

Thunder looked back at her. "I get the feeling you're gonna ask it even if one of us says no."

"Right. Well, is there– hey." She frowned. "How much time has passed since we were here last time? Eight, nine months? Less than a year for sure. That being the case, what I wanted to ask is, is there any reason the palace has deteriorated like this? I'm no expert on interior upkeep and all, but doesn't that seem kinda fast?"

"Hm. That's actually a good point." Hunter turned to Thunder and Logan. "I'm assuming that this palace's previous resident may have employed certain magical elements for the decor elements? Perhaps even for the building itself?"

"It's likely," Logan nodded. "One common theme in most, if not all, of the readings about his rise to power was how fast it was, so it wouldn't be farfetched to assume the construction of this palace was less than manual. The amount of degradation you see here seems to be in line with that kind of hypothesis, too."

They walked farther, before stopping in the main throne room. Given what had transpired here the last time, it wasn't a surprise that there was visible damage to the room; that being said, there seemed to be much more than anyone who was present could remember. Perhaps it made sense for the formerly white walls and columns to be stained with black dust from when The Dictator met his demise. But the frays on the curtains near the windows, the holes in both the curtains and the carpeting– likely from fire– were almost definitely more recent. Everything generally felt darker, but that could also be because the only light in the room at this time was the torch-like pole Logan was currently holding.

"But wait a minute. When we were here last, and I rubbed one of the flower petals I saw, I accidentally rubbed off some of its magic," Mishaela recalled. "I guess I'm trying to ask how magic can be used to build something so solid if it's that delicate."

"Well, as you can see, it ain't really that solid after all," Thunder gestured to the room they were currently in. "While, yes, generally magic can be used in much stronger quantities than are found in that flower petal, it's not the best thing for a person to use for anything that's meant to stand long-term. Remember how we were just discussing conjuration longevity last night."

"*And* in case your next question is about the longevity or stability of our world, given that it itself is made of magic; this is different because structures built with magic like this one are made with the hands of men," Phoenix explained further. "The magic that ordinary people use is miles different than that of the goddesses. With your newly gifted powers, think of how long you're able to produce a constant flow of magic before you begin to feel tired."

"Not very," replied Jasiela, remembering the night out in the woods. "I think I'm starting to get it now. Emphasis on *starting*."

Thunder chuckled, just a bit. "All right, I stopped us here because I think it'll be smarter if we split up. This is a big palace, and to search it all as one group would probably take days. If we divide ourselves into teams it'll be more efficient."

"Okay, but we only have one light," Jaiden pointed to the light to emphasize her point.

"Oh, that? That's the least of our worries." Logan smiled before taking the light Thunder had and, with a little effort, splitting it into four even pieces, each just as perfectly lit as the one piece had been when it was together, and handing one to each of the official members of the Resistance. "Now, I'm gonna start looking over there," he pointed back toward where they'd come. "Probably gonna find myself on the higher levels. If two of you would accompany me, that would be great."

Everyone turned to each other. "I don't mind," Spencer-Lynn volunteered. "Logan and I have already established we work well together, so."

"I think I'll come with you guys," Madeline said then. "See you guys in a few!"

Mishaela waved to the group as they departed.

"Right, so..." Thunder quickly counted everyone who remained. "Three of y'all can stay with me, and the rest can split between Phoenix and Hunter. We'll meet outside at the top of the stairs when it gets dark, unless someone finds something interesting."

When everyone left the area, Thunder remained in the throne room with Lisandra, Brecken, and Jasiela.

"Thank ya kindly for stayin' with me, ladies," Thunder gave them a nod. "Now, where do we start? Jasiela, I think you're the only one who's been here for an extended amount of time before. I think it makes the most sense for you to lead us in our investigation."

"Me? Little old me? Hehehe." Jasiela giggled mischievously, loving the wash of pride she felt come over her from being named the leader. "Well, if you insist. I mean, if you guys would just be *lost* without me, I suppose I have no choice–"

"Jasiela. Can you cut the shit." Lisandra frowned.

"I'm cutting the shit, of my *own volition*," Jasiela replied as she began to walk around. "I need to get reacquainted with this room before I can have any real thoughts on it, so give me a minute. Hmm... yeah, right over there is where the magic happened, figuratively speaking of course. Uh, okay. I notice that those two potted trees over by the windows are the only things here that aren't on a massive decline. Why don't we take a look at them?"

"These trees don't look like anything I've seen since I've been here, Thunder," noted Brecken. "Are they native to this area?"

"Not at all. One thing all rich types seem to all have in common is they're usually predisposed to... uh, importing, that's what it's called. Y'know, paying people to collect things far away from their home and bring them back. I wouldn't be able to tell ya what kinds of trees these are or where they're from exactly, but what I can say is, they ain't from any city in the nearby area. You can tell by how dry they are that they're not used to the climate."

"Hm. You know, it makes sense for there to be more cities and towns here, but the thought never occurred to me until just now." Brecken mused as she examined the leaves on the nearest potted tree, taking the lowest one in her hand. "Oh. That's interesting."

"What's interesting?" Lisandra had asked, but all three heads turned toward Brecken, almost in unison.

"U-um, it's just that..." Brecken lost her composure for a moment, unnerved by the amount of attention that was suddenly directed at her. "I remember Mishaela mentioning, not very long ago, that she was able to touch a flower petal and have magic dust rub off on it. Are all plants here supposed to do that?"

This time, everyone turned to Thunder, who took a pause to think before answering. "Yes and no. It varies by plant, but whether it be from a single touch or a little more vigorous rubbin' and such-yes, ya should be able to eventually rub some magic dust off of just about any plant."

With this response, Lisandra plucked a leaf from the tree and scrubbed it against the back of her hand, as if she was using it to exfoliate her skin. The shimmering, iridescent, golden hue of magic dust would have been easy to see against the contrast of her brown skin... if there had been any. Instead, when she removed the leaf, her hand was unchanged aside from a bit of redness from the force of the leaf rubbing against it so harshly.

"Oh!" Jasiela gasped. "That's not... are the leaves fake, then?"

"No, I don't think that's it," replied Lisandra. "Fake leaves have that sort of thick, plastic-like texture, and are usually harder to pluck from their branches because of how they're manufactured. This is definitely a real leaf."

"If it doesn't give off magic powder, the only place this could've come from..." Thunder stared at the tree. "Is it possible? Did he know a way to reach between the two worlds?"

It wasn't long before Logan's group hit a dead end, and with that realization, he sighed. So much for appearing to be a capable and very cool leader.

"Well." He turned around, where Madeline and Spencer-Lynn were patiently waiting for his next directive. "It would seem we have reached a dead end. In the name of democracy, I am now taking suggestions for what our next move will be."

A silence fell with all three of them pondering.

"Oh!" Madeline raised her hand. "So, when we passed the stairwell back there, remember how it was blocked off by some kind of collapse?"

"Considering that happened less than five minutes ago, yes." Logan nodded, only lightly teasing her.

"Right. So we couldn't go up that way. *But,* what if we got upstairs another way? Like so?"

Madeline pointed above their heads at a hole in the ceiling, more than adequately sized for a human to fit through. There was just one problem: the trio would have to come up with a plan to get up to it. The ceilings were a standard nine feet high, which meant that even Logan– the tallest of the three– would have to account for just over three feet of height to get to the hole, and that was before trying to figure out how to get *through* the darn thing.

"Okay. We have an objective. Now we just need a method..." Logan began to survey the immediate area again, this time looking for something tall or sturdy enough to serve as a platform. When he looked up at the hole in the ceiling again– the hole which, at this very moment, seemed to be mocking him just a tad– he noticed there was the end of what looked like a rope, not very far from the opening of the hole.

"Oh! I have an idea!" Before either of the girls could ask what it was, he'd grabbed a nearby candle holder off of one of the walls and put all his strength into chucking it at high speed toward the hole, right around where the rope was. Sure enough, the rope unfurled... just not to a length that seemed very helpful.

"I think that'll do. Thanks, Logan." Spencer-Lynn smiled before taking a few steps back, getting a running start and jumping, just barely grabbing onto the rope and slipping just a bit, but then climbing until one of her hands touched the marble of the second floor. But the remainder of the rope fell then, and the resulting scream from Spencer-Lynn could probably be heard throughout the first and second floors.

"It's okay! It's okay!" Logan hurried to where her legs were dangling from the hole. "We can fix this! Don't panic!"

"I think it's a wee bit late for that!" Spencer-Lynn's voice came from the second floor.

"Then don't panic any more than you already have! Help me give her a boost, Madeline."

"Yeah." The two were able to easily boost her up to the second floor, and from there, Logan was able to toss the rope back up so he and Madeline could climb up as well.

The second floor of the palace was where The Dictator's quarters had been, as well as a few rooms dedicated to literature and various amenities. This room that the trio currently found themselves in looked to have been some kind of closet at some point; although there was very little light in the room coming from a singular window, the light that shone through revealed that there were multiple expensive-looking garments hanging from clothing racks, all with a relatively generous coating of dust from the general condition of the palace. At one point, this room had probably been worth more than the sum of the most money all three of the people currently in it had ever held in their lives. But how much would it be worth now? Did it matter? Had it ever mattered?

"Logan, you had blueprints on this place way back when, right?" Madeline asked. "Do you know where we are?"

"Kind of. There were alleged to be two rooms like this, one at either end of the second level. I'll be more certain once we explore more of the surrounding area; but before we do that, I think we should survey this room. You can never be too sure about what kind of information a person had in their pockets."

His two companions wordlessly agreed, and with that they all began to search the room for anything that looked interesting. However, since the room was pretty much completely comprised of clothes hanging from racks, it was easy to quickly look through them all. There was, sadly, nothing in this room of importance.

"Of course this room is a bust. That would have been too easy," Logan complained to himself as the three left the room. Louder, he said, "The benefit to getting into that room first, is that it was at the end of the hall. Let's just go into the rooms as we come up to them, yeah?"

The next room's opening was partially blocked by part of the wall caving, but the opening still looked wide enough to walk through.

As it turned out, it was deceptively narrow; a truth that the trio only learned when Spencer-Lynn was the first to walk through and got stuck.

"Why is everything happening to me?" she asked, in a more resigned way than anything else.

"It is the hazard level accepted by those who volunteer to go first," Logan replied. "Stay put. What's making you stuck?"

"I think it may actually just be my leg, here. There's still quite a bit of space in the doorframe, see," she reached out and touched the fallen wall with her right hand.

Logan nodded, bending down on one knee to get a closer look at the problem; it wasn't long before he noticed the pesky slab of wood that had nestled itself into Spencer-Lynn's pants leg. "Oh! I think I see the problem now. Madeline, I'm going to go to the other side and whack this wood panel into place, and I'm gonna need you to do the same on this side."

"Gotcha!" She nodded. "Holler when you need me to do it."

"Yeah." Logan then stood, taking very much care to not get caught on the panel himself, which meant he had to hold the higher part of the beam for support, his arm snaking around Spencer-Lynn's waist. It was fortunate that she had such a tiny waist to make it possible to do so, without their bodies rubbing together *too* much, but even then, this was a bit awkward. *Just* a bit.

"On three. One, two..."

When Spencer-Lynn was finally free of the beam, all three stepped inside of the room, which seemed to be a dilapidated planning room. "All right, more interesting stuff!" Madeline cheered, already running off to rummage through an opened chest.

"Right," Logan nodded, still the tiniest bit flustered from the way he'd had to get into this room. "Uh, let's see if we can find some sort of map in here, or blueprints or something, that'd be really helpful as we continue to search this floor."

Phoenix's group consisted of Mishaela, Gavin, and herself; they opted to take their search downstairs, into the storage areas of the palace. After all, the Resistance kept their records in their basements. It wouldn't be too much of a stretch to check the basement here too, right?

"There's a lot of strange knickknacks and junk here..." Mishaela said as they arrived in the main storage area. "Where do we even begin?"

"It is overwhelming, isn't it?" Phoenix asked. "I have an idea. Why don't we start in one corner of the room, and gradually make it to the other side? So, let's start in that corner right over there, and continue to the left. Sounds good?"

Clearly, Mishaela and Gavin were not in a position to disagree, since they had no other ideas. So, the three soon busied themselves with opening and looking through the many boxes and barrels that were strewn about the storage area. After looking through a few of them, though, all three of them began to notice a pattern...

"Phoenix, Gavin," Mishaela said as she hopped down from where she'd been standing to peek inside of a tall box. "I have a question. Have either of you, so far, encountered a single box that actually had anything in it?"

"I thought it was just me." Gavin turned to her, placing the barrel he had tilted toward him upright again. "That's so strange. Why have a room full of boxes and barrels just to keep them all empty? Unless... unless it's part of a strategy."

"What do you mean?" Mishaela asked curiously.

Gavin held an arm out, gesturing around the room. "Hiding in plain sight. If you wanted to make sure something really important to you wasn't easily pilfered, what do you do? You place it in one specific box, maybe put that box inside of a box, the most inconspicuous, unassuming box you can get your hands on... and then you surround it with a bunch of bait boxes that look exactly like it."

"So that, if anyone comes looking for it, they get so discouraged from opening so many of the empty boxes that they assume there's nothing in *any* of them!" Mishaela nodded. "Very smart observation, Gavin! But that does mean that we're going to have to look through all of these just in case, doesn't it."

Gavin shrugged. "A necessary evil, I suppose. Now let's get back to it."

Just as Gavin prepared to get back to his box investigation, a large, distant thud sounded throughout the room. Both teenagers looked up abruptly, in the direction it had come from. "W-what was that?" Gavin asked. "Phoenix... are you there..?"

"Am I where?" she asked, popping up behind the two. Gavin nearly jumped out of his skin.

"Aah! Don't do that! You might give someone a bit of warning before... approaching them so quietly and suddenly," Gavin replied. "But... if you're over here with us, then that noise... oh, I do hope it wasn't a... a *ghost*."

The terror with which he whispered the word "ghost" revealed an interesting truth about Gavin: he believed in the existence of ghosts, and was not only afraid of them, he was *terrified*.

"Is investigating this room going to be too much for you?" Mishaela asked. "If it is, there's no shame in asking to investigate with Thunder. I'm sure he'd be okay with swapping out one of his team members with you."

"No, that won't be– I'm fine, I assure you," Gavin replied. "All the same, I don't think any of us would object to getting out of here as soon as possible, in a productivity sort of way–"

He turned ever so slightly and screamed at the sight of what he thought was certainly something otherworldly, stumbling a bit, all but falling into Mishaela and grabbing her, holding her close for support. "On second thought, forget it. Forget I said anything at all. I need to get out of this place before I lose my mind."

As he stood back up, he and Mishaela stared at each other for a few moments more. "Oh, no," she whispered.

This certainly didn't help Gavin's current mood. "Oh no, what?"

"Oh, it's not– I just had a thought that was completely unrelated," she explained. Mishaela wasn't a good liar, so it was easy to tell she was telling the truth about that. "Now, why don't you just stay really close to me and Phoenix? I'm sure she has the knowledge to protect you from anything that could hurt you here."

"That I do," Phoenix agreed, noticeably farther away than before. "Aside from Logan, I don't think anyone here is more knowledgeable about the ghosts, spirits, and specters of this world than I am... and that's not to brag, but to assure you of your own safety."

"I... suppose that's a good point. I'll follow you, then," Gavin nodded, not feeling very reassured, but enough that he felt confident he would get through this alive. "And if there's anything that can be done to ensure we get out of here as soon as humanly possible, you needn't hesitate in asking me to do it. I insist."

Hunter, Jaiden, and Chiara's group remained on the first level, combing through as many rooms as they could, the first few being largely unremarkable. There would occasionally be the odd interesting decor element, but otherwise, the search was beginning to feel a little grim. That was, until they came across what had been the Dictator's art gallery.

This room, unlike all the others, maintained a certain level of structure; the exhibits also seemed to be mostly unharmed, aside from the generous coatings of dust on everything. It was interesting to come across this area; previously, none of the present three would have ever guessed that the former tyrant of this land had an eye for art. Then again, there was the possibility that he hadn't, and all this art was just bought to showboat... or even that it was stolen; the possibilities were many.

Now that she was awake and more or less recovered, Chiara seemed to move at a slightly faster pace than before. She couldn't quite put words to how she was feeling, but it was like her mind was battling itself, trying to decide if she wanted to give up on helping everyone, or prove to them that she could be useful. There was a part of her that wanted to hide inside headquarters until this was all over, but there was another, growing part of her that wanted to defy her fears; to prove that she could learn to be an adequate fighter, detective, and whatever else this mission needed her to be. The thought of doing that– of being a big sister that Mishaela could be proud of, and that the younger charges could look up to her because of it– was an idea that, as she matched her paces with Jaiden and Hunter, felt closer and more possible with every step they took inside this castle.

As Jaiden searched the drawers of the lone desk in the room, and Hunter investigated the hanging art, Chiara walked about aimlessly, waiting for something interesting to catch her eye. "The designs on this rug are very similar to those from the Italian renaissance," Chiara said softly, to herself. "That's very interesting."

"Yeah, I guess it makes sense if the people of this world share some history with us," Jaiden said then, surprising Chiara.

"Oh. I didn't think you'd... hear me."

"I've gotten pretty good at hearing you." Jaiden smirked. "Don't worry about it. Hunter, finding anything that will blow our minds?"

"Actually... I think I might have found something, yes. If you'll come over here, I think I need more sets of eyes to be able to tell for sure."

"Exciting!" Jaiden whispered as she and Chiara hurried over to where Hunter had been inspecting some of the framed curiosities on one of the walls.

The earth-toned walls were adorned with many a poster, tapestry, and artwork, but the one Hunter currently stood by was the longest artwork in the room, the frame being at least six feet long. The art was of a green, hilly area... not unlike what Deity Hill might look like if the plant life here was in better shape. Nothing seemed amiss about this particular art, though, or about the plain wooden frame that was mounted to the wall.

"This... looks shockingly normal," Jaiden noted. "What am I missing? What's making it so interesting to you?"

Hunter pointed to the corner of the wooden frame that he was standing closest to, before running his finger along a fine crack that Jaiden and Chiara hadn't seen until they'd gotten closer. "It's something that I might be being overly meticulous about... but if you take a look at this crack here, and you touch it, and you know a little bit about wood and how it behaves... this type of hairline fracture is usually caused by a sort of blunt force being used on or near it. If you were to drill a hole or hammer a nail into it, in other words. But here, at the corner, you'll notice there's no hole; it's still completely smooth. It is my belief that the blunt force came not from hammering directly onto the wood, but directly *behind* it, to remove it from the wall."

"You'd need a hammer to do that?" Chiara asked, confused.

"Depending on how it was affixed to the wall, yes. There's a certain type of method that ensures your wall decorations will not fall of their own volition, for better or worse."

"Interesting that this place has its own version of Krazy Glue," Jaiden chuckled. "Okay, Hunter. I'm getting what you're saying. But I guess now my question is, why go to so much trouble to take it back off the wall?"

Hunter and Chiara then said at the same time, "Hidden compartment!"

"It is my understanding that after The Dictator was defeated, there was a period of time in which the palace began to rumble, as if there was an earthquake. And I am aware that some of the personnel here fought to defend their home and their monarch, but I also remember reading that there was a rush of people escaping from the castle around that time. It would not be farfetched to assume that some of them may have tried their hand at looting before running for their lives."

"Right! It all makes so much sense!" Jaiden nodded, remembering all the secret stashes of snacks, trashy romance novels, and many other things hidden around her bedroom, in places her parents would never look. Or, at least, they hadn't looked yet... or hadn't brought it up yet. "Need a hand getting that down?"

"I'd very much appreciate it, yes."

Both grabbing one end of the art display, Hunter and Jaiden carefully lifted it from its place on the wall. The wooden frame made the whole thing heavier than expected, its lesser-affixed portions creaking as the duo carefully placed it on the floor in front of where it had been.

As expected, in its former place there was a small, dark, round hidden compartment, an indentation within the wall.

"I think I'm the only one of us that's tall enough to see into here. I just need a better source of light..." Hunter patted his clothes before he began to look around.

"Oh! Hey! Since I haven't been using it, I think I should still have enough juice left in this thing..." Jaiden reached into her pocket for her phone. "Here. It's one of the newer smartphones, so try not to break it. My parents would kill me."

"Uh..." Hunter stared blankly at Jaiden's hand. "This is... a light?"

Jaiden frowned in confusion, before realizing what was happening. "Duh. Of course you wouldn't recognize a phone. Don't worry about it, then. Get in there, I'll turn on the flashlight and hold the light steady."

"Oh! Right." Hunter nodded, reaching into the small cave. "It's still too dark to see. Might we shine the light at a different angle?"

"A different angle." Jaiden had to think about that– but not for long, before she noticed Chiara scurry off to another part of the room.

She quickly returned with a fragment of what was formerly a mirror, making sure to hold it carefully so as not to cut her fingers as she used her shirt to clean the dust off. "Here we go. Shine the light here, and I'll move it around a little, until we find the best angle for Hunter's search."

"Hey, yeah!" Jaiden grinned. "Excellent teamwork, Chiara. Let's do this!"

The next few minutes were spent configuring the angle of the light, but even with the best angle, it was still difficult to see inside of the secret compartment. After some making sure that there was nothing hazardous inside, Hunter gave up on trying to investigate visually, and just stuck his hand in there.

"There... doesn't seem to be anything here. I suppose it *is* more than likely that someone thought to raid this room when the palace began to tremble after the defeat of... wait! I was mistaken; I do very clearly feel something!"

Jaiden and Chiara were both filled with excitement as Hunter pulled out a black, round case of something and sat it on a nearby table. It had a generous coating of dust on it, so he picked it up again and turned away before blowing the dust off, and sitting it back down.

"What is this?" Jaiden asked.

"Um, I... I can't be sure... but it looks like one of those really old film reel cases," Chiara said, squinting to try and notice anything she hadn't before. "You know, like the ones that were used to play films in theaters before we had our current style of projectors."

"This does indeed appear to be a projector reel," Hunter agreed. "It's not compatible with the particular style of projection player that we have back at headquarters, but I think I saw a projector somewhere in here, back toward where Thunder and the girls were. Let's make haste in that direction, that we might see what secrets we uncover with this."

When everyone had been rounded up and gathered in the throne room, with a projector, Hunter explained where and how his group had found the projector reel before he relinquished the case to Thunder.

"Have you opened it yet?" he asked.

Hunter shook his head. "Not yet. I assumed that we would all want to be together when it came to investigating potential pieces of evidence. Fresh pairs of eyes and all that."

"I taught you well." Thunder smiled. "We got a table here? Something we can sit this projector on so we can watch this?"

"We're gonna watch it here?" Jasiela asked.

"It makes sense. If we watch it and there's nothing of use in the footage, we know to keep looking, rather than having to circle back," Gavin replied.

"Boy's a bright one," Thunder said as he began to open the film case. Almost immediately after it was cracked open, a piece of paper fell out; Lisandra was the first to get to it, and sat it on the table. Logan then shined a light on it.

"I think it's a bit too old to be read," Logan said, "but I can tell something important was written here. Look, you can see where the note was written with black ink, and when it was written in red instead. I just wish there was enough to get the gist of what was happening, but as it is now, I can only distinguish a few words here and there. Look, 'wards,' 'nature,' 'people,' 'creation...' and 'danger.' It's very ominous."

"Well, if that's it, then that's it. Keep it just in case, but don't go worrying about it too much," Thunder replied.

Thunder was the person to begin setting up the projector. During this time, the room was completely silent aside from the sounds of the projector being set up, the reel being put in place, and finally, the projector being turned on.

The winding sounds of the projector punctuated a flickering, dimly lit tale of what one could assume was magic being cast. Although the setting was dark, the magic was beautiful; sparkles and curls of vibrant colors, swirling around harmoniously as if it were perfectly in tune with both the setting and the silhouettes of people.

When the scene changed, those beautiful swirls and sparkles of magic began to burrow into the ground, evoking clouds of darkness, giving way to more foreboding, brooding figures; still shaped like humans, but the sickly blue-gray of their skin were a clue that "human" would not be an accurate descriptor for them. These creatures ran after the humans; the humans started to flee, before they began to fight back.

Amidst the battlefield, similar clouds to the ones that had appeared began to formulate, but these were different because they were pitch-black and *much* bigger. The ground began to rumble. Dust began to formulate in a menacing twister, the whooshing sound becoming almost uncomfortable.

"Wait! This is just like..." Madeline started.

Before she could finish her sentence, the film confirmed her observation; that the figure the twister gave way to was none other than The Dictator.

"So is that... is that how he came to be?" asked Brecken.

"It appears so," replied Hunter. "It is the answer to a question the people of this world have wondered for many years. It's helpful... but is it enough?"

"It also shows us the creation of our current problem," Thunder pointed out. "That particular section where the magic goes into the ground. But it wouldn't be able to do that on its own... something feels strange about this, somehow. Let's take it with us; I wanna analyze it by myself, in a more comfortable setting."

"Right. Are we heading back, then?" Phoenix asked.

"Let's. I know this isn't a whole lot, but I strongly feel that this will be vital," Thunder replied as he placed the film back in its case. "Back to HQ. We got everyone?"

Phoenix was the one to take on the duty of doing a headcount. "Yep, that's everyone. Let's get out of here; with all of this dust, I'm going to need a nice, hot bath."

"No kidding," agreed Jasiela, "you read my mind."

The winds passing through the palace began to pick up as the troupe left the premises.

THIRTEEN

In Need of an In-Depth Analysis

The return to headquarters was one of a tired accomplishment; that everyone was happy to have made some progress in figuring this whole thing out, but at the same time, were tired from all of the effort it had taken to do so. With a murmured proposal to make dinner, Hunter disappeared into the kitchen to survey the materials he'd have available to cook. With the night's chef decided, everyone dispersed. Thunder remained behind, staying near the door even after he had removed his shoes.

Something felt odd about those projector slides. But what was it? Why did viewing them make him feel as uncomfortable as they did?

He realized, then, that there was only one way to find out: to watch them again. And again, and maybe even again. As many tries as it took for him to find out what invisible issue it was that was bringing him down.

"Everything okay?" He was met with Phoenix at his side.

"Huh? Oh! Yeah, I just need some good food in my gullet and some studyin' before bed," he replied. "I'll be right as rain by then."

"Of course," Phoenix laughed a bit. "I'll see you when dinner is ready, then?"

Thunder nodded wordlessly before making his way to the conference room. If he didn't hash this out now, it would eat at him until he did.

"What is this you're making?" Brecken asked, occasionally picking up a shaker or bottle from the counter where Lisandra had placed them all. She hoped she wasn't being too disruptive; but all the same, she placed her hands in her pockets to deter herself from grabbing anything else.

On the other side of the counter, Lisandra was busy combining a bowl of spices. "Hunter decided we didn't have the right ingredients to cook what he wanted to, so in his place, I'm gonna make you guys the best pulled pork you've ever had in your lives, just like how my mother makes it. I won't be able to make her rice, because

I don't think we have enough time, but the pork alongside the fried plantains should be enough to take your tastebuds on a journey."

"I see." Brecken nodded, smiling. "Do you study your mother's recipes often?"

"Not often, but enough to keep family traditions going. Mami's food always has a way of making you feel like you're at home, no matter where you are. Comfort food, you know? Food that touches the soul. What about you, do you cook with your mom?"

Lisandra instantly noticed the look of disgust on Brecken's face, even though she did try to hide it quickly. "I can't say I can stand to do much of anything with that woman."

"Oh. I won't pry." Even though she really, really wanted to. "But that sucks. I can't imagine not having the relationship with my mom that I do."

Lisandra said this, but she also was well aware of the times the relationship between herself and her mother was not good. Of the times where she'd yell at her for having a perfectly reasonable negative reaction to bad news, about objecting to all the extra studying that was forced upon her ever since she could read. Why was she so complacent with her husband, Lisandra's father, throwing things at her if she couldn't remember everything she'd read? Maybe she could understand Brecken's visible reaction to being asked about her own mother.

"Anyway, you're welcome to help me if you want to." Lisandra tried, then, to push that all to the back of her mind.

"Thank you. I think I will." Brecken grabbed another shaker of seasoning; its label said "mustard citrus," and she put it back down, unfamiliar with the idea of combining the two. "It'll distract me from worrying too much."

"You too, huh?" Lisandra asked. "I don't think I've worried this much about anything ever in my life. I've done more worrying since I got here than I could ever conceive in my mind, and about so many things. Mostly, though, I worry about Thunder. The guy's been through so much– not even just this week, but in general."

"Did you notice his reaction to watching that projection?" Brecken asked. "It was subtle, but there was a noticeable stoicism that overtook him. Do you know how you make yourself steel your gaze when something's happening that's dealing a heavy emotional blow, but you don't want to draw too much attention to yourself? It was like that."

"I didn't notice, no." Lisandra sighed. "We need the big guy. The last time we handled things without him, progress slowed like molasses. But even more so than that... we were scrambling. We were lost. What is a resistance without its leader?"

Brecken hesitated. She wasn't sure how to answer that, but after a few seconds of thought, she was able to come up with an reply that she believed was satisfactory.

"In that case, we should work hard, together, to make sure this is the type of meal that makes everyone's worries melt away."

"One of the things that really sucks about being here is being completely disconnected from our lives at home," Madeline complained as she sat at one of the kitchen tables with Jaiden and Mishaela. "It's not something that's so inconvenient that I'd complain to anyone else about it, but even with whatever time-bending shenanigans are pulled when we go home, last time it still strangely felt like I'd missed something, you know?"

"Oh, I thought I was the only one," Jaiden agreed. "It's hard to put words to, but like... last time when we got home, my mom was nicer to me than she's been in years. And then that day when I went to school, one of my classmates sincerely asked me about hearing one of our mutual classmates use they/them pronouns for me; a classmate who's usually a real turd about that kind of thing. The best way I can explain it was that it was like some kind of elaborate inside joke thing that everybody was in on except for me."

"Right! Exactly!" Madeline pointed a finger. "And you know I hate being left out!"

"Is it that you don't like being left out, or that you like being nosy?" Mishaela asked.

Madeline paused before answering. "Well, hey. Come on. It's within my nature to be at least kind of a chismosa. Surely you wouldn't deny me that. Plus, if I don't know the general gist about what's going on in our area at all times, the opportunity to finally track down concrete proof of alien activity could slip right under my nose!"

Jaiden and Mishaela just exchanged a look. Somehow, even in a world full of magic and strange zombie-like creatures, Madeline managed to be one of the more distinct personalities around.

"Where's Chiara, by the way?" Madeline asked then.

"Oh, she went back to her room for a nap," Mishaela replied. "She mentioned being tired when we were on our way back, so I kind of nudged her toward resting before dinner. After all, she's still recovering, even if she's mostly mobile now."

"Right." Madeline nodded. "Well, in that case, I'm gonna go track down Jasiela. I just realized I haven't seen her in at least five minutes, so now I'm curious. I'm on the case!"

Madeline hopped out of her seat, pointing toward the kitchen door before hurrying to it, barreling through it with such force that it swung back and forth a couple of times, like a saloon door. Jaiden chuckled, before turning to Mishaela, who seemed to have something on her mind. At this point, it was second nature for the two to recognize this state in each other.

"Okay. What's on your mind?" Jaiden finally said.

"Too much, which I'm sure you know by now is usually the problem," Mishaela replied. "But you probably want to know what's weighing heaviest on my mind as of this very moment, and I... am kind of having a bisexual crisis right about now."

"Oh! Again?" Jaiden asked.

"It's just that– wait, what do you mean, again?!" Mishaela nudged her. She lowered her voice before continuing. "Well, we have our lives to return to after this, lives in which I cannot deny a very cute girl is involved in mine these days. But today– don't mention you heard this from me, by the way– I learned that Gavin is afraid of ghosts, and, well... if only you could see how pitiful he looked as he was convinced some type of specter was going to pop into the room we were in. It was adorable."

Jaiden gasped. "So when we were discussing if there was something between you and Gavin last time..."

"You did what?"

"Oh, wait... that's right. You weren't actually a... part of that conversation. Whoops." Jaiden chuckled nervously.

Mishaela frowned. "Anyway, you're wrong. I never had any thoughts like that back then. Or at all really, until today specifically. Gavin's built a stronger friendship with my sister than with me, I'd think, but I'm firm on not actually wanting anything from him, that isn't the friendship we have now. Even so, it's still really inconvenient to have the thought that someone is cute creeping up on you like that, you know? Especially at a time like this. There are matters at hand that are so much more important."

The one thing that Jaiden was sure of regarding this topic was the very last thing that Mishaela had said: right about now was not the best time to be despairing over attractive people. There were much more important matters to deal with. Besides, if they didn't get out of this alive and intact, whatever was going on with Mishaela and Lulu would never be resolved. Jaiden, personally, had invested too much time and effort into introducing them to not see a resolution.

"So, what are you going to do then?" Jaiden asked.

"Exactly what I'm doing now: nothing," Mishaela replied. "On the outside, at least. I wish you could hear the amount of screaming that's happening internally."

Silently, Jaiden was grateful she couldn't.

"Anyway, should we go over and help Lisandra and Brecken with dinner? It looks like they're making lechon," Mishaela said then.

"Oh, I love lechon!" Jaiden agreed, nodding as the two stood up to walk over to the counter where the others were cooking.

Outside, Gavin noticed the moment he stepped into the training area that Spencer-Lynn was sitting out here as well, in the grass.

"I see I wasn't the only one with a mind to get a bit of fresh air," Gavin said as he approached. For the first time, he was able to see Spencer-Lynn's cool exterior crack as she jumped a bit in surprise, before registering who he was.

"Ah, Gavin. Aye, the atmosphere inside is just a bit too tense to be comfortable," she replied. "I'm certain we're on the cusp of a grand discovery, which means the time is coming where we won't have much in the way of rest or leisure. Have you ever sat out here before? The grass is intriguingly soft, more like cotton or moss."

"Yeah. It adds to the ethereal nature of this place," Gavin agreed.

The wind blew softly then, a nice cool breeze to offset the residual warmth of the area.

"Stay a while," Spencer-Lynn held a hand out toward the empty space beside her. "Have you got something on your mind?"

Gavin obliged, sitting beside her. "Not anything particular, I suppose. Just a few... jitters. You'd think this would be easier the second time around."

Spencer-Lynn looked extremely confused at hearing that. "Why would I think that?"

Both fell silent as Gavin pondered that. She had a point; these weren't exactly circumstances one could get used to.

"How bad was it, before?" Spencer-Lynn asked then. "I've spoken with just about everyone here in the Resistance when it comes to what life used to be like, but in doing that, I've noticed there always seems to be some level of resignation whenever they speak to me about it, the kind of resignation that comes from a person who's spent their entire life under such oppressive conditions, you know? ...Or maybe you don't know. I am talking to an Englishman, after all." She added under her breath, "More likely to be doing the oppressing."

"Oh, I..." Gavin blinked; he was speechless. "Oh. I'm sor–"

He was cut off by the sound of Spencer-Lynn's laughter. "No need to apologize; just a bit of banter. I wasn't expecting you to be so gentle-natured. Life's been full of nothing but surprises for the past couple weeks or so, but surprises *are* what keeps things exciting."

"They are." Gavin nodded. "To answer your question, it was... while it wasn't the worst of it based on what I've heard, it was a very desolate place. Everything was so lifeless compared to now. I suppose there's still a considerable amount of lifelessness about, but there was barely any color; it was like a desert. To your point about the resignation in everyone's voices, it was like so many here had given up."

Spencer-Lynn was quiet for long enough that Gavin began to wonder if he'd upset her somehow. "Are you all right?"

"What? Oh! I am, I was just... lost in thought for a moment, I suppose," she replied.

"Would you care to share?"

"It's just..." Spencer-Lynn hesitated. "You know I've been here with the Resistance for a little while now, and in that time, I've become fully convinced that they're all some of the kindest people I've ever met. I suppose it weighs on my conscience a lot that, even though they've all been putting their hearts and souls into their operations for years– some of them from quite a young age, too– I'm feeling a wee bit of despair that it still wasn't enough. That, even with the best of intentions and with all the strength you have, bad things will still happen."

Gavin was silent, noticing the shift in Spencer-Lynn's demeanor. Where it hadn't been so long ago that she'd tried to crack a joke at him, it felt like, now, if he were to try to make her laugh, he'd only earn the smallest of chuckles. It was as if she was as resigned as the people here had been back when they'd lived under a dictatorship. He accepted, then, that there was not only a lot he didn't know about her, but that it was all of a magnitude so great that she wouldn't want to speak of it right now if he asked.

She then said, "I've sometimes, as a result, wondered: is it worth it to fight? And of course I know it is, but you can't help but wonder if it's worth it sometimes."

"That I can understand, albeit on a much smaller scale," Gavin said. "It's kind of similar to when your siblings decide they're gonna tease you over something they made up, and then even when you prove them wrong, they continue to do it. Heavens forbid if more than one of them is in on it."

This got a smile from Spencer-Lynn. "An example many of us with siblings can relate to, aye."

"I'll keep fighting as long as you do," Gavin said then.

"Ah, so it is." She smirked. "Then I guess there's no giving up from me, then. I can't let you outdo me like that. My ancestors would weep from their graves."

This time, both of them laughed.

Thunder had mentioned wanting to eat, but he hadn't left his seat in the conference room since he'd first sat there.

With pen and paper at his side, he feverishly wrote down notes that he felt may be of use, watching the film, and rewinding it to watch it again. He didn't notice how much time had passed until he saw Phoenix in his peripheral vision, placing a plate and a glass of water at his side. Wordlessly, she nodded in understanding before heading back to where she had come.

There had to be some explanation for why Thunder had such strong feelings about this film. If there was one thing he believed, strongly, it was that these deep feelings he sometimes got– the type of feelings that resonated deep within one's belly, simmering through the veins, and buzzing throughout one's head– were always a precursor to something more. This was the type of feeling that had led him to his wife. That had led him to found the Resistance, after he'd lost her. And to trust the five teenagers from the other side, when the Resistance had a task that was entirely over their heads.

They were in over their heads again, and here that feeling was. What other choice did he have, than to follow it?

By the time the house had become noticeably more quiet, signaling that everyone was winding down to go to bed, Thunder had been able to pinpoint a certain stretch of the film that caused him to feel uneasy, so it was a little easier to form hypotheses around why it may be. This stretch covered the entirety of the time in which those menacing creatures appeared, but cut off before The Dictator became a problem.

It was perfectly logical to be upset and disturbed by the appearance of the current thing causing him so much stress that he wouldn't be surprised if he was going even more gray than before, but somehow, he could sense that there was more to it than that.

"Goddamn it. There's something here. I know there is." Thunder sighed, and accidentally knocked his notebook into the projector, making it stop. He gasped, afraid to breathe for a few seconds, before noticing that, thankfully, both were unharmed. A sigh of relief resounded around the conference room, before he began to re-orient the projector. He picked up his glass of water, ready to get back to work.

"Wait a minute." Now that the film had paused, Thunder stared at the frame that it had frozen on. With the movement and shadows halted, he now noticed a blur in one of the crevices of the buildings. It stood out because it was a light, almost mint green, unlike many of the dark and somber shades of the silhouettes and people that were more noticeable.

He'd seen that shade of green before. In his home. In his nightmares.

The sound of the glass of water hitting the floor and shattering echoed throughout the halls of Resistance headquarters.

FOURTEEN

If Only, If Only

In the levels below ground of headquarters, most of the lights had been turned off. This didn't stop a few people from jolting up the moment they heard that glass shattering upstairs, fearing the worst. Phoenix, as usual, was the one to come around and reassure everyone, and was able to talk them down; or into their own rooms, at the least.

"This isn't good. That sounded like glass. If someone's gotten close enough to break one of our windows..."

"Phoenix! Are you unharmed?" She turned to see Hunter hurrying down the hallway toward her.

"Hunter. Yes, I'm okay. It seems that everyone heard that noise upstairs, so I just got through doing damage control," she explained. "There was a lot of work to be done, but all are accounted for in this area. Is everyone in your corridor accounted for?"

"Yes, thankfully. I saw to it personally." Hunter nodded. "How will we be approaching the situation, then?"

Phoenix glanced toward where her room was. "Give me two seconds to grab my weapon. We're going in."

Since Phoenix was the close range fighter, she took the lead, with Hunter closely following. The two carefully tiptoed up the stairs to ground level; this was the only path to the lower levels, so the fact that they'd yet to see any intruders was a good sign. At the top of the stairwell, Phoenix looked from left to right before being perplexed at the lack of sounds and movement.

"Where should we go from here?" she whispered to Hunter.

"The only windows are in the foyer area, the conference room, and leading to the courtyard," Hunter explained. "Our odds are greater if we head toward the front of the building."

Phoenix nodded, taking one last careful look before heading toward the conference room.

It was a short walk, and both were shocked to see Thunder still sitting at the table, not moving, not even blinking, it seemed like. Hunter was the first to notice the broken glass near his seat. Before either of them could say a word, Thunder stood.

Without a word, he walked past them. There was nothing behind his eyes, as if he were in a trance. He didn't notice them as he passed.

"I really am fearing the worst of things, now," Hunter said softly. "I'll do a sweep of this floor just to make sure nothing is amiss. Would you mind checking in on Thunder?"

"Of course." Phoenix nodded, feeling that she would've done that even if she hadn't been asked.

The next morning, Phoenix made sure that she was present at the very beginning of training, to ensure that everyone she needed would be in the same area. At the time she found everyone, they were gathered in the courtyard, stretching and getting ready for whatever the day was to throw at them.

"I am so sorry to have to tell you this *again*, but late last night Thunder made a discovery that has shaken him to his core. Because of this, he's expressed that he needs some time to run an errand that will take him more than one day to complete. Until he's returned, he's specifically entrusted management of our current situation to me."

The air was tense, now.

"Well, I guess there's not much we can do about that, is there?" Jasiela asked. "Especially since he's already gone. So then, what's the plan, boss?"

"I... am not the best at making plans like this, admittedly. However, I've consulted with Hunter about what we should do. Do you mind taking over?" Phoenix turned to Hunter, looking up at him. She admired how good he was at keeping his composure; she'd initially thought during times like these, before realizing he was *always* composed like that.

Hunter took a step forward. "No problem. To get you all up to speed, we have deduced that our hypothesis was correct; that our current problem is the result of a witch's magic. The issue would be finding this witch, which we've fortunately also got a good idea about, since we've already been able to deduce that there's been something sinister happening in the nearby woods for a few weeks now. I do believe our best bet is to undertake another expedition into the woods to hopefully find the base the witch operates from."

"Would that not be dangerous?" Mishaela asked. "Witches are supposed to be extremely powerful, aren't they?"

"Magically. As one could assume, they suffer in physical strength because of it," Hunter replied. "There are ways to protect oneself, even so– but also, I will mention that we are very open to revising the plan, especially if Thunder rejoins us by the time we're ready to undertake it."

"Which is something I'm sure we're all hoping for," added Phoenix.

The area fell into silence again, in a rather somber way. There was only so much the troupe could do if they would be facing a witch. More than half of them had never actually seen one, only heard of their legacy, so the plan didn't instill a lot of confidence in anyone. It did a better job at instilling worry, or fear, or even panic. Would they be able to live through being directly attacked by a witch? They'd barely gotten through a skirmish with holzomen.

"Does this plan include us training more?" Jaiden asked. "I can't speak for everyone here, but I personally think I'd feel a lot more confident if I had more practice."

Hunter nodded. "And that is exactly why, if you'll notice, Logan is not currently present. He should have everything in the training area set up; even though this will be a bit of a crunch session, all practice is good practice, as they say. Let us gather our wits, and meet him there."

Scattered sentences of confusion, complaints, and resignation sounded from the crowd before they were all ready to meet Logan. Walking through the back doors, they found him demonstrating a move to a Resistance member who, by the looks of things, fought with an axe. The other man didn't look much older than Logan, and yet, his hair was a striking snow white, braided into two low braids, a stark contrast to his skin of burnt sienna. By the time the group had caught up, the two were laughing together, the type of laughter that came from knowing someone for a while.

It was a pleasant sound to hear, given the general lack of laughter within the Resistance ever since the battle in the square had happened.

"Oh, there you all are!" Logan smiled. "Good to see you. This is Forrest; he's going to be heading the crew that will be accompanying us into the woods to search for our witch."

Forrest waved. "Pleased to meet you all."

A few members of the group waved. "We have backup?" Madeline asked. "Any reason why?"

Hunter was able to answer that. "For two reasons. Do you remember when I mentioned the defense mechanism needing to charge after it's been running for a few days? But even if it didn't, its reach doesn't cover all of the wood. It would be foolish to think we won't be running into any holzomen while we're out."

"Right," Logan agreed. "Precautions are the name of the game from here on out; we've come too far now to be taken out by mistakes that are easily preventable. Forrest, can you gather a group of people and start preparing them for tonight?"

"Yeah, sure," he agreed. "Good luck out there!" he added as he ran back toward headquarters.

"Thanks!" Jaiden yelled back, as she waved.

Now that the area was clear, Logan picked his sword up again. "Well, then. Are we all ready to get sweaty?"

If a witch didn't want to be found, that witch was not going to be found.

Logan remembered reading this in a book once, and was getting frustrated with the amount of truth contained in the statement. Days went by, and there was no sign of their witch. He had begun to doubt the possibility, but Phoenix and Hunter then shared with him the reason Thunder had been so confident in there being a witch involved, and he ceased his complaints.

As training began a few days later, Hunter and Logan both found themselves getting more confident in their ability to not sustain any serious injuries tonight. Hunter had asked Brecken's assistance in creating ice pillars that were fairly human-sized, so he could use them in his tutorials with Chiara. It helped that he had graduated from bow and arrow to crossbow to shotgun anyway, so he was familiar with the weapon; after sharing tips regarding ergonomic and comfortable weapon wielding, he guided her through an exercise to help with teaching her to shoot while moving, using the pillars as targets. As he demonstrated, dodging and dashing through the pillar maze, he had to admit: this was actually kind of fun.

Since possessing magic aligned with the element of light meant being predisposed to healing abilities, Lisandra had taken it upon herself to teach Spencer-Lynn how to use a few of them. However, it didn't take long for Lisandra to finally realize what all her magic teachers meant when they'd say that not every person was meant to learn every spell. Every time the two would try to cast healing magic– even when it started out very promising, and she could practically feel the healing properties, it would fizzle into electricity, and Spencer-Lynn would let out this yelp, like she was being shocked. Which didn't make sense, because one was always immune to the spells that they themselves were casting, but after a while, she asked to rest and Lisandra gladly waved her off. Trying to figure out why she was so bad at this was too stressful.

Logan was happy to see that the five from before managed to remember the tips he had given them when it came to basic hand-to-hand combat; for some of them, like Jaiden and Mishaela, this helped them when it came to wielding a weapon. There was more work to do with the others though, particularly Gavin and Brecken.

"Hey, Logan? Or Lisandra, whichever of you can answer," Jasiela said as she was resting to catch her breath. "You know how, in order to summon our magic, we have to build that feeling in our center, right, and then toss it? What happens if we just keep building it up and you don't throw it?"

"You get chest pains, in my experience," Logan replied as he tightened the tie of his ponytail. "But I don't think that happens when the goddesses share their power, since the dynamic is different. Why don't you give it a try? If it starts to hurt, we have our healing prodigy right here," he held out a hand toward Lisandra.

Jasiela stared at him. "Do I have to?"

"No, but it's the only way you'll get an answer," he replied, without missing a beat.

This made Jasiela frown. "You're right. Hey guys, can someone do this with me? I don't wanna be the only one accidentally incapacitating myself."

Everyone abandoned their current tasks then, all forming a huddle; closing their eyes, summoning all their magic to their center, and building and compounding upon that initial ball. After a few moments, there was this strange feeling, as if one were slipping out of their own body, during which Jaiden was the first to open her eyes again as a knee-jerk reaction.

"Hey! My clothes are... sparkly?" Mishaela was the first to notice, prompting everyone else to look down at themselves as well. Indeed, there was glitter of varying colors adorning everyone's clothes.

"Oh! This is interesting!" There was the light of wonder and amazement in Logan's eyes.

"Do you know what this is, Logan?" Chiara asked.

"I do, but I'm not sure if I have time to tell you about it," he replied. "Also, even though I know the 'how,' I guess I'm also a little confused about the 'why.' From what I know, though, there's no need to worry. It'll go away on its own. Now, why don't we try to get a little more training in before it's time to get the ball rolling?"

"Logan, might you take over Chiara's instruction?" Hunter asked. "I have to let our captain know the circumstances behind tonight, since he may not have realized so many days have passed already. We don't want anything too horrible to come to pass."

Logan nodded. "Yeah man, of course. We'll be more than happy to have Chiara. Come on over, we can start studying your magic more."

Chiara smiled, always feeling warm when Logan's kindness was extended to her. "Okay. Thank you, Logan."

Hunter gave them both a grateful bow before heading back into headquarters. He wasn't sure how this talk would go, but he was hoping it was smooth.

"Thunder-"

"Charging night?" He asked, after being approached by Hunter. The two had crossed paths in the kitchen, which was otherwise empty. It was rare for the kitchen to be completely empty during the day, so the silence of the room felt a little eerie.

"Wow, you're good." Hunter replied, but almost immediately bit his tongue. "Of course you're good. You're literally the founder of the Resistance. That was a dumb thing to say."

"You're too accomplished to worry about things like that," Thunder said in an attempt to calm Hunter down, but he could tell by the look on the redhead's face that he'd only made it worse. "Now, what did you wanna tell me?"

Hunter nodded, as if to regain his composure. "Right. So, tonight is the first night you're here that we won't be able to use the defense mech I created, because it has to charge. Which means we're back on the field until its energy is restored. One or two nights."

"Right. Which means we can't take Phoenix with us, and we should think hard about whether takin' Lisandra is a good idea too." Thunder nodded.

"The good news is that, since we've had a few days to recover, the combatant division is at 100%; which hasn't been the case in quite a while. I spoke to Logan about this earlier, and he is optimistic about our combat power this evening. I've drawn up a few diagrams for tonight's approach to defense, and they're ready to be reviewed for your approval."

"Right, right. Hunter..." Thunder turned to Hunter then, placing a hand on his shoulder. "I wanna give that responsibility to you."

Clearly, Hunter was surprised by this statement; for a moment he was unable to speak. "U-uh, um. I- are you sure about that?"

"Yeah. In the time since you've been promoted to strategist, you've only grown. Only a damn fool wouldn't be able to see that you're mighty fine at your job. Permission from me won't change that in any way." Thunder smiled at him. "Talk it over with Logan if you want a second opinion, that boy's brain is amazing. I gotta go talk to Phoenix and the kids. Wait, no. Actually... come with me once you find Logan. I have an update y'all will need to hear."

"Oh. Certainly. Front of house in ten?"

Once everyone had gathered in front of headquarters, ready to head out, Thunder began to speak. "Glad to see y'all. I'm told you already have plans in place. Good stuff. But I..."

There was more he wanted to say, it was easy to see. But after more than three unsuccessful attempts to get the words out, Thunder could only sigh.

"Don't worry about it. Let's head out, all right?"

When night fell, there was no moon. It was difficult to see in front of oneself, and even more difficult to avoid any obstacles in the road. Even so, everyone continued down the road, recharged, prepared and ready to defend their town. It was a little scary– especially when it came to walking through the forest, which was even darker once they progressed beyond the intermittent lamps on the path– but even so, they persevered. Turning back was no longer an option, at this point.

"Are we ready, troupe?" Logan asked, placing his sword behind his back, holding it in place with the sole of his shoe so he could readjust the scarves around his hips.

"I don't think not being ready is an option," replied Jaiden.

Logan smiled at her. "There's that sensibility and spunk I remember from you! Glad to see it back!" He put up a fist of encouragement. "Now, then, while we have some considerable downtime I think it'd be best if you all got ready now."

"Right." Jasiela nodded. "Let's do this thing, guys!"

"How exactly are we doing this thing, again?" Brecken asked. "For clarity, you know. Are we prioritizing fighting or searching?"

"Searching. If the horde gets large enough that it renders searching impossible, that becomes our focus for a time, until it's back under control," Logan explained. "That's why we have Forrest and the guys here, to hopefully carve us a clearer path."

Logan waved to the white-haired man, who waved back before leading a group of about fifteen people ahead of them, all with their weapons drawn. They fanned out a bit, until the way they stood and marched in front was reminiscent of a shield.

"A shield. Somehow, I feel a lot safer now," Jaiden smiled. "So I know we had that talk regarding how to spot a witch and all, and there was that one time we came out here and found nothing, but remind me: is there any other kind of evidence we should be keeping an eye out for, or anything? Like, is there a certain type of plant, a certain smell? Smoke? Lights?"

"I'm glad you asked that! In addition to our witch, since we are trying to determine if this area is where all the magic is happening, literally, there would have to be some kind of base around. So maybe all of those. Just keep a lookout for anything that suggests a person has been living here any time within the past few weeks," Logan explained.

Someone in the shield shouted something indistinguishable, pointing farther out, which made the rest of them draw their weapons. This made Logan and Thunder grab theirs as well. Hunter did too, albeit a bit later. Any further conversation would have to wait.

As the horde of holzomen approached, the air growing tense with the stench of battle, everyone sprang into action. While the shield was more active than anyone else, the amount of adversaries meant that everyone was going to have to defend themselves. This was where the ranged fighters shone, able to stop any enemies that were getting too close for comfort. And although Logan was perfectly capable of fighting off the few that still weren't picked off any other way, he quickly gained the support of Spencer-Lynn and Brecken. He smiled; realizing that, as many times as the three of them had fought together now, they were a team, and having the two of them beside him felt comfortable in a way.

The assault dwindled after about fifteen minutes of fighting, and everyone took some time to catch their breath. Hunter went to speak to the defense force, thanking them, and commending them on their technique. Logan was complimenting Brecken on how much she was improving with her spear. Thunder was reloading his guns. With all of the Resistance members busy, disaster could have easily struck, if Madeline's sixth sense hadn't activated; she quickly turned, launching a rock at high speed in the direction of the figure she felt watching.

"Ow! Watch it, jerk. Who gave you the right?"

Everyone abruptly turned toward the sound of the voice, and were surprised to see a person perched on a branch of one of the sickly gray trees. Even from this far away, it was easy to see that they couldn't be much taller than Chiara, if at all. Dressed in a lolita-like dress of pastel blue, purple, and green with cap sleeves, adorned with several bubble-like adornments, and with hair of a seafoam green that faded into blue at the ends, bangs falling just before their magenta eyes, there was no doubt about it.

This was their witch.

"You!" Thunder pointed one of his pistols at the witch, but in more of a pointing way than an attacking way. "I knew you were behind all of this! What's the matter, decided ya didn't ruin my life enough yet?"

"What..?" The witch feigned ignorance in a sickeningly cutesy way. "Why do I feel as though I should know what you're talking about... hmm... oh! Ga- ah, Thunder is what you go by now, right? Hm. To your credit, you haven't aged as much as I thought you would."

There was dead silence.

"So incorrigible of you to not respond to an obvious compliment. What in the world am I to do with you and this band of children you seem to be rather attached to? I certainly hope they don't become collateral damage in these fights. As I recall, the last time that happened, you didn't take it very well."

Rage flashed before Thunder's eyes, but Hunter was quick to stop him. "If we kill the witch before we ensure the end of the spell, things could get even worse than they have been," he said quickly. "I know it is easier said than done, but you *must* control yourself!"

"Someone's got a temper even after all these years, hm? Interesting."

"What is your *problem*?!" Logan finally said. "What did Thunder even do to you, for you to continue to torture him like this?"

The witch was genuinely confused this time. "You think this is about your friend? Oh, no, no, you poor confused child. It is as if you never considered that it wasn't anything personal, and I was simply... having a little fun. What a self-centered assumption, but I cannot say it surprises me. No, the witches of my former coven thought similarly. It is their fault that those with knowledge of witches refer to me as 'Threnhette, Sewist of Discord...' but that is simply a misunderstanding. I'm no more fond of discord than any of you."

"Then what *is* your whole deal?" Jasiela asked.

"I love the world. Perhaps too much." Threnhette began to kick their feet, their legs swinging under the branch they currently sat on. "But people misunderstand me when I say that, too. To many people, loving this world means they wish to keep it pristine, unmarred. To that I say, how can one claim to love the world and all its intricacies, if their actions seek to eradicate any of its natural states? I fear I am the only person who will ever love this world unconditionally, which is why I wish for it to experience both prosperity and ruin. Life and death. Fortune and poverty."

"Wait. So was that why you created The Dictator, then?" Mishaela asked. "So that there would be a constant source of misery in the world?"

Threnhette shrugged their shoulders. "No. That was an accident. An annoying one, because the amount of magic that went into maintaining his form meant there was no way to continue to create any more fun little creatures like this. Honestly, I'm glad to see him gone. To plunge this world into such despair... even something of my own creation could not comprehend the beauty of *all* the world's states of being. It truly is a shame that if one wants something done right, they have no choice but to do it themselves. Well, by themselves and with an undead army."

Jasiela frowned. "I don't get you."

"You are not required to. The world understands me. It thanks me for encouraging its myriad ways of expression. I suppose this puts us at odds yet again... well, if it's fate, I cannot contest it. Gavin and your accompanying forces, return here when you're ready to fight, if you so fiercely stand by your beliefs of eternal peace, or whatever it is you fight for. Or don't. Doesn't matter to me, really."

With another shrug, and a leap into thin air, Threnhette was gone.

"Why me specifically?" Gavin asked, confused. "What did I do?"

"I have no idea, but we can worry about that later," Logan replied. "We got what we came here for. Let's head back home so we can start planning out how we're going to deal with it."

There was even more haste in everyone's step as they started the walk back to headquarters.

FIFTEEN

Witch-Hunting Night

The next afternoon, the brisk progression into the conference room felt tense, but there was also a rousing feeling in the air. There was obviously a lot at stake, but the resulting unity between everyone in the group felt a bit like defiance of one's fate. Like standing up against uncertain odds, and being confident they'd come out on top.

Like revolution, once again.

As everyone filed into their seats, Thunder took his position at the head of the table to lead everyone in discussion. "All right, y'all. I firmly believe that we got enough information to formulate a strong plan. Let's throw out everything we're thinkin' onto the table, and hammer it into a plan that'll get us our lives back. We'll start with recapping the facts we have so far. Hunter, ya wanna give us the rundown?"

"Certainly." Hunter pulled out a notepad.

"The adversaries that we have been facing for the better part of the past month, the holzomen, are created by way of a constant stream of magic being funneled into the souls of the recently departed. Because of this, their ability to be recreated is almost infinite, and they do not abide by the physical limitations of a human body, or any usual corporeal form. This phenomenon has been brought on by, in part and as far as we know, the elimination of The Dictator. Something we thought to be a good move– and that, ultimately, I still maintain as one– but we were not aware that his presence was stopping this from happening, in a way. It also brought about the actions of the spurned witch Threnhette."

At this point in his synopsis, Hunter took a deep breath.

"The very same witch who is responsible for the loss of our leader's family. We did not know her–"

"Their," Thunder corrected.

"Thank you. Their motives then, and even now our knowledge of them is kind of dubious at best, but that isn't necessarily detrimental. What we *do* know is that they will be the largest roadblock between us and our goal of peace for our town. As we learned during our last excursion, they've made some kind of operational base somewhere in the woods. After a bit of reconnaissance work last night and this morning by some fine members of the Resistance, I am confident that the exact location of said operational base is behind the waterfall further into the woods. This is a location that will *not* be easy to reach on foot due to its distance. Please be aware of that."

Hunter then snapped his notepad shut, the resulting slap of paper against paper echoing around the room. "That is the end of my preliminary notes."

"Thank you kindly." Thunder nodded toward him. "So, with all of that in mind, I'd like to open the floor. I wanna hear everyone's thoughts on what we can do about the situation, even the smallest little tidbits you can think of. I only ask that we let each other speak, so we can hear everything."

Logan was the first to eagerly raise his hand.

"I expected that," Thunder chuckled. "Start us off, Logan."

"Right! Thanks. So through all of this, I think something we haven't yet touched base on is the time of day that we do this. They both have their merits: if we go during the day, we don't have to contend with the horde, but we also risk them rising again without their master, which could cause all kinds of problems. If we go at night we can extinguish most of them with our fighting and the special powers of our favorite friends here, but that'll be more taxing than if we did it during the day, so whether or not we'd still have the necessary strength to fight a witch... well, that becomes a lot more nebulous."

"Normally I'd be against any extra work, but you know what I think?" Madeline asked. "If we go during the day and just merk the witch, that means that for all of us that don't live here, our job is done. Which means we'd go home and leave you all with a pretty big mess to clean up. And, respectfully, as I recall... you guys weren't doing too great with cleaning it up before we got here."

"We weren't," Thunder agreed.

"Also, if you're all here as we're disposing of our tormentors, that means you can help us ensure they never come back," Hunter added. "To do so would require us to extinguish all of them, as well as require us to utilize a particular spell that not many know how to do; but luckily, we know someone who does."

"We do? Sweet! Who is it?" Jasiela asked.

"Lisandra." Thunder nodded toward her, before turning to fully face her. "Y'know, I really don't wanna put you directly in the face of danger. I made a promise to Fulvio that I wouldn't."

Lisandra just shrugged. "Eh. Who said he had to know?"

Even though Thunder gave her a look that was clearly disapproving, it was also easy to tell that he was proud of her ambition.

"What we have so far," Hunter had pulled out a different notepad, "is a loose plan to disembark at night and face our enemies head-on before pursuing the witch. That is almost definitely going to take more manpower than the thirteen people in this room, even with magic. Logan, this is where you'll shine; do you have any combat formations that are conducive to this plan?"

"Almost definitely, but I can go get my book of strategies if you want me to be absolutely sure. I'll be back in a jiffy." Logan hopped onto his feet, hustling past everyone to leave the room.

"While he's going to procure that book, I believe we should delve into further detail about the type of terrain we'll need to traverse in order to reach our destination," Hunter said next, standing up himself, and walking over to one of the storage baskets in the room. "Please give me just a moment to find the particular map we'll need... ah, here it is."

He picked up a rolled-up map, unraveling it on the table so that everyone could get a visual of the area. Before beginning, he picked up a few pins to mark important points off. "Our current location is here. At this point, you are all likely familiar with this path, here–" he traced the curving path toward the forest with his index finger. "That is the path that takes us farther into the forest."

"Is this the forest, then?" Jaiden pointed to where the path was leading: an area sparsely dotted with tree-shaped stick drawings. "I mean, obviously 'cause that's where the path is leading. But I ask because I don't remember this being there."

Jaiden was currently pointing to a drawing of a solitary building with a fence around it.

"Oh! I recognize that. It used to be a farm." Lisandra was the one to recognize it. "I remember reading about it in school. Fairly culturally significant if you're into things like agriculture and livestock, but like so many other things in this area, it became abandoned. I think the family that tended to it died out or moved away or something, but I don't remember the specifics."

"How long ago was this? Would we be able to find anything to help us there?" Jasiela asked.

"I doubt it, outside of providing cover if anyone needs to take a breather," replied Lisandra. "Still, that's an awesome thing to have, so maybe we can implement it into our plan somehow?"

"We can establish it as a base while we're clearing out the horde," Thunder suggested as Logan returned to the meeting. "Not only does it give us a safe haven in case things begin to get overwhelming, it's also near enough to our final destination that we can recover there before pressing forward."

"It also keeps us in a centralized location, which would avoid anyone getting pushed away in the undertow, like the one time that happened," Jaiden pointed out. "So it's worth it just for that, in my opinion."

"Right. So here's what we have so far: we go, at night. Set up a base on the farm. Kick these things' asses to high hell. And then we go get us a witch." Thunder nodded. "Logan, full manpower?"

"As full as possible," Logan replied. "It just makes sense to leave a few people here, in case the worst happens. Not something we want to think about, I'm aware, but even so. Also, one more concern from me: how soon are we wanting to execute this plan?"

"I would think as soon as possible, due to the gravity of the situation," Phoenix pointed out. "And I know you know that, so there has to be another reason you're asking."

"There is." Logan nodded. "If we were to go out and execute this plan tonight, if I'm being completely honest, I'm not too confident in our chances to win this thing. Remember, amidst our plans to rid our home of the holzomen infestation, we need to make sure we're also eradicating our witch so that we don't find ourselves in the same position a few months down the line."

An indistinguishable sound came from Thunder, and everyone turned to him. With the encouragement he felt from that, he tried again. "I agree. I'm not gonna blame myself, but objectively speaking, we'd not be in this situation if I had just ended that witch the moment I saw them in my house. I wouldn't be able to live with myself if I let that chance pass me by again."

"Completely understandable!" Madeline agreed. "But, uh... how exactly do you kill a witch? Make sure a witch is dead? It can't be easy, right?"

"Yeah, I know the other day we were talking about how it'd probably be easier to attack one with physical means– but even so, with how magically attuned they are, I wouldn't be surprised if they're able to cheat death," added Gavin. "Is there anything we'd be able to do?"

Thunder turned to Lisandra. "I remember reading once that there's some kind of magic spell that doesn't necessarily kill some-one, but sends their soul directly to the goddesses. Would you know anything about that?"

"Not offhand, but we have a giant library in the basement that I can consult," she replied. "I'll go sample the literature after this meeting is over."

"Yeah." Thunder nodded again, crossing his arms. "You go do that now, actually, and I'll start to deliver the word to everyone else."

The two left then– without adjourning the meeting.

"Hey, so, one thing we haven't touched yet," Jasiela said. "You guys made it sound like the place we're going to is a long way out, and that there are hills and stuff. Are we gonna be expected to walk all the way there?"

Hunter put a hand up. "Actually, I had an idea about that too."

"So just out of curiosity…"

Logan, Hunter, and Phoenix turned at the unmistakable sound of Spencer-Lynn's voice. The four of them were in the kitchen.

"When the three of you went over the plan with us, you mentioned using Thunder's lorry– ah… truck, right."

"Right. I'm on my way to go speak to him now," Logan agreed, nodding. "We'd never take it without asking him first."

"I'm quite certain." Spencer-Lynn laughed. "That wasn't my concern. It's more of… exactly what kind of… *truck* is it really? It's just that the lack of roads and cars here have me wondering who's going to be the one to drive the thing. I can't imagine driver's licenses being a common item here."

Phoenix looked from Logan, to Hunter, and then the boys looked at each other. "We were hoping Thunder himself would drive it; that would be the best course of action because it belongs to him, he's driven it before," replied Hunter. "But even in the unlikely event that he refuses, I mean, how hard can it be?"

Spencer-Lynn stared at him like he'd just confessed to murder. "Oh, no. We're not doing that. Where are the keys? I'll have to take a look at it. I've never driven anything that size, but I've driven *something* before, which puts me at a more knowledgeable spot than all of you. I'll be back. Do *not* get into the driver's seat of that thing."

Hunter and Logan just looked at each other again before shrugging. "I suppose she has a point; it is a rather large mechanism,"

Hunter admitted. "It is just another way in which we would be lost without our valiant captain. Make your speech as convincing as possible, all right, Logan?"

"Ah! You are in luck, my friend! Being extremely convincing is what I do!" Logan replied, grinning, before heading off to find Thunder.

"He's right," agreed Phoenix. "I almost hate how aware he is of how logical and charming he can be."

"A deadly combination," agreed Hunter. "Are you at all opposed to me being the person who oversees tonight's training session?"

Phoenix smiled. "I was actually hoping you'd say that. May I borrow Lisandra? I want her to help me work on our stockpile of medications and such. If this is such a large-scale attack that we're going to have almost everyone here on the field, we need to be prepared for the aftermath of that scale of operation."

"Indeed. She is your responsibility for the evening, then." Hunter nodded. "Is there... anything I can pick up for you before you begin? There are still a few hours before we need to head out. I wouldn't mind the trip."

"Oh! Well, if you insist, I do have a whole shopping list of herbs and spices I've been meaning to pick up, but I've been perpetually busy. Wait right here! I'll go get it."

Phoenix hurried away, leaving Hunter to wonder if it would've been better to have not asked.

Meanwhile, Logan wandered the halls of headquarters until he found Thunder, speaking to a group, before they dispersed. "The ones that will be staying here," Thunder explained, not even looking back at Logan. "I was trying to prepare them for the worst. Never hurts to be prepared for that kinda thing, right?"

"I guess," Logan admitted.

"What brings you around? Shouldn't you be busy with training the kids?"

"Hunter's going to be doing that tonight. I wanna use today for formation instructions for our permanent personnel," Logan explained. "It just makes more sense to train them first; since they're accustomed to battle, they'll be able to practice among themselves after the initial demonstration. That's something we don't get with our visiting friends."

"Right, right." Thunder nodded. "So then, what's happening?"

"I wanted to run an idea by you." Logan sounded uncannily nonchalant when he said this, as if they were discussing dinner. "We travel up the path for a few minutes, right? On a good day, but the length of the path means we risk getting tired on the way. We obviously don't want that, so I've been thinking, wouldn't it be really cool and awesome if we used your truck to get to the farm, and then continued on?"

When Logan finished that sentence, it felt as though all noise in the world had ceased. Thunder's expression was unreadable, almost blank. This went on for almost two minutes, and just when Logan had decided it would be best to rescind the question, Thunder spoke.

"Well hell, that does make a lot of sense, huh? Add it to the itinerary."

Waiting for the defense mechanism to recover meant optimal training conditions.

Being able to spar with each other was one thing, but to be able to spend a few nights battling holzomen meant gaining real-life experience, and between the two, there was no debate about which was preferable.

On the first day, Hunter was the person to oversee training, and did so about half a mile outside of town with a few other Resistance members venturing farther out as a kind of safety net to somewhat cull the numbers, or at least make them more manageable. He disclosed that, like many other members of the Resistance, he was not adept at magic, so this would be a more weapon-focused training; however, he also wasn't good at melee battle, and settled for doing his best. His strength was instructing Chiara, since she also used a ranged weapon; he remained by her side for the duration of the battle, instructing her on how to aim for both long- and short-distance targets, make quick evasive maneuvers, and verbally encouraging her between all of her correct shots.

Being taken under Hunter's wing like this instilled a certain level of confidence in Chiara that she couldn't quite explain, but she was sure that it was partly because he was also a mild-mannered bookworm like her. He also obviously knew her weapon the best of anyone in this group, so practicing beside him felt almost effortless. The more they aimed and dispatched holzomen together, the more she was beginning to believe that maybe, just maybe, she was good at this after all.

The following day, Logan was ready to take control of training, and knew he'd have to do so while not only using weapons that were less familiar to him than his double-edged sword, but he'd also have to switch between them depending on who was currently under his tutelage. On this night he'd adopted Mishaela and Brecken; he was, at least, pretty familiar with rapiers and spears, so it wasn't a horrible night– but absolutely more strenuous than usual. Still, at the end of it, both girls eagerly thanked him for the lesson, both expressing that they felt not only more competent, but more confident that they would be of use in the battle to come.

And so, this was the way things continued for about a week. Learning weapons, learning magic, and becoming more familiar with the terrain surrounding and within the woods. At the end of it, Thunder issued an official statement to the Resistance, and everyone was in agreement with the main sentiment expressed: it was time.

SIXTEEN

The Battle on the Abandoned Farm

When anyone in the Resistance would allude to Thunder's truck, the general consensus of those not in the Resistance was that they should expect a pickup truck, or maybe even a box truck, enough to transport the entire group with a little bit of room to spare. This was not, however, what awaited when everyone ventured outside, to head out to what could possibly be the most important battle of their lives.

Instead, what they were faced with was an almost inhumanely tall pickup-esque truck complete with suspended turrets on either side, and a storage area that would comfortably fit the entire group and their weapons, and then some. This was something that the laws of gravity shouldn't have allowed to exist. It was something that many of the group's members– if not all of them– were struggling to perceive.

"I have multiple questions about this truck," Mishaela was the first to speak.

"Well, they're gonna have to wait until we're on our way. We're moving with a finite amount of sunlight," Thunder replied. "Hunter, Chiara, y'all mind taking the turrets? As it happens, you're the only other ranged fighters that are planned to be in this vehicle."

Hunter turned to Chiara. "Are you confident in your ability to do so? If you are not, we won't hold it against you; we will simply find another way."

This caused Chiara to think to herself for a moment. *Can I do this? My first instinct is to say no, but... why not? I've been practicing so hard. Plus, being higher above ground would make me feel a lot safer. If I had a vantage point like that turret would provide, it would also ensure I could see a lot better, too. Visibility isn't the best for people of my overall stature.*

"Yes, I think so. I think I'm as confident as I'm going to get," was her answer.

"Wonderful. With me, then; I'll help you up," Hunter volunteered, holding a hand out. Chiara took a deep breath before joining him.

"Do ya... think it's the best idea that you come with us?" Thunder asked Phoenix. "I mean, when we were at our lowest, it's not unreasonable to say that we'd have lost a lot more of our ranks if we didn't have you. And that's not even touching the fact that so many of us love you and your continued presence in the Resistance. The thought of something happening to you... so many of us would lose ourselves."

"I know. That's why I'm going to make sure nothing happens to me," Phoenix replied confidently. "Come on, Thunder, have a little faith in me. We've been working together long enough for you to know what I'm capable of."

"I do. But I also know what our enemy is capable of." Thunder then shrugged, "But I *also* know how all y'all Oliveiras are when you've made up your minds, so I won't waste any more time tryin' to convince you. In front."

Once the truck had been turned on and started down the path, two more old-fashioned wagons– one on either side– approached, with other members of the Resistance riding along. It felt riveting, rousing. It was as if everything had been building up to this mo-ment.

The truck drove down the road at a comfortable speed, the wind blowing into everyone's faces, but not in a way that made any of them uncomfortable. The combination of sounds of the engine and the tires traveling down the road weren't so loud that it was impossible to have conversation, but even so, everyone remained quiet for the first few minutes of the ride. It was as if no one wanted to disrupt the deep concentration of the moment.

Until Madeline had a thought she couldn't stop herself from sharing. "How in the world did we not see this truck the first time we were here?" she asked softly, almost as if she wasn't expecting anyone to hear her.

Despite this, most of the people surrounding her laughed. "If I'm being completely honest with you all, I'm not entirely sure where he keeps it when it's not being driven," Logan replied. "It's a mystery. Even with the extensive underground network of our headquarters, I don't believe we have any rooms that are large enough to house such a behemoth."

As the sun sank closer to the horizon, the road began to change; once dusty and bumpy, the trail into the woods became more compact and somewhat smooth, as if it had been traveled down frequently. The wheels of the truck rolled down the road with ease, making the trip feel simultaneously easier and that much more tense. The sooner they arrived at the farm, after all, the sooner the thick of the fight would begin.

When the last rays of sunlight dwindled over the horizon, the cover of the trees began to make everything relatively dark, anyway; however, it was at this time that the first creatures were sighted. The plan was then set in motion.

Since there were still very few of them around at this point, the ranged fighters began by dispatching them as the vehicles continued along the path. As formal and tightly wound as Hunter was, there was something undoubtedly cool and effortless about seeing him point and aim his shotgun with expert-like precision. He had the steady, composed hands of someone who had been with his gun for a long time, and watching him was like taking a lesson from an artisan. It was a stark contrast to Chiara's nervous handling of her crossbow. She had very good eyesight, so her aim was good... when she finally was ready to shoot an arrow. Her loading process was painfully long, to the point where– inevitably– the creatures were able to get closer and closer to the truck.

"Hey! Get away from here!" Madeline yelled, summoning her strength to conjure a few vines and whip them at their pursuers, "Are we close to that farm base thingy?"

"Uh, I think we're anywhere from five to ten minutes out still," Logan replied from where he was holding the map. "There is a chance we might not make it all the way there before it becomes difficult to move, but I was reassured that there was a Plan B for that," he raised his voice toward the end of the sentence so that Thunder could hear him.

"There is! Don't start worryin' too much, young gun," Thunder replied.

"Straight from the captain," Logan said then, sitting up on his knees– wobbling a bit– so that he could see over the walls of the truck. "Oh. Uh, guys, if you ever had an intense desire to start throwing magic around, this would be the *perfect* time to act upon those impulses."

"Awesome!" Jasiela agreed immediately, sitting straight up. "You tell me where to point the fireballs and I'll throw 'em!"

As could be expected from drawing closer to the point where all of the creatures were composed, the onslaught became more dense as the truck and wagon brigade ventured deeper into the woods. The old barn was in distant view when the horde had become so dense, it was impossible to make any progress down the road, swarming the unfamiliar vehicles. The Resistance members that had come along in wagons had since hopped out to fight off their pursuers, but it seemed that it was all they could do to get them off of the wagons. There was not enough bandwidth to even think about clearing a path.

"All right! You all asked for it!" Logan was the first to hop out of the truck to try and make some headway through this crowd. When his feet touched the ground, they did so with enough of an electric shockwave to make some space for him to both gain his footing and draw his sword, and the nearest creatures to him had been stunned by the electricity enough that it was easy to subdue them.

Jaiden was the first person to realize they should probably follow Logan, and so she stood, ready to take on this crowd with him. Seeing her stand roused everyone to action, and they all hopped out of the truck, ready for battle.

As the battle officially started, the strategy was to first focus on crowd control; so that no one would get swept away or trampled to the ground, Logan had advised everyone fighting to focus on attacks that could hit a crowd of enemies rather than one, magic that covered a general area rather than a target. And so, the battle began much like the first few had; everyone combining their best efforts to clear out enough space to eventually continue down the road. Even after ten minutes of the most crafty combinations of spells and weapon usage, though, the way through wasn't looking any clearer.

"So about that Plan B," Logan shouted, clearly winded. "Things are really looking a lot like that should be Plan A right now!"

"He's got a point," Hunter added, still seated up in the turret. "Even with my vantage point, it is difficult to see an end to the current onslaught. If we wish to have any strength left to face the mastermind, it is imperative that we change our approach."

"So I see." Thunder nodded, before reaching to turn the truck back on. As it rumbled with the beginnings of life, he turned toward the passenger's side. "Hunter, Chiara, Phoenix, stay put; and hold on tight."

"Sure. Wait, hold on to what..?" Phoenix asked.

However, Thunder was already turned to yell out of the window. "Logan! Have everybody trot about 15 feet back!"

Logan looked, perhaps, the most confused he had in all his nineteen years of life. "We're retreating?!"

"By stepping back a few feet? You gotta trust the process, kid," Thunder replied. "Now hurry!"

He just shrugged. "You heard the captain! Bring it back!" He yelled, waving his arm in a beckoning motion. "Come on back! Clear the area, quickly!"

Thunder nodded, before pressing a few buttons on the dashboard of the truck in succession. He then switched into reverse, backing up just a bit before parking and pressing one final button; there was an instant intensification of the rumbling of the truck. This was when he held tightly onto the steering wheel.

"What's happening?!" Chiara strained her voice so that Hunter could hear her, as her hands held the railing of the turret so tightly her knuckles were devoid of all color.

He turned to her, an uncertain look on his face. "I cannot say I have any idea, but the captain seems to be quite sure of himself!"

The rumbling continued to increase in potency until a bright light formed just in front of the engine. This seemed to attract the creatures to it; a deliberate action, because after about three seconds, the truck fired a blast so potent that it caused the surrounding area to tremble like an earthquake. Some of the smaller people were knocked off of their feet by the potency of the blast, and those on their feet did stumble.

It was worth it: when the light cleared, the size of the horde had diminished greatly.

"Just like we rehearsed, everyone!" Logan's voice rang throughout the woods. "Now, while the enemy is scrambling!"

The members of the Resistance that had arrived via wagon charged into the fray then, wasting absolutely no time in bringing the fight to the creatures that were still around; although the blast had cleared out a large amount of them, there were still a legion of them around, as could be expected from being so close to their origin point.

"Let's go!" Jaiden yelled, running towards the creatures, brandishing her scythe.

"Hey! Hey, Jaiden, be careful!" As usual, Mishaela was hurrying after her, making sure she didn't get herself into too much trouble. This was enough to get everyone else into gear, and with that, the fight had officially resumed.

The sounds of blades slicing and bullets flying through the air, among other things, filled the air as the Resistance fought to gain ground in the forest. Thunder parked the truck again and fired at some of the holzomen in the general area by leaning out of his window and shooting. He had a quick thought about using the weight of the truck to run over some more of them, but quickly determined that the crowd was now too sparse and it was too dark. The last thing he wanted to do was accidentally hit one of the Resistance members instead.

"Are we still clearing a path for the truck and wagons?" one of the Resistance members asked, somewhere in the distance.

Spencer-Lynn was the first person to hear the question. "We are, I'd believe. The abandoned barn we were aiming for isn't far at this point, it's over thonder–" she pointed– "so we should get there before going through another major strategy change."

"Got it. Thanks!"

With that, those who were more comfortable with fighting up close brought the fight to the creatures in almost expert ways. There was Logan, of course, who seemed intent on not letting anyone forget that there was a reason he was in charge of the combat training in this organization. The constant battles of the past month had clearly taught him even more than before, though: it was noticeable that he didn't move as quickly as before, sacrificing some of his speed for more intricate and precise swipes with his sword. There also seemed to be more strength behind his moves, but of course, that could be expected. After all, the best strength training was actual combat.

What *was* a surprise was how easily he and Spencer-Lynn continued to be able to fight together. At this point, it almost felt natural for the two of them to drift together and time their movements for maximum damage. It worked because Logan was taller and had the weapon with more range, so it made it easy for him to follow up behind the creatures that Spencer-Lynn had either already hit, or that were near the ones that had been hit. In this way, they were able to move with each other quickly, and clear the immediate area.

As for the portion of the group that was new to handling weapons, Mishaela was shockingly graceful with the rapier that she'd chosen; although none of her swipes were particularly potent, she was very good at staying on her feet and avoiding strong attacks. However, she wasn't very quick, and ended up sustaining a few swipes from her pursuers. This was similar to how Brecken was faring; she had the advantage of having more distance between herself and her enemies because of the nature of the spear she used, and the tips she'd gotten from Logan were helpful. But she was, by nature, not a fast person, and found it difficult to avoid strikes.

Jaiden was mostly hindered by the fact that she'd chosen such a long weapon; it hindered her speed as well as her longevity. Even so, after a while Madeline noticed this was happening, and hurried to her side to help her with defense. Madeline had tried to use a lot of the weapons that the Resistance had on hand, but had ultimately decided that none of them were more efficient than her own hands and feet. This did mean she was incapable of actually killing any of the nuisances, which meant it made even more sense that she paired with someone with a strong weapon like Jaiden; or Gavin, who was trying his best to wield the mace he'd picked up without injuring himself too seriously. So far he'd been moderately successful, but it was still obvious that he was struggling.

The arrival at the barn made things much easier because it opened up the possibility of environmental attacks and strategies, and Jasiela was the first person to take advantage of the opportunity. Where before she had been a lot more guarded due to her small size, not wanting to be overpowered by the larger creatures, she was now faced with a myriad of possibilities, and found it in the form of a large tree beside the barn. This barn was two levels high, so she hurried up to the second floor to make it easier to climb the tree. Once up there it not only gave her time and space to summon the magic she needed– bubbling through her veins with the intensity of adrenaline, so warm that it began to make her sweat– and launch some fireballs at the remaining creatures; which seemed to be getting even more sparse.

When the crowd had almost completely been dealt with was when Thunder, Phoenix, Hunter, and Chiara emerged from their safe position in the truck, wasting no time in doing away with some of the stragglers that were running around. Lisandra had been busy helping with a few small injuries that various people had sustained, but she was also trying to be mindful of how much of her energy she was expending. She needed to be able to continue to do this, of course, but there was also the matter of the larger, more powerful spell she'd have to conjure.

It was about two hours later when the area had become noticeably more quiet, so many people took this time to catch their breath and rest.

"Whew... nice to be able to breathe again!" Madeline said, panting, as she leaned on one of the old farm fences for support.

"I can't help but agree," Gavin replied, standing opposite her, placing his mace on the ground. "The stitch in my side feels permanent at this point. I certainly hope the worst of that wave is over."

"I hope the wave is over, period," Madeline said. "I don't know how much I can– Gavin, watch out!"

There had been a stray creature running for the two, lunging to grab Gavin; but, just as Madeline yelled for him to watch out, it was shot once, twice, three times and fell to the ground.

Thunder gave them both a reassuring smile. "Pay a little more attention next time, all right, kids?"

"Yeah. Sure. Of course." Madeline nodded, still panting, and clearly shaken up as well.

It had grown much more quiet than it had been for the past hour, the woods almost completely dark aside from the old street lamps that were situated along the path of the woods. There was not the sound of approaching footsteps or weird grunts anymore, so all signs seemed to point to the area being officially cleared.

"Did we do it?" Jaiden asked then, her voice barely a whisper.

SEVENTEEN

Et Tu

The resulting silence from having cleared out the area of the nuisances that had been tormenting the area for the better part of a month was less rewarding than everyone involved had expected it to be; likely because they were so tired from having to fight off such a large horde, that the silence was difficult to be noticed amidst the thundering of their hearts against their eardrums, and pants and gasps for air.

After several minutes of this being the case, Logan was one of the first to recover, and luckily, his mind was as sharp as ever.

"Lisandra! A magia!"

Lisandra turned to him. "Oh! Right! Everybody, give me a minute!"

She then ran off toward the abandoned farmhouse, but there wasn't enough time for anyone to question why she did so before there was a grand beam of light that shot out from behind the farm-house, up into the sky; and the unmistakable sound of Lisandra screaming. Logan's first instinct was to run in that direction, but he was almost immediately stopped by Phoenix.

"You can't interrupt, it would make things even worse!" Phoenix explained, clearly struggling to hold her larger brother back.

"I can't interrupt? Did you not hear our little cousin screaming in pain?!" he asked.

"Of course I did! It's not a painless spell, but she knows what she's doing; I *promise*," Phoenix replied. "Don't mess this up just because you're getting too emotional! Think about what it would mean for everyone else if we go through all this effort and still are unable to get rid of the holzomen infestation!"

This was what convinced Logan to stop squirming in her arms. "Okay. Fine. I'm trusting you with this. Please don't let it be a mistake."

Phoenix gave him a dry smile. "When have I ever steered you wrong?"

Everyone began to draw closer to one another then, to be certain they'd all regrouped before heading farther on. "If Lisandra will be in pain following this, that means she'll need time to recover, right?" Gavin asked. "Should some of us wait out here with her, then?"

"I didn't account for that in the battle plans. No one *told me* this would be something we'd have to *consider*..." Logan gave Phoenix a glare. "But that being said, I don't think there's any reason all of us have to chase down that witch. There's already going to be a few guys out here anyway to make sure they don't get away, so we can leave the split up to them as to who stays this far back."

"We ready to continue on?" The two were approached by Thunder.

"As always," Logan nodded, but before he could say anything else, they were all distracted by the sound of Lisandra's footsteps approaching, slowly. Her hair was stuck to her face with sweat, and the dress she'd been wearing had clearly seen better days; and, clearly, she'd been hit more than once by the enemy crowds. With the state she was currently in, it was impressive that she was able to stand, let alone walk.

"I hope... you guys... weren't trying to leave me behind."

"We weren't *trying* to leave you behind, we *are* leaving you behind," Logan corrected her. "Have you seen yourself? You look like hell. You're in no position to fight any more than you have."

The moment Lisandra opened her mouth to complain, Phoenix added, "No one is underestimating or demeaning you, Lisandra. You've helped us more than we could ever fathom with words, but you have to remember that we're all responsible for you. Don't make us be the ones to give your parents bad news when this is all over."

"Besides, what would be the point of helping us finally make it through all of this, if you were not here with us to enjoy the world at peace?" Logan asked. "Se saiu bem, mas agora precisa descansar."

Lisandra sighed softly before nodding. "Fine."

"Gavin, could you wait here until she's in better shape?" Logan asked then, handing him the one potion he'd had with him in case of an emergency. "Take this. I think she'll need it more than I will."

"Don't worry, she's in the best of hands," replied Madeline, putting an arm around both Gavin and Lisandra. "We'll hang back. Now head on over there and kick ass. And don't forget to save some for us!"

"Of course." Logan grinned, before heading for the waterfall with everyone else that was leaving.

This cave, much like the last one this group found themselves in, was beautiful.

The interior was almost perfectly round, lined by a marvelously clear pond that cast everything inside in a bluish-green light. The jagged walls of terra-cotta rock were occasionally dotted with brilliant gemstones, and glowing blue flowers that were shaped similarly to buttercups sprung through the cracks of the ground.

And there, further ahead, was the perpetrator of this entire scheme.

The air was thick as Thunder approached the small, raised part of the plateau that Threnhette was currently standing on. Despite the intensity of the situation, their face was curiously nondescript. It was as if they were only mildly intrigued as to what was to happen.

"You gonna try to do anything to prevent me from turnin' you into Swiss cheese?" Thunder asked, with a level of calmness that surprised even himself.

Threnhette looked up at him, with that same expression. "I don't believe that will be happening anytime soon."

"Why's that? Gonna unleash some of that witch magic on us?"

"Hm." They shrugged one shoulder, holding out one of their hands in a carefree expression. "Not at all. I have no intent to try and stop you; to fight for one's morals is the way of the world, I suppose. I don't think we're so different in that regard. However..." They turned their back to the crowd and began to walk away, "I think there are other circumstances that will give you pause. For example, there's a gentleman that might get *very* upset if I were to come to any harm."

Thunder frowned, reaching for one of his guns. "What are you talking about?"

Before he could pull the gun to his level, it was knocked out of his hand by a flying... what *was* that?

"Show yourself!" Jaiden yelled, having picked up a nearby rock, and was poised to throw it. "I've got 20/20 vision and a need to throw things!"

The cave was tensely silent before the figure did, indeed, show itself in the form of a familiar large, dark-haired man. The members of the Resistance instantly recognized him.

"Tornado?!" Phoenix and Logan both said. Logan added, "I knew it! I *knew* that guy's vibes were rancid!"

Tensions seemed to build even farther as Tornado walked closer, into the light, where he could be seen more clearly. There was absolutely no mistaking it was him, even with the change of clothes that came with the post-Dictator era. He did look a lot more comfortable in his loose black t-shirt and pants, even with that being the only comfortable thing in the area at this point in time.

"Son, what are you doing?" Thunder asked, confusion in his voice clear, but even more so than that... disappointment.

"I think we both know the answer to that," he replied simply. "There's been enough carnage for the past month. Why don't you all just go home and forget about whatever plan you had and... have yourselves a nice dinner and a show, or whatever it is you all get up to these days."

"But why?" Hunter asked, trying to take a step forward but finding that his feet were stuck to the ground. This prompted everyone to try to do the same– and, sure enough, they had the same issue. Hunter just sighed, and continued to speak from where he was. "Were we not brothers of the rebellion? Did we not surmount one of the greatest challenges of our collective lives, together? Why would you not only throw that all away, but do so in an effort to join enemy forces?"

"What was the point in helping to save the world in the first place if you were just gonna help destroy it a few months later?" Jaiden added. "It doesn't make any sense."

Tornado simply drew a menacingly large sword from its case on his back. "Like you would ever understand," he replied.

He charged then, directly at Thunder, who was able to react in time by using one of his guns to block the swipe. "What in the world has gotten into you, my boy? I don't wanna have to fight you!"

"Then I suppose you wish to die?" Tornado asked. "Because those are your only two options!"

He then readied another strike, which Thunder was lucky enough to parry. He sighed then, resigned to having to fight someone who he cared strongly about, and drawing both guns. Regardless of the circumstances, Thunder would never be the type to go down without a fight.

"All right. I think we've gone through enough emotional banter," Threnhette finally said from their perch, farther away, near the center of the cave's interior. "But now I'm bored. We ought to do something to spice things up, wouldn't you agree?"

Almost instantly, small, sparse fireballs began to fall from the ceiling. The startled yelp from Jasiela echoed around the cave as Brecken pulled her out of the path of one. At least everyone seemed to be able to move again.

"I thought you weren't going to try and stop us?" Jaiden pointed out.

"Oh, you think I'm trying?" Threnhette laughed. "How adorable! Fate has played out in such an amusing way this time, I see."

Logan huffed exasperatedly. "That's it! I'm tired of this haughty half-pint!" He pulled his sword off of his back and charged.

"Logan, no!" Phoenix and Hunter both called after him, but they both knew it was too late.

When Logan had covered enough ground to, ideally, be close enough to strike, he did so and was knocked off balance by the sudden disappearance of his adversary. Of *course* there would be teleportation magic in play. He was foolish to have not considered that. Fortunately, he was still on his feet, which meant he could recalibrate and try this again. He'd have to try again. There was no turning back now.

"Okay, we're obviously not going to get anywhere if Logan's going it alone," Mishaela pointed out. "If we all spread out, I think our chances are a lot higher. That witch can't dodge us all, right?"

"Right! Good thinking," Jasiela nodded. "Let's spread out. I'll go to the left, Mishaela and Brecken to the right, and then Spencer-Lynn and Jaiden can go long. Chiara, could you give us some cover?"

"Mm." Chiara nodded. "I'll stay here with Phoenix and Hunter."

"With Hunter," Phoenix corrected. "There's no way in hell I'm letting Logan go this alone."

And with a mighty screech, she had gone after him.

"I suppose it runs in the family..." Hunter said after everyone had run off. It was difficult to tell if he was amused or confused– or perhaps both. He merely shrugged before preparing his gun. "Very well, then. Chiara, let us show our friends as well as our adversary what happens when we are threatened!"

"Right!" Chiara readied her crossbow as well. "On your count, Hunter."

While everyone else venturing around the area to execute a more spread-out attack plan, and Thunder contended with Tornado, Phoenix had been able to fall into the rhythm that Logan had established when it came to trading blows with Threnhette; when he would come close with one of his attacks, she was quick to follow up with one of her own. It was not unlike how it had been when they had just begun learning to fight with their swords. Matching each other's pace, in a way that only siblings could.

"Isn't it... nice, that you two are finally on the same page," Threnhette half-complained, winded. All three of them had seen better days at this point. "It wasn't so long ago... that you were at odds with each other, was it? Why was desperation the only thing that caused you to finally believe in your baby brother, Phoenix?"

"You shut your mouth!" Logan yelled as he took yet another swipe with his sword, one that was strong enough to temporarily get the blade stuck in a crack in the ground when he, again, missed. He frustratedly grunted with effort as he pulled it free, before assuming his stance again. "I'm not gonna let you sow the seeds of doubt into either of our heads! Now why don't you just stay still and take this ass-kicking!"

"My, are we angry. Defensive, almost. Insecurity doesn't suit a combatant too well," Threnhette replied, as they sidestepped a hefty swipe from Phoenix. "If you're so good at what you do, you wouldn't be so hostile, now would you?"

Logan didn't speak before taking his next swipe, one that went egregiously wide; it meant that Phoenix wouldn't be able to follow up effectively. However, both were surprised when another blade sliced between them.

"*Back*, you nuisance," Spencer-Lynn said, before turning to Logan, giving him that wry smile that almost always coaxed a smile out of him in return, whenever he saw it. "Come on, man. You can't possibly let someone who probably can't even reach the kitchen counter take the piss from you that easily."

For the first time in about twenty minutes, Logan indeed smiled–a much longer time than he usually went without smiling.

"Well, if it isn't our favorite Irishwoman. Glad to see you join the show." Threnhette smirked. "I'd say it's a bit cowardly for you to wait until other people have already gotten it covered, but your hesitance is understandable. Things didn't go so well the *last* time you were pulled away from everyone you knew in a foreign land, did they, Spencer-Lynn?"

Immediately, Spencer-Lynn's face drained of any and all color. "What? How would you know about–"

Her sentence was interrupted by the most ear-piercing screech most of the room had ever heard; in split seconds, Madeline had kicked Threnhette with enough force that they flew away from their standing position and rolled a bit. Indeed, Lisandra and Gavin were at the entrance to the cave, the former leaning on the latter for support.

"Take that, you vile person!" Madeline said triumphantly, before waving to Logan and Spencer-Lynn as if nothing had happened. "Hi, guys."

Logan could only laugh. "Good work, Madeline."

She saluted. "Here for the people."

Meanwhile, Thunder and Tornado were both still embroiled within their own fight, both adeptly avoiding each other's attacks in a round that, at this point, was clearly depleting both of them of their energy. "I don't understand… why would you forsake us like this, Tornado? After we extended our home to you, called you family?"

"Don't you say that word!" he all but yelled. "What do you know about family?! Do you think that keeping a small army of people around you that are willing to fight for whatever cause you choose really means you're a family all of a sudden? Do you think that could ever replace the ones that we lost? You think you could ever mean to me what my mother did?!"

He swung his sword again, and it swiped closely enough to Thunder to cut one of his sleeves open. It was likely that the swipe had also broken his skin, but at the moment, his adrenaline was running too high to have felt it.

"I did… once. But I was stupid to believe that, and you were stupid at best to enable me, make me believe that righteous causes would ever fill the hole that her death left within my soul!"

Another swing, which Thunder was able to avoid this time. He was clearly at a loss for words. "You…"

"What else could I do? If saving the world couldn't grant me peace, what could? If the world would only continue to beat me down, who was it that determined I can't beat back?!"

"So ya decided to do it by allying with the person who took *my* entire family away from *me?!*" Thunder asked, his voice cracking, trying to find the sense in any of this.

Tornado was visibly taken aback by this. "What?"

"Damn good kick..." Threnhette muttered as they got back up onto their feet. At this point, they were nearest where Chiara was standing, on top of a rock formation, at attention and ready to fire at any time.

She narrowed her eyes. "If you move, I have no choice but to aim for your heart," she said. It was impossible to miss the slight tremble in her voice. Threnhette certainly didn't, and knew that this was their chance to, possibly, drive a rift through this entire group. It was a chance they'd sooner die than not take.

"Oh, so you're here as well, Chiara? What a surprise; I thought everyone else would have left you behind a long time ago. You've done nothing but slow them down, after all. Are we not certain that this excursion would be over by now if your little episode in the forest hadn't happened?"

Chiara was visibly hurt by hearing this, if her wince was of any indication.

"Let us not forget all the anxiety attacks you've been close to having, as well. I don't understand why they brought a weakling like you along– you're clearly much more trouble than you're worth."

Tears were now forming in Chiara's eyes. She fell to her knees, dropping her weapon.

"Chiara, don't you dare cry!" Jaiden's familiar voice darted across the cave, as if it were an arrow of kindness piercing through the fog over her head. "I've known you since Mishaela and I were ten, and you're one of the strongest people I've ever met! You've been kicking ass the entire time we've been here!"

She swallowed a sob. "But... but the forest..."

"You just got separated from everyone else, it wasn't your fault," Lisandra joined in. "You were overwhelmed with the number of mutants because of the way we spaced ourselves out, so if that's on you, that's on all of us! Besides, the same thing happened with Brecken and do you see *her* beating herself up about it?"

Chiara looked across the room at Brecken, who waved and gave her a reassuring smile.

"You're right. You're all right." Chiara stood again, picking up her crossbow. "I can't beat myself up for every mistake I make... because you all make them too..."

The crossbow clicked.

"And I'm going to start by forgiving myself for making the mistake of listening to you!"

The following sequence of events happened so quickly that, for a moment, it was a bit difficult to parse the order in which they happened: Chiara's crossbow fired an arrow, and the sound alerted Tornado, who ran as fast as he could to intercept it. However, he didn't time his leap correctly, so instead of intercepting the arrow and clearing Threnhette, he crashed into them and sent them both falling to the floor. This did accomplish the main goal of avoiding the arrow, which went sailing into the water behind the ground that everyone now stood on, but such a large man tackling such a tiny person meant that there would be some time before they would get back to their feet.

"Oh…" Tornado breathed softly when he realized what he had done. His job, as he knew it, was to protect Threnhette from any harm that might come to them as a result of their actions; and if he performed this task in a satisfactory way, he would know peace when it came to his mother's death. At no point was it ever discussed what would happen if *he* ended up being the one to cause them harm, but based on the stakes of their deal, he couldn't imagine this going over too well.

This was bad. This was very, very bad. He took a small step back, then another, then one more…

It was shocking to see a man of that size run that fast, but when he ran out of the cave, Gavin instinctively entrusted Lisandra to Hunter before running after him.

"This… is why I work alone… the big man, the other witches, they do nothing but slow me down…" Threnhette was on their knees now, and they began to laugh, a dry, joyless, almost chilling laugh. "I don't understand. Why do you continue to resist the natural progression of the world? Do you really think there can ever be an end to living strife? And do you honestly think *you* can be the ones to end it?"

At the very end of their sentence, the sound of a gunshot rang throughout the area; Threnhette grasped their chest with both hands, gasping for air. Some yards away, Hunter continued to point his gun at them.

"Next one's going into your mouth if you don't *shut up!*" he screamed, in a manner staunchly unlike him.

"The sealing, kids!" Thunder said, now able to assess the situation. "Now!"

EIGHTEEN

Securing The Future

I f one were to consult a magic textbook, they would learn that there is more than power, more than determination, even more than desire, or a combination of all three when it comes to the proper way to subdue a witch.

There would be, of course, the initial subduing, which Hunter had just taken care of seconds prior. Witches had always been and would always be powerful beings, regardless of the situation; but they still retained their humanity in many ways. And powerful certainly didn't mean bulletproof.

The more important part, the sealing– the only known way to permanently take a witch out of the equation since there was never a sure way to know if time-bending shenanigans were a part of their magical repertoire unless they'd used that ability before– it had always been a tricky thing to pull off due to its highly variable nature. Not only that, but for various reasons, it wasn't something that could be practiced because the particular moment was so integral to whether or not the spell would even be successful.

One would need power, of course; a level of power to surpass that of the witch at that current point in time, which is why the spell was usually done in groups.

One would need determination, and focus. For every person who was a part of the spell, their mind would have to be not only entirely focused on the spell, but confident in its outcome. They would have to truly believe, with every fiber of their being, that it would be successful.

One would need, perhaps most of all, desire. More than believing the spell would be successful, one would have to truly want it to be. To desire the spell's successful outcome would be to give one's entire emotional bandwidth to it, in that moment. It needed to be the biggest, maybe the only, thing to sate the caster's aspiration.

But– as previously stated– even with all three of these things, with these alone, it wouldn't be enough to truly defeat a witch. If one wanted to be absolutely sure they've surmounted their witch, and said witch would never come back, when casting the spell...

One would need love.

Love for the world and all its people and all its living things, however flawed they may be. Love for the world's smallest things, and its big things as well, and for the way they interacted with one another. One could argue that not all these factors were not present in this current group; but it could just as easily be argued that there was a special kind of leverage from there being more than one world in play. Whatever the case may be, within all the magic flowing between all thirteen people present, came a large burst of light, and a thundering twister of darkness, gradually shrinking, until it was sealed tightly within the most pristine, clear, crystalline stone anyone present had ever seen.

The amount of light in the room slowly died down to a level that enabled everyone to see again, and with that came a heavy sigh of relief from everyone involved. Thunder was the first person brave enough to breach the circle they'd all created, and bent to pick up the mystic stone. It was still possible to see some of Threnhette's figure amidst the dark clouds within.

"The bane of my existence," he said, staring directly into it. "May the goddesses have much less mercy for you than I ever did."

Meanwhile, everyone around seemed to be recovering from the magnitude of the spell.

"Oh man. I haven't used that amount of magic in so long, I had no idea it would take so much out of me," Logan complained, bent at the knees. "No offense to the magicky types here, but I'd like to ask that I strictly be a combatant from here on out?"

"I don't think any of us could ever blame you for feeling that way, Logan," Brecken gently patted his back to comfort him.

"Quitting when the going gets rough, huh? That's so unlike you, cousin." But the tone in Lisandra's voice made it very obvious that she was joking.

Lisandra felt a very strong sense of dread upon breaching the topic of cousins, so she turned to where she remembered Phoenix was stationed, and noticed her tightly clutching her stomach for some reason. When Lisandra was close enough to see her clearly, surely about to ask why, Phoenix slowly moved one of her hands, revealing the blood on it and her abdomen.

She'd been shot.

Lisandra screamed, "Taylor!" before running to close the gap between them. Phoenix fell gently into her arms, causing Lisandra to stumble a bit under her weight. Her screech had been enough to alert everyone else that something was wrong, so they all hustled over. They were all worried, but Thunder looked especially so.

Phoenix must have noticed this, because she looked up at him and gave him a half-smile. "So much for not getting hurt, huh?"

Thunder was so torn between hoping she would be all right, and being frustrated that she hadn't listened to him and stayed back home, that for the moment, he couldn't speak. He closed his eyes, tightly, visibly frustrated with the situation.

"There's only two gun users here, and Thunder didn't shoot his in this direction... is it possible that the bullet that Hunter used to shoot Threnhette could have passed through and hit her?" Madeline asked.

"You mean I... shot her." Hunter looked distraught.

"By accident," added Jaiden. "You didn't know it would happen. No one did."

That clearly didn't help any, as Hunter dropped to his knees and held her. "It's all my fault. Please forgive me."

"Hunter, I understand the magnitude of the feelings you must be feeling right now, but this is no time to be mopey!" Lisandra scolded him. "I just have to do a few healing spells, and it'll be like nothing ever happened. Be strong."

"Yeah, but have you ever healed a gunshot wound before?" Jasiela asked. "I would think the process is different."

"And *I* would think we've all been through enough at this point that you guys wouldn't keep questioning the extent of what I can do, but here we are," Lisandra replied shortly. "Now, after these quick initial healing spells, we need to get back to headquarters as soon as possible for the best chances of a quick and painless recovery. Guys, could you give me a hand?"

Thunder nodded quickly, already bending at the knee to help lift Phoenix whenever he needed to. "If there's anything I can do to help with the spell, just give me a holler."

"Of course." Lisandra had the smallest smile on her face. "I'm almost done... there, let's get moving!"

"Right. Guys! We're moving out! Let's go!" Jaiden shouted, as loudly as she could. Finally, the voice that people often complained about being too loud could be put to use. "To the vehicles!"

Upon the return to Headquarters, the level of activity in the halls was higher than it had been in a long time.

When everyone had exited the cave and returned to the farm, Gavin had stood triumphantly with some of the other Resistance members beside one of the wagons, revealing that they'd all worked together to subdue Tornado; he was still alive, but tied up securely in the wagon and awaiting orders. It was hastily decided that he'd be taken to the outpost house and detained there, until there was time to decide what to do with him. At the moment, there were more pressing issues at hand.

Since Phoenix was currently out of commission, Lisandra took over the role of head medic; there were other older and more experienced medics that were willing to take on the role, but she insisted this was her job, and she was the correct person to get everything running again; she did this in a way that was so confident and direct that it felt foolish to argue with her. Perhaps the fact that her own flesh and blood was in dire need of care made her more intense. Surely, it would have that effect on most reasonable people.

Of course, Phoenix was not the only person in need of medical attention after such a large fracas. Having become relatively familiar with potions and remedies at this point, Brecken eagerly volunteered to help, and it was needed. The party had scattered at this point; those unharmed trying to help in any way they could, and those who needed care holding on as best as they could. Gavin had collided into a tree trunk at full speed sometime while he had been chasing after Tornado, and still now didn't feel as if everything was properly aligned there. Jasiela was showing a few signs of mild dehydration. Chiara had slightly twisted her ankle from a fall around the time of the large spell Lisandra had cast, but had kept quiet about it so that she could continue to fight with everyone. Spencer-Lynn had also kept quiet about cutting her hand at some point, but she'd at least known to wrap it if she was going to go the silent route.

"But I still wish you'd told someone," Logan said, half complaining, half teasing, as he prepared the gauze to give her a clean wrap on her hand. The two of them were alone, in Logan's room; he had remembered having the materials there to treat this kind of injury, and thought that it would be helpful to lessen Lisandra's load of patients by taking care of this one himself.

"Maybe I should've. But everything happened so quickly. It was like the moment I fixed this, we found out your sister got shot," Spencer-Lynn replied. "This isn't the first time I've cut myself, and it won't be the last; I'll be sound after the new bandages."

"Can you at least *try* to make it sound like you'll be more careful in the future?" Logan asked, a bit of a laugh at the end of his sentence; and so, they laughed together for a moment. He reached for the first aid cream then, suddenly realizing that it may be a good idea to clean the wound before it was wrapped again. "Hey, uh... if you're up to talking about it: what was that, back there?"

"Back there?" Spencer-Lynn repeated.

"Yeah, right around the time you stepped in to help at close range," Logan explained. "It almost sounded like you have some deep, dark secret."

Spencer-Lynn heaved a heavy sigh— but when Logan opened his mouth to retract his question, she put a hand up to stop him. "It was already alluded to. If I don't tell you, your imagination will just go off and imagine even worse things." She took a few deep breaths. "Do you remember that talk we had right before we first started training? The one where I told you I was afraid of lightning because something really horrible happened to me?"

Logan nodded. "Yeah."

"Okay. When I was eleven years old, my mother and I were out and about, doing some shopping, in the streets of Tokyo– you'll recall I lived there for some time when I was younger– and we lost each other on the way home. I remember, I stopped to tie my hair back because it was bothering me, and she... she couldn't hold my hand because both our hands were full with the bags, and she must not have noticed that I wasn't still beside her. I was scared, obviously. I didn't know the streets by memory, I was a child. When I finally started to remember the way home, I remember being fernenst a park– I was grabbed from behind. This group of teenage boys, or maybe even young adult men found me, three of them. It's been seven years, you know, and I don't think I've ever forgotten the way they touched me, and threw me aside when it started raining too hard, and I started bleeding– and how awful and dirty and used I felt, and how no one aside from my family seemed to be bothered to give a fuck because I was just some gaijin, anyway. Amazing what you can get away with in so many countries if the victim is a foreigner. I think one of them even kept my underwear as a trophy, because I didn't have it when I finally made it home."

She sniffled. "Can't say it gets easier to tell that story, either," she admitted, wiping her eyes. "But it was around then that I asked my father for a connection to any self-defense classes he had ties to; I wanted to be able to protect myself, or anyone else I was around. I never wanted it to happen to any other person. And he was able to find what I was searching for in one of his eccentric friends' sword training classes."

Logan was silent, unsure of what to say; but he knew he should say something. He settled on, "Thank you for trusting me enough to tell me this."

Spencer-Lynn shook her head, her bangs bouncing. "Nothing to thank me for. Just a bad memory, that's all."

"Just a bad memory? Spencer-Lynn, querida, you were a *child*. You had something happen to you that even adult women have trouble processing. I don't understand how..." Logan stopped himself. "This is probably the way you cope, but I sincerely hope it's not truly how you feel. You are allowed to be hurt five, ten, even twenty years later."

"Aye, so it is." Spencer-Lynn wiped her eyes gently. "But enough about me. How is Phoenix faring, do you know?"

"She's seen better days, but I've heard she's seen worse ones too," Logan shrugged. "Those Resistance days when she was new, before she became a medic, were apparently really gritty. I've always been in awe of the lengths my sister will go to if it means protecting others. I suppose the two of you are not too different in that aspect."

"Suppose not." Spencer-Lynn smiled.

Logan smiled back, lifting her freshly wrapped hand and giving it the softest of kisses. "Shall I escort you to her room? Lisandra was pretty confident that she'd been waking up soon."

Now that things were calming down, and there was time to breathe again, Brecken took a moment to visit Thunder– a moment that was slightly delayed by how difficult it was to actually find him, but she eventually tracked him down seated in the library. There were a few books on the table in front of him, but none of them were open; he was staring at the candles lit opposite him, in a trance.

"I hope I'm not disturbing you," Brecken said softly, sitting a cup of hot cinnamon spice tea on the table. "But I know that this whole ordeal was very personal for you, so I wanted to be sure you were okay. Is... everything okay?"

"Yeah. Yeah, you know, everything is more okay than it's been in a while," Thunder nodded. "I'm just thinking about a lot of stuff."

"I'm sure," agreed Brecken. "Would you like to share?"

Thunder sighed, nodding, placing one of his elbows on the table, resting his chin in his hand. "Just ponderin' the fallout. What'll happen in the town now. How we're gonna handle our captive. Dinner. You, even."

"Me?" Brecken asked, surprised.

He nodded. "When I first met you– or should I say, when I was first able to speak with you– there was this feeling of a sadness, a longing, and I didn't realize why at first, but now that I've had time to think about it: you know that I once had a family of my own. And the more it bounces around in my head, I think about how much you remind me of my middle daughter."

"Oh." Brecken nodded, but then thought about it some more, looking down at her fair-skinned hands and her light blonde hair. "Uh..."

This made Thunder laugh. "She wasn't my biological daughter. My wife and I found her abandoned on the farm grounds when she was no older than six months old, so we took her in and named her– Cheyenne, but as she got older she preferred Enna– raised her as our own, alongside our other two girls. She was always more soft-spoken than her sisters; we always made sure she knew she was one of us, but there were some times she felt she didn't belong because she looked different. But as time went on... we didn't get much time together in which she knew she made our lives better by being there. She was seventeen when she died, the same age you are now."

Brecken gasped softly, taken by surprise. "I understand. That must have been so very hard to bear."

"Never good to learn a child has died," agreed Thunder. "You know, these past few weeks have been the most I've ever been able to speak of my family in years. It hurt so much... to accept that they're all gone, even now, more than a decade later. But now I realize... that I've gained a family here, within the Resistance. Maybe in the beginning I was their leader and they were my subordinates, but that concept doesn't feel right when it comes to describing the relationship we have today. And I could extend that to everyone who's visiting, too. The way y'all have continued to make sure I was all right mentally, and looked after each other, and cared for one another; is that not what a family does?"

Brecken nodded. She understood the point he was making; and indeed, even though she had only recently made the acquaintance of this group of people, she already thought of some of them more fondly than some of her family members back home.

"You're a good person," she said then. "And based on what I've seen here, I bet you were a great father too. I don't know if you'll ever be enticed to find your person again, but if someday you are, if it makes you feel any better, I have an aunt in Brooklyn that's probably around your age, and she's single!"

Thunder laughed at that. He wasn't sure if Brecken had intended for it to be funny, but for the past years he'd been so busy with Resistance things he'd never given it any thought.

"I'll... look into it if I ever cosmically find myself in your world," Thunder replied. "Thank you, Brecken."

Nineteen

A Time of Rememberance

A few days later, Thunder woke up early, much earlier than usual. There was still one very large loose end he had to tie before he would consider this whole debacle over and done, and it was one of the ones that he wished he didn't have to deal with. But this was the burden he bore as the leader of the Resistance, he reminded himself as he made his way to the front door.

"You showed. Guess there *is* still some integrity left in ya."

Silently, Tornado looked down at his feet. "I deserve that, I suppose."

"You do." Thunder nodded. "But... I didn't ask you here just so I could berate you like an angry father. Why don't we take a little walk?"

The two men made their way to the river, both silent against its lively, rushing current. It was perhaps the strongest either of them had ever heard it be, or at the least, the strongest since the Resistance had moved its headquarters near it. The closer the two got to the riverbank, the more details were visible: the different plants that were beginning to sprout, the tiniest of flowers blooming as well, and the minnows heading upstream. It was reassuring, in a way; this pointed to the region continuing to regain its health, and its magic, the way it had been before those creatures had appeared.

"Times are a-changin," Thunder finally said.

Tornado nodded. "That they are."

"I don't think things have ever changed as rapidly as they have this past year, in all my 43 years of life. Think a lot of people here have been struggling because of that. After all, it wasn't long ago that it was impossible to believe we'd be living in a world where this place was no longer a dictatorship, and that the environment would improve this way. How do you adjust your life to a world you'd never known could exist? You know, some... misguided, but strong-willed young'un said something like that in his resignation letter, can you believe that?"

Another silence passed between the two.

"I can't berate ya because I can't say with confidence that I'd never find myself in your position," Thunder said then. "I *can* say that I was dangerously close to it, honestly, and for a person who's been through something like that, it ain't hard to understand that mentality. When you lose somebody that meant everything to you, that level of hurt... is something that I don't have the poeticism to put into words. But it's so immense, so crushing and devastating, that I don't think a single person who's felt that can claim to have never– not for even a second– felt a resulting desire to inflict that hurt onto other people, especially when life is going on as if nothing has changed. It feels almost insulting in a way, don't it? I remember what it was like to feel that way. How dare everyone keep going on, the world keep turning, like I didn't just lose the most important person, or people, in my life?"

"But even so, you didn't hurt anyone. You did the opposite when you founded the Resistance," Tornado pointed out. "Why? And how?"

Thunder shrugged. "Anger. A whole lot of anger and resent. When you think about it, it's almost like the Resistance is a round-about way of me getting my revenge, focusing my hurt on someone who kind of had nothing to do with it. I had no way of knowing where to find Threnhette back then, or of knowing if they were even still alive. But if I couldn't hurt them, I could hurt the man... thing... whatever, who treated my hurt like it was nothing but an inconvenience. Thinkin' of it that way... are we all that different?"

"Yes. I still believe getting rid of The Dictator was a positive thing, and I think everyone here would agree with me on that. But in my actions, all I did was hurt people that had nothing to do with it... as well as the people who showed me nothing but kindness," replied Tornado. "I've been a fool."

Thunder nodded. "You figured that out by yourself?"

"Had no choice but to. There wasn't a lot of entertainment in the room I was locked in."

This made Thunder chuckle.

"So it's true, then? Threnhette was responsible for you losing your family?" Tornado asked. "I had no idea. I would have never even guessed they were old enough to have been alive back then. I assumed they were around Logan's age, but when I think about it more, why would I trust such a young witch to be able to help me? Looking back, I made it so easy to manipulate my emotions. I really did get played for a fool."

Thunder shrugged. "It happens to the best of us. And maybe I'm a fool myself, but I do believe in the good of people; and that would include you, Anton. Now that you've had time to reflect on all of this, have you started to do any thinking about what you want to do from here?"

"I already know. Could you meet me in the market plaza in three hours? Bring the Resistance kids along, if you want."

For the souls that departed too soon. May the goddesses greet them favorably in the afterlife.

Near the entrance to the market stood a monument made of stone, its inscription visible from a few feet away. When one ventured closer they would be able to see the names carved into the monument, the names of not only the people who had died in that battle in the marketplace, but all of them who were killed much too soon in this town. Also visible close up, at the foot of the monument, were the first young leaves of plants that would, in time, grow to be beautiful flowers.

"I planted the flowers here not only as decoration, but as a reminder that everything is always reborn. That, every time we had to lay a soul to rest, we looked forward to their return to this world in another time, in another form. None of these flowers are perennial, so they'll be reborn every year with some upkeep."

So Tornado explained the monument to Thunder, Hunter, Phoenix, and Logan.

"How did you get this done so fast?" Logan asked. "I don't even think I could've done that."

The shift in Tornado's body language indicated a significant amount of pride. "I started my work while I was imprisoned. I asked one of the men watching me if he could bring me the death records when someone else took over watch, and he was kind enough to oblige me. I was also able to do some research on which flowers were best to plant here, and where to find the appropriate stone, neither of which were very far away, thankfully."

"Oh." Logan nodded. "Well, it looks nice. Very eye-catching."

There was a brief silence then.

"When we last spoke, you were pretty insistent on leaving the Resistance," Phoenix said then. "I'm sure you already know– due to all that's happened– that very many of us wouldn't feel comfortable having you back within our ranks, either, so... what will you be doing from here on?"

There was a halt in conversation as Tornado began to form the sentences in his mind. "You know, during my time with the

Resistance, I always felt welcome, but... there was always this feeling that it wasn't the right way to apply myself. I never thought much about it, because back then it was *the* way to apply myself, you know? But now that those restrictions don't exist anymore, I think I know of a better way to do that."

"Really? And what would that be?" Thunder asked.

Tornado held his hand out toward the empty expanse of land outside of the market. "Look at what this town looks like. It's desolate. It almost looks abandoned, especially with the state the old palace is in these days. This is supposed to be the magic capital of the entire *world*, and look at it, a hollow shell of itself. This town deserves to be a city again, like back in the old days. Wouldn't it be nice to restore it to its former glory?"

Everyone pondered this.

"Well, as a person not originally from this area, I can only say that I would absolutely love that," Hunter replied. "To think that I could someday live in the place I've only seen illustrations of. The intricacies in design, the colors, the textures... it would be like a dream come true."

"It would be nice, wouldn't it?" agreed Phoenix. "That's a hefty job to take on, though; there's so much work to be done before it gets there."

"We all have to start somewhere, right?" Tornado pointed out. "Well, at any rate, that's what I've decided. While I was out here chipping away at this stone, I was even able to find some of my old crew that also left the Resistance to help me out. We'll have a storefront somewhere in the market in a week or two for information and donations and stuff of that nature, so... feel free to come down sometime, if you ever want to help out with any rebuilding."

"Yeah." Thunder nodded. "Best of luck, then."

The two men waved each other off, before they began to go their separate ways.

As the four of the Resistance made the walk back to headquarters, Hunter was the first to speak. "You know, that conversation has made me start thinking."

"Yes, Hunter?" Thunder asked.

"What are *we* going to do from here on? We've worked so hard to eradicate hardships in this region twice now, but– figuratively knocking on wood– there cannot be much else here to resist against, can there? Is continuing to be a resistance feasible? Sustainable?"

"I hadn't thought about that, but these are good questions," agreed Logan. "At this point, it's probably a good idea to at least restructure what it is we stand for. I mean... not change completely, because– although in different specific ways– we've always, at our core, been in the business of helping the citizens of our fine town live the best lives they can. We can still continue to do that, but it's gonna be in a different way than we have up until now. I mean, Hunter said it best: we're not really resisting against anything anymore, so can we really call ourselves the Resistance?"

The walk grew silent. Thunder was deep in thought.

"You both make a good point, one I don't disagree with. And at this point you'd have to be completely unaware of your surroundings to not understand that, for better or worse, the people of this town look up to us now. So no longer doing what we do has never been an option, and I'm glad y'all agree on that.

"Who's to say what the future brings? We have no idea of knowing what's gonna happen tomorrow in this unpredictable world. That's how all this happened: peaceful one day, ancient magic creatures the next. If anything dangerous ever threatens our home, we'll be there to defend it, and I think this is the best way to focus our efforts from now on. Still a resistance, in that now, we're resisting anything that may threaten our right to a safe and peaceful life, and an equally safe and peaceful life for anyone that decides to call Compositora home."

Thunder then looked over at his three companions, who all had various sized smiles adorning their faces.

"How beautifully stated," Phoenix said then, her smile growing even bigger.

"It is an admirable goal, one that I would be honored to continue to lend my efforts to," agreed Hunter.

Logan added casually, "Well, considering how much I pissed my parents off by coming here, I might as well ride this train until the wheels fall off, huh?"

All four of them laughed.

"I'm grateful for you kids, especially you, Oliveiras. You both sacrificed your youth for this old man and his cause, and I'd never be able to overstate how much I admire y'all for it. And Hunter, the amount of growth you've gone through in such a short time can only be commended." It was Thunder's turn to smile. "Now enough being sappy. What are we thinkin' for lunch today?"

"You guys can have that out," Logan replied. "I still have half a sandwich left over from yester– my sandwich. I didn't put a claim on my sandwich. Oh, no. I gotta get back there!"

The three older adults could only laugh as Logan ran off at high speed to ensure his sandwich would still be in the refrigerator when he got back.

TWENTY

The Return Home

There was a point in which Mishaela suddenly became aware of the weight and existence of her own body; too much so, at one point feeling so overwhelmed that she felt almost compressed. It was at this point that she opened her eyes.

Her mind swam with confusion as she was slowly able to pick out familiar parts of where she now found herself. She'd seen that ivory popcorn ceiling before, and those peach-colored curtains with the embroidered purple flowers on them... yes, this was Madeline's house, wasn't it? But why was she here all of a sudden?

As she slowly sat up, Mishaela realized she was lying on a mattress in the middle of the living room. Her eyes slowly adjusted to the low level of light in the room, and with this came the sight of all of her other friends as well. Madeline and Jaiden were both asleep on the couch, which let out; Jasiela was out cold on the loveseat; Gavin, perhaps the worst off of the bunch, seemed strangely content on his makeshift bed of the couch's cushions. And of course, beside Mishaela on this double mattress, was Chiara.

This wasn't too unlike the first time she'd been brought back home, especially now that her body felt normal again. The quietness of an early morning, the almost uncanny silence. The mysterious serenity of it all. She couldn't imagine Madeline's parents sleeping very much if she'd disappeared for as long as they'd been in the magic world. The goddesses were so cool, the way they always looked out for this group of wily teenagers.

She heard Chiara stir on the mattress next to her, and turned to see that she'd tried to sit up, but almost immediately fell back onto her pillow, a hand lightly on her forehead. "So dizzy..." she whispered to herself.

"It goes away after a little while," Mishaela reassured her, as quietly as possible so she wouldn't wake the others.

Chiara looked over at her, startled, but immediately relaxing when she realized who it was. "So it does."

The sisters remained there in silence, then.

"That was... that was absolutely an adventure," Chiara said after the silence had gone on for some time. "Was it like that the last time, too?"

"Not at all. I don't think I could've ever imagined things being that big and exciting last time," Mishaela replied. "This was scary at times, lots of times, but... I can't say that parts of it weren't also fun. That's something that *did* happen last time, in contrast."

"So I see." Chiara smiled.

"You know, Chiara, I... I don't think I got to say so while everything was going on, but I really loved seeing your growth from the time we arrived at the Resistance's headquarters up to now. It's been sometimes subtle, sometimes in spurts, but it made me– *continues* to make me– really proud of you," Mishaela confessed. "You gave it all you had. You were insistent. You were brave."

"Brave? Really? Do you think so?" Chiara asked, surprised. "It was scary, but I... everything I did was what I felt I needed to do, so we could all survive and make it through. I don't know if I would call myself brave for that."

Mishaela nodded. "Maybe not. But with that, I'd ask you: is being brave the act of accomplishing great feats? Or is it when the mountains in front of you begin to look more like hills?"

Chiara sat with that for a moment. The last time she'd been in this house, she'd had to give herself a pep talk for three minutes to convince herself that it was okay to go outside, where Jasiela and Gavin might see and start conversation with her. There would be barely any psyching up needed, now. She even found herself looking forward to when Gavin woke up, so that she could talk to him about his opinions on American food and to expand on some of the conversations they'd had before via IM.

Maybe, from where she was at this very moment, her view was looking a bit more hilly now.

"Just wait until you guys see this! I made a whole itinerary scrap-book full of things we can do while you're visiting! Of course we've gotta hit the touristy areas like the bean and the Sears Tower, get you some hot dogs and deep dish, but there's also some other really cool stuff we can do together too!" Madeline dropped the scrapbook on the table, making a cloud of pink and orange glitter fly out from its underside.

"Will we really be able to get through all of this?" Gavin asked, clearly having his doubts.

"Wait, how did you make this so quickly?" Jasiela added. "We weren't able to give you a ton of prior notice about us coming here. How in the world..?"

"I have my ways," Madeline replied elusively. "Oh yeah, and I think we were talking about the beach last time, right? A heads-up that if we go there, my sisters are gonna want to tag along too, but they're good people."

"Yeah, why not?" Jaiden agreed. "More the merrier, as the old saying says."

"Speaking of that old adage..." Mishaela said, raising her hand just a bit. "If we go to the beach or one of the museums, are there any objections to me bringing a, um... friend?"

Madeline immediately caught on to her hesitation. With all of the delicateness of a freight train she asked, "Oh? *Just* a friend?"

"Just a friend." Mishaela nodded. "I'm not entirely sure that things have progressed enough for us to consider each other more than that, just yet. I don't want to rush things."

"But you *do* want them to happen?" Jasiela asked.

Mishaela nodded bashfully. "I certainly wouldn't mind if they did."

"Then how can I say no to a couple of budding lovebirds?!" Madeline agreed loudly. "Just say the word and I am completely on board with being your third-wheel photographer, ready whenever you give me a holler! You guys will have the cutest couple pictures as long as I'm taking them. Total 'most liked picture on Instagram' material, I tell you!"

"Madeline, you'd just end up making all the pictures look like they'd been dipped in neon-colored acid," Jaiden teased her. "I've seen your posts. Besides, third wheeling those two is already my job; I've been doing it for almost eight months already, might as well start taking pictures too."

"I guess that's a good point. All right, so I guess we can officially add the beach to our itinerary. Let me write that down so that I don't forget," Madeline pulled out a pen with the most obnoxiously poofy and showy pink feather tip. While she was busy writing, Mishaela noticed that Gavin was now sitting in a much more closed-off manner than before, his hands folded in his lap.

She gently nudged him to get his attention. "Is something wrong?" she asked softly, so that *certain people* wouldn't hear her and make this conversation into a big deal.

Gavin nodded, not speaking or making eye contact. After a moment, though, he whispered. "Everything is as it should be."

Mishaela nodded then. She wasn't sure what he'd meant by that, but he didn't seem like he was in the mood to elaborate, so she left him alone for the moment.

"Okay. That's all settled and notated." Madeline smiled, feeling very accomplished of herself. "But there's one thing we still need to settle on. What exactly are we gonna end up doing today?"

They may have all been able to call it the best summer ever; or at least so far.

It started with a dinner out at a neighborhood pizza parlor, one recommended by Madeline's parents, where everyone was able to introduce Jasiela and Gavin to the culinary wonder that was deep dish pizza. Both of them agreed that the spectacle of the whole thing was more exciting than the pizza itself; and, honestly, none of the Chicagoans present could debate that. It was still a tasty dinner, though, and Gavin dedicated an entire page to it in his food journal. Prior to this, no one present had known he even had a food journal, but he insisted that it was the most comprehensive piece of literature he could ever amass; and that, when it was in a state that he was comfortable sharing it in, he'd publish and share it with the world.

Then there was the visit to the bean downtown, an architectural marvel that Gavin was so captivated with that he asked the group to go get hot dogs without him as he stared at it, as long as they brought him back one with the works. Mishaela had been the one to oblige him, because, in her words: "if something is so interesting that Gavin is choosing it over food, it must be really important to him." Jasiela was evidently surprised that the people around the bean were dressed so plainly, when the mirroring/reflective nature of the bean's surface meant that there were so many interesting fashion choices one could make. Nobody around seemed to know what she was talking about, though, so she let the matter drop.

In the last few days before Mishaela and Chiara were due to fly to Italy, the group went to the beach alongside Madeline's twin sisters and Lulu; they were there almost the whole day, splashing in the waves and playing volleyball where the nets were set up, and of course taking breaks to eat, and play cards on the sand. Watching the sunset on the beach was something that no one present would forget; while it was a simple occasion– one that happened every day, in fact– these kinds of occurrences always felt more significant when they were experienced alongside good company. Mishaela, particularly, would never forget how happy she was to see Gavin and Chiara talking and laughing like they'd been lifelong friends, or the moment where Lulu tightly held her hand as they all headed back to the parking lot.

They also all went to the aquarium the next day, marveling at all the different kinds of sea life. Neither Jasiela nor Gavin had ever actually been to an aquarium (or at least neither remembered going), so there were some things that blew them away, like the dolphin show and the absolutely massive size of the beluga whales. Gavin insisted he couldn't go home without a souvenir, and ended up leaving the gift shop with the most adorable octopus hat. Jasiela preferred the charm bracelet option, picking up charms of a sea turtle and penguin.

After the Pagliardi sisters had gone on their trip, Jaiden was the person to escort Jasiela and Gavin to the skydeck at the Sears Tower. She did this alone because Madeline asked to not be a part of things beyond a "reasonable altitude," and she knew that Mishaela would have had a similar reaction if she'd been around. Still, they had the opportunity to eat lunch up there with Jaiden's parents and marvel at the view. It was an experience none of them would forget anytime soon.

All good things were destined to come to an end, though, and when it was time for the duo to go back to New York, Madeline had to talk herself out of scheming up ways to stow away on the train. It was a bittersweet goodbye, but all the same, all four of the teenagers present were certain of one thing: that they would all have the chance to be together again.

Hopefully, next time, it wouldn't be because of impending disaster in a magical world.

Spencer-Lynn still felt disoriented when she woke up after the transport back home. As she descended the stairwell to get to the kitchen in her house, she needed to grip the handrail tightly; it was difficult to tell which way was up, but when her bare feet touched the cold tile of the kitchen, the sensation was surprisingly grounding. And so she looked around, walking toward the front of the house, somewhat surprised to see that life was always as it was in the Cambridge house. Her two youngest siblings, Colin and Nicole, were in the living room watching cartoons. Her brother Vincent was seated on the couch, reading a book that she couldn't see the cover of from this angle, but she was able to see it was quite thick. Mumford, the final sibling who still lived here, didn't seem to be around– but she recalled seeing his door closed when she passed his room, which usually meant he was still asleep.

She was, then, suddenly very conscious of the sound of someone cutting something in the kitchen, so she turned back around and saw her father slicing some vegetables. It wasn't too surprising that she'd missed him when she'd first come downstairs; she was taller than him at this point, and it made it easy to lose track of him, especially in places like the kitchen where there were appliances that could hide a person's entire form.

He looked up when she pulled out one of the chairs at the island, his brown hair falling down his forehead. "Du er våken."

The only thing he received in response was a blank stare. His mother, Spencer-Lynn's grandmother, was from Norway, but it wasn't often that Norwegian was spoken in the house, and she was in no way fluent. She had thought for sure that "good morning" was a completely different phrase.

"You're awake," he translated then.

"Then why didn't you just say that," Spencer-Lynn said flatly, with a bit of a laugh, as she grabbed a red apple from the bowl of fruit on the counter. "You know the only one of us who can hold a conversation in Norwegian doesn't live here anymore. How long have you been up? That's a lot of vegetables."

He laughed then. "I'd be surprised if I slept at all, but it's not a bad thing. The baby's here."

The eldest of the Cambridges, Liam, had been expecting a child with his wife any day now; they lived in Dublin, which meant they had to have called here when they were on their way to the hospital. Why did babies always seem to arrive at the most inconvenient times?

"It's a boy, and he's nice and healthy," he continued as Spencer-Lynn took a bite of her apple. "They named him Samuel, Samuel Ryan Cambridge is his full name. I'll tell the little ones that they're uncles and aunts when we all sit down to breakfast. Mumford already knows; he was awake with us. We're surprised you didn't wake up. You're usually such a light sleeper, Lynn."

Interesting— so, here, she'd been asleep the entire time that had been transpiring. But she couldn't have been asleep for the entire time she'd been in the magic world, or else her father would be questioning her a lot more than he was. How was this possible? If only she'd have had more time to learn about how the two worlds interacted with one another. "I... was really tired, is all. You know, all the studying I was doing up until a few weeks ago. Has anyone let Maceida know she's officially an aunt now? Oh, wait— time zones, right? What time is it in Montreal, anyway?"

"Doubt the sun is up yet." He shrugged, but Spencer-Lynn knew that he was practically itching to call. Her older sister had always been her dad's favorite. "Hm? What happened to your hand?"

Spencer-Lynn's eyes darted to her hand; the gauze from when Logan had wrapped it was still there. The goddesses could transport her back home and pull some magical time-bending nonsense, but they couldn't fix her hand? Inconvenient. What could she have done that caused her to wrap her hand this way? Fallen? Done it just for the aesthetics? She settled on, "I burned myself the other day when I was baking." Plausible. Reasonable.

"Ah. Be more careful next time, aye? That being said, it looks like you did an amazing job securing that."

She nodded. If she placed her hand close enough to her face, she could still smell that faint minty scent from the first-aid cream that Logan had used. He had been so gentle with her, and had wrapped her hand so meticulously, that she was sure she'd never forget it. It was strange– such a mundane action, why exactly was it staying in her mind like this?

When Brecken first awakened, after feeling like she'd been dropped from the sky into her bed, she took a few moments to stare directly up at her ceiling. The sun was just now rising, so slivers of gold stretched across the smooth white paint. Despite the abrupt awakening, she felt more rested than she had in a long time. That was partly her fault for staying up late– usually reading her comics– but everyone had their vices, and she'd accepted this as one of hers long ago.

Speaking of comics, she then sat up and looked around her room, the familiar posters grounding her. Yes, this was her room. The multitude of comic-based posters assured her of that, particularly the large one from her favorite series, Evil Scientist Schiller, which she'd gotten signed by its creator a couple of years ago at New York Comic Con. When it came up in conversation, she'd refer to it as "the best day of her young life." The other poster that stuck out wasn't comic-based at all (which was partly why it stuck out); it was the largest one in the room, of girl group 2ne1. Brecken's cousin Elise had bought it for her as a birthday gift right before she'd moved to Germany; both girls had promised each other that, someday, they would see their favorite girls in concert together.

And that certainly felt possible now, after what Brecken had been through.

Coming from the Resistance headquarters, which was always a little noisy, to her quiet home felt a bit disconcerting. Here, it was just Brecken, and her parents if they were home. Her father, Raphael Islington, was a very likable man; he was respected by everyone who worked with him, because he was not only a man of his word, he was also humane, which wasn't very common in the entertainment industry. He was a playwright, which meant that he often traveled around the country to assist with putting on different productions in various theaters. Her mother, Mary Anne, traveled a lot as well as a real estate agent. It was for this reason that Brecken didn't have any friends here in Portland, even if it was where she was born and raised for the most part— by the time she ended up getting settled in one place, they were moving again.

Brecken carefully stepped out of her room, with a glass in her hand; she was thirsty, and decided that a drink of water would do her well. She wasn't expecting to see both of her parents in the kitchen when she got there, though, and for a while she could do nothing but stand there.

"Are you here to apologize for ruining our vacation?" was the first thing her mother said.

"Now, now, dear. It's not like Brecken intentionally got sick. No one would do that." Raphael rounded the corner around the island to place a supportive hand on his daughter's shoulder. "There's saltine crackers and gatorade in the pantry if you're still not at a hundred percent, Brecken. You rest as much as you need to, all right?"

Brecken didn't remember being sick, and she certainly felt fine now– but then she remembered that, before she'd gotten pulled into the magic world, she and her parents hadn't been at home. They'd been in San Francisco. But they were home now, which meant... well, she wasn't sure what it meant, but she was sure that it had something to do with the magic world and its goddesses. What an interesting place that was.

"Thanks, Dad," she said softly, the way she would usually speak if she was sick. "I'm going back to my room again to save my strength."

And while she was saving her strength, she could also devote some of it to researching the existence of her new friends, to be sure they were real... just in case.

Not long after she was back in her bed, there was a knock on her door, and her father peeked in. "Hi. I know this probably isn't the best time to breach this topic, but I meant to tell you before we went on vacation–"

"Are we moving again?" Brecken asked. Whenever her father put this much effort into trying to be tactful, it was always moving.

Defeated, he sighed. "Yes, we're moving again. But it'll be fine! You'll love the house we have picked out."

Brecken could only sigh. Now that she was back home, she'd really like it if things could stop happening to her for at least a calendar day.

How We Rebuild

"**D**o I *have* to go home?"

Two weeks after Threnhette's defeat, the Resistance was more or less back on their feet; almost all of their personnel had recovered, including Phoenix; and the building itself was back in working order, fully stocked with potions, antidotes, and food. This meant that it was now time for Lisandra to return to the City of Garnet.

"Are we sure, Thunder?" Phoenix asked. "I mean, it's been nice having someone here that I can offload some of my work onto. With Lisandra gone, I don't know who else could fill that void."

Thunder's arms were folded; he wasn't intending to appear shrewd or intimidating or stern, but he was also clearly not budging on his decision to send Lisandra back home. "Now, we all knew that this little arrangement was temporary from the start. I made that very clear to both of y'all. I didn't think there would be this much difficulty when it came to saying goodbye; for crying out loud, y'all act like you're not family. You'll be seeing each other again, I'm sure."

Phoenix nodded. "Right. I guess that would be easier these days, now that we don't have to hide underground, huh?"

"Yeah. Are you just now figuring that out?" Lisandra asked. "I only say that 'cause Aunt Tania has had some very *not nice* things to say about the fact that you and Logan haven't visited her at all now that you can."

This made Phoenix frown. "She could've just as easily come to visit us. She's the adult in the picture. You know, I was going to visit her and Dad on my way back, but now I'm reconsidering. Why is she like that? Why does she always have to..."

As she continued to rant– more to herself than anything– Logan entered the courtyard, where they had all gathered. It was easy to tell he had been resting, because it was one of the rare times his hair wasn't in its ponytail, instead flowing freely past his shoulders and down his back. "Who's responsible for this little meeting?" he asked.

"I'm surprised you weren't one of the first ones here," Thunder replied. "Remember, we're shipping your cousin back today?"

"Oh, yeah, yeah! A joyous occasion," Logan nodded, smiling. "Well, I got sidetracked. When I was getting dressed, I noticed that at some point, some of my hair got cut. Not surprising, given how close I've been to multiple blades throughout this entire excursion; but it was like after I'd seen it, I couldn't not see it. You know? So I'm going to have to cut it even later, I guess, but that can wait. I've got a parting gift for you, Lisandra."

"For me? Oh, you shouldn't have!" she replied, clearly exaggerating as she accepted the small box that Logan was handing to her. Inside was a singular, pristine apple cinnamon muffin, along with a note.

Read this note whenever you feel like everyone and everything is beating you down. I believe in your ability to become someone that people look up to. With everything that rests on your shoulders, I have no doubt that– if it were me– I'd have been crushed a long time ago by the weight of it all.

I'm proud of you, Lisandra.

"You really... shouldn't have," Lisandra said, much quieter, fighting the tears that tried to form within her eyes.

Logan merely smiled. "Safest of travels to you both. I'll be praying to the goddesses for your safety, as always. And make sure you guys tell everyone back home that I'm cooler and more handsome than they remember me being."

Everyone in the area laughed at this. "See you when I get back, Logan," Phoenix replied. "Try not to cause too much trouble for the captain, all right?"

"Wouldn't dream of it!" Logan replied. "Bye, guys!"

The girls waved, getting into the wagon that would take them to the next town over; from there, they would be able to take a train into the city. Once they were seated, they began to wave again until they were out of sight.

"Now that that's taken care of..." Logan turned to Thunder. "If you're not too busy, I could use some help making sure my hair gets cut evenly."

"But of course, now that all of that is over and done with…" Thunder said to himself a few days after Lisandra had gone home, as he sat in the back area of Resistance headquarters, that small area between the training grounds and the riverbank.

"Something troubling you?" Logan asked, sitting beside him.

Thunder glanced at him, surprised he had heard him. "Yeah. Now that we have the time to breathe, I think it's really sinkin' in just how underprepared we were for a situation like this. Not that I'm willing to let it happen, but what can we do to make sure something like this doesn't happen again?"

"A good question." Logan nodded. "I think this is the part where I remind you that this isn't something you have to ponder alone. Hasn't this entire adventure, in a way, been a lesson in trusting our friends with our burdens?"

It had, hadn't it? The thought that things were much easier to bear after he'd let his friends know about the heavy pieces of his heart had occurred more than once to Thunder. "Y'know, youngin, you got a good point there." Thunder chuckled. "But do you have any ideas?"

"I don't know what's worse: that we've all settled into a dynamic where everyone in the Resistance expects me to constantly have ideas, or that every time you guys ask me that, I actually do have one." Logan laughed. "Anyway. To get back on topic, I'm thinking of how there were never any particularly scary happenings like this in the City of Garnet, or at least not that I was ever aware of in my fifteen years living there. An interesting phenomenon, when you think of how many people live there compared to here."

"Right. City of Garnet's a lot richer than these parts too, which undoubtedly factors into it somehow," Thunder pointed out. "It's been so long since I've been there that I'm not too familiar with the infrastructure over there. Mind jogging my memory?"

"The infrastructure? Sure. It's... well, I guess one way it's different is that there's an actual governing body. A police force. I would assume there's some kind of government funding system..." Logan was thinking now.

"There has to be, or else it wouldn't look so exquisite," the two men heard a familiar voice behind them, and turned to confirm that the man they were expecting to see was approaching.

"Of course," Thunder agreed. "What are your thoughts on the matter, Hunter?"

Hunter took this chance to sit between the two men, making himself comfortable on the grass. "I believe this discussion harkens back to the one we had a while back regarding what will become of the Resistance, now that we have effectively and directly contributed to the betterment of the quality of life here in Compositora twice now," he replied. "It would be beneficial to consider the safety and security of our home our main priority, especially now that we are aware of Tornado... of Anton's plan to lead the restoration effort. It would be more than a shame to have that effort go into making this place beautiful like the days of old, if someday it was razed to the ground in an instant. So... I suppose now the question is how we structure our efforts to ensure that the quality of life for the average citizen of Compositora only improves from here on out."

"Indeed." Thunder nodded. "In addition to aiding the efforts of the restoration as much as we can, there should also be some sort of security detail, but what bothers me about that is, do y'all remember what it was like the last time this town had any sort of security detail? It was when the Dictator's guards were still around. Remember the way they all abused that power? I even... remember what it was like to be employed by the ruling class, and turn a blind eye to the suffering of the average man until it affected me personally. That's not what I want this organization to become, but I have no idea how to avoid it. It just feels like human nature at this point, and you can't avoid that."

"Can't we?" Logan asked. "This is a big, big world. Surely there has to be some place in it that's been able to find some sort of balance between government and civilian."

"Is there?" Hunter asked, his voice full of curiosity.

"Is there." But when Thunder repeated it, it was not with the inflection of a question; rather, it was a statement of reflection. This was something he had to think about for a while, but slowly yet surely, an idea began to formulate in his head. An idea he'd need a little outside help for, from an old friend of his.

"Logan, could you do me a favor?"

As always, Logan responded with a high level of exuberance. "Of course! What can I do for you, chief?"

"If you could track down a bird to send a message, that'd be great. I have to enlist the help of a very knowledgeable friend of mine; like you said, we don't have to face these things alone, right?"

Logan then grinned in a very infectious manner, one that enticed Hunter to smile himself. "You got it. I'll have it ready to fly in a few hours."

Thunder nodded. "Then I need to get to writing the message."

In almost no time, Thunder had tracked down a quill pen and paper; he'd opted to use paper of a more sepia tone for contrast against the bird that would be carrying the message, and also to signify the message was important enough that he'd given thought to writing it on paper that wasn't plain white.

After taking a few minutes to mentally walk through the words he'd use, he put pen to paper and began to write.

Dear Herman,

It's been a while, hasn't it? I'm very sorry that it's taken so long for me to contact you, but I'm sure you know that the situation hasn't been the best here in Compositora for the past few years. How are things? Hope the wife and son are still doing well. Are you still in government? I ask because I'm in need of your expertise when it comes to maintaining a peaceful environment in a sizable city. Could we meet for lunch sometime to discuss the future? The sooner the better, for various reasons. I'm sure we have a world's worth of things to catch up on.

Looking forward to our reunion,

Gavin

About The Author

Michelle Rivera is an Afro-Latina writer from Chicago, IL, where she currently still resides. As a child, she was drawn to narratives that involved groups of friends banding together to fight gods, magic, and impressively complicated wardrobes that no one would actually wear in their day-to-day life. These themes would, in time, come to be elements of her own writing.

Writing wasn't the first occupation she ever wanted to pursue as a child (that would be gardening), but it is undoubtedly the one that stuck with her the longest. Whether it was about the characters she'd grown to love, or the friends she'd wished she'd had, it wasn't long before pen touched paper, ready to create yet another world.

If not writing, she can be found drawing, crocheting, sewing, or playing video games.

Also By

Don't forget to read the first book in the series!

Revolution is available online at most major book retailers. You can also keep an eye on Michelle's website www.iridescentofraynu.com, to find out when and at what locations she will be selling copies at in person!

Join Us Online!

Are you a fan of the Revosaga series? Would you like to join a space to talk about it and meet other fans? You can do so by joining Revolutionary! The Revosaga Server, on Discord!

To do so, use your smartphone to scan the QR code below. We're excited to see you there!